LATE SHIFT

First Published in the UK 2014 by Glastonbury Publishing. This edition published 2018 by War Stories, an imprint of Mention the War Limited, 32, Croft Street, Leeds, LS28 5HA.

Second edition: 2018

This book is a work of fiction. All names, characters, locations and incidents are products of the author's imagination, or have been used in a fictitious context. Any resemblance to actual persons living or dead, locales or events is entirely coincidental. I'm not sure where the Grim Reaper fits into this however; perhaps he'll sue me.

A copy of this work is available through the British Library.

ISBN: 978-1911255307

LATE SHIFT

by

Simon Hepworth

Sarah,
Don't have nightmares!
Best wishes,
Simon

WAR STORIES

To Mandy, my wife,
and William, my son.

Thanks for putting up with me wittering on to anyone who
will listen about how much I enjoyed writing this book!

Author's Note

This book is obviously a work of fiction. No one knows what happens after death. The story was, however, inspired by my experiences as a police officer. When dealing with sudden deaths, it has often occurred to me that the person who has passed on now knows what, if anything, happens next.

The idea for the story came from an experience I had whilst being trained as an Authorised Firearms Officer. I was taking part in an exercise which involved following a fleeing vehicle on a dark and wild evening. It stopped, and a figure emerged carrying a double-barrelled shotgun. He aimed it at me and fired. It was, of course, loaded with blank ammunition. However, for an instant, the scenario seemed horribly real, and the memory stayed with me. The rest of the story flowed naturally.

Most of the locations in the story are entirely fictional, though the major ones, such as Cardiff, Bristol, Newport and Penarth are real. So, of course, is the Clifton Suspension Bridge. The events are fictional however. All the characters are imagined.

No offence is intended to readers holding religious beliefs. I just hope St. Peter sees it that way.

It is, of course, entirely possible that the Grim Reaper really is a nice guy with a great sense of humour, just doing a difficult job. If not, I'm stuffed.

PROLOGUE

Christmas is never a nice time to kill someone.

As a cop I had been well-accustomed to dealing in misery; we used to refer to our clientele as the Bad, the Mad and the Sad. Over the festive season the suffering seemed even more poignant and it is especially hard when the job involves seeing a family torn apart. But whatever the time of year, the objects of our efforts are never likely to be particularly enthusiastic, at least initially, but they do tend to see the light eventually, accepting the necessity of what we have to do. When all's said and done it's their own fault they are in that situation.

So there we were that Boxing Day afternoon, working at a time when in the past we would have been celebrating with our families. There were the inevitable garish decorations, as many adorning the doors, window frames and even bushes in the gardens as there were shining from those rooms in which the curtains remained open. Danny was peering through the kitchen window of the target's house as I loitered near the back door. He gave me the thumbs-up. 'He's put the kettle on now and is going to the fridge. What do you reckon this time, Nick? Electrocution or heart failure? It's your turn to choose.'

'His file says he's survived four heart attacks so far, and he's still smoking, drinking and knocking back the pies. He's been taking the piss so no one will be surprised if he succumbs to a massive coronary.'

'Yeah, I expect he thinks that he's untouchable. As I read it, the third one should have done for him, but they had a defibrillator on hand at the shopping centre and some enthusiastic member of staff who'd paid attention to their training brought him round. The fourth time he was even luckier as he was in A&E at the time having cut himself while making some chips. Knowing his luck, I wouldn't be surprised if there's a doctor in the house.'

'On this occasion there's just his wife, who is asleep on the settee. I hope they enjoyed their Christmas lunch. Probably as well for all concerned that she's out of it; she'll sober up pretty damn quick when she goes to the kitchen.' I checked one more time through the window, the target now helping himself to another can of beer and some mince pies. 'Well, old son, you can run but you can't hide. Let's go, Danny.'

I went into the kitchen, Danny ambling along behind me, hands in his pockets. I wished he wouldn't do that, it looked slovenly and unprofessional, but when I'd mentioned it before, Danny told me that in his old job they had to blend in, and very few crims marched smartly around the place. That's the difference between spending a career in uniform, and specialising in undercover work, I suppose. Anyway it didn't really make any difference as the target wouldn't see us till it was too late, but I had never shaken off my desire to see standards maintained. Old habits die hard, and at least he didn't stand around in briefings chewing gum, one of my pet hates.

The unwitting subject of our attention was forty-eight years old, and weighed eighteen stone. He wasn't hugely obese, by modern standards at least, but smoking sixty cigarettes a day and spending most evenings in the pub hadn't helped. I was surprised he'd lasted this long, but that was probably a testament to his good fortune and reluctance to accept that his time here was up.

I walked past the target and leant against the kitchen door, to deter him from going through. He couldn't see me, of course, but my negative vibes would make him strangely reluctant to leave the kitchen till Danny had done the hit. My colleague took his hand out of his pocket, holding his stun gun. Very similar to the devices we used to have when we were back here, this was designed to interrupt the body's natural electrical impulses and stop the heart. Simple and effective, it caused an immediate, massive and irremediable heart attack, one that wouldn't be questioned as the cause of our target's apparently untimely demise. He'd certainly had his chips.

The target turned from the work surface and Danny was waiting for him. A swift jab to the centre of the chest with the

2

Taser and our overweight chum looked stunned. He dropped the plate of mince pies and beer as his hands went to where Danny had zapped him. Eyes wide in shock, he collapsed, subsiding almost in slow motion to the ground, where he then lay in an untidy heap on the kitchen floor. For such a big bloke, he didn't make much noise at all once the plate and can had bounced off the laminate flooring. His wife slumbered on, oblivious to the imminent onset of widowhood.

'Excellent hit, Danny. I'd expected him to make more of a racket.'

'You are observing a true master at work. Watch and learn, young man,' Danny grinned. 'Not the griefiest of jobs, though his family might not use that term.'

All we had to do now was to wait for the target to come through to our dimension and then we could take him with us to the Afterlife.

CHAPTER ONE

On my last day on Earth I was working as a police officer. The change in my personal circumstances was sudden, terminal and totally out of my control. Shortly before nine o'clock one cold, wet and windy autumn evening, I was on traffic patrol. My colleague Mark was new to the Roads Policing Unit, so still highly enthusiastic. Eager colleagues can be a mixed blessing, but it meant that our performance figures were good, which kept the sergeants and the bosses off our backs. He was also very diligent and had been paying attention when observations were requested for a blue VW Golf GTi which had been seen earlier doing something it shouldn't. In this case, it shouldn't have been lurking around the high street checking out a cash-in-transit crew busy collecting the takings from some of our town centre supermarkets. We tended to take dim view of that. Fortunately some diligent member of the public also thought it was not on, so rang it in.

We mooched about for a while, trying to spot anything that looked like a dodgy Golf without seeing anything that might fit the bill, so gave it up as a bad job and went to look for drivers not showing proper respect for the Road Traffic Act. Given the weather conditions, though, I couldn't get too excited about getting in and out of the car to dish out words of wisdom and traffic tickets to errant motorists. Fixed Penalty Notices go soggy in the rain and are difficult to write on, and in any case I didn't fancy getting wet, even though the taxpayer had thoughtfully given me some waterproof clothing. Eventually Mark conveniently remembered he had to finish some paperwork so we headed for the nick.

Another crew was working late and wanted to take our car when we got back to the office, which suited me fine. If I sound a bit jaded it's probably because I had been in the job for nearly twenty years and I had long since exhausted the supply of adrenaline that gives younger-in-service cops so much of a buzz. Don't get me wrong; I still got a lot out of the work and had no plans to leave it just yet. Unfortunately our own intentions don't necessarily get taken into account in the greater scheme of things, as I was just about to find out.

Mark had got himself a brew and settled down to throw the book at some half-witted driver who hadn't been able to keep his vehicle shiny side up on the tarmac. I didn't have any outstanding paperwork to dive in to so I had a word with the sergeant to see if she had any bright ideas about how I might protect the community for another hour or so prior to clearing off for the evening. Being a sergeant, naturally she did, and suggested I take an unmarked vehicle out and about. I actually liked going out in a plain car as it let me sneak up on unsuspecting wrongdoers. It appealed to the ruthless bastard in me.

It was sod's law, of course, that it took me about five minutes out there on my own to find the Golf. It pulled out of a side road without the driver considering the option of giving way to the oncoming traffic, namely me.

19:35:05 'Control from Mike Whisky Seven Six.'

19:35:11 'Mike Whisky Seven Six, pass your message.'

19:35:17 'Mike Whisky Seven Six, was there a definite registration for that blue Golf from the suspicious incident in Stambridge earlier?'

19:35:26 'Checking for you now, standby... (lengthy pause)...Mike Whisky Seven Six partial registration only, Yankee Zulu Five Seven, no other letters.'

The Golf wasn't hanging about so I set off after him, as you do. I shouted control and let them know what I was up to as the Golf headed out of town up towards the forest. He was going like a bat out of hell, I'll give him that.

19:36:05 'Seven Six roger. Blue Golf partial registration Yankee Zulu Five Seven, rest is obscured, making off from Stambridge, North West A4583 towards Severndale Forest. I'm following it, speed varying seven zero to nine zero miles per hour. Vehicle about two hundred yards ahead. Request back up. Is the helicopter available?'

19:36:37 'Seven Six, I will call NPAS but it was a negative when I checked earlier, I'm afraid. Cloud base below is limits today. Any units free to back up Mike Whisky Seven Six, A4583 Stambridge towards Severndale Forest? Vehicle making off.'

The sparse details on the Golf's part-registration suggested it was initially registered somewhere in the North of England which was probably irrelevant. Blaggers aren't generally in the habit of using their own legally-registered motors as they go about their work so it would have been nicked or on false plates. It might have been a two-in-one burglary: they see the car on the drive, having probably spotted it a while back; kick in the door, grab the keys and the next time anyone sees the car it's been torched after some job. That meant that I had absolutely no idea who was driving, or who else was likely to be in the car if I actually managed to pull it over and start asking searching questions of whoever I found in it.

19:36:56 'Mike Whisky Nine One from the office, we'll start travelling.'

19:36:59 'Mike Whisky Nine One thanks, any other units.'

19:37:06 'Sierra Bravo Two Zero, I'm not pursuit trained but we'll make for the area.'

19:37:12 'Sierra Bravo Two Zero thank you. Mike Whisky Seven Six.'

19:37:17 'Seven Six, go ahead.'

19:37:20 'Seven Six further units backing up. Location now please?'

19:37:26 'Seven Six I'm four miles out of Stambridge just past Parker's Farm.'

19:37:32 'Seven Six roger.'

19:37:48 'Control from Mike Whisky Seven Six, vehicle has turned left, left, left onto an unclassified road. I think it's the one that leads up to Stoney Fold. Speed five zero miles per hour. I'll try and get a complete registration number for you.'

19:38:10 'Mike Whisky Seven Zero roger. Mike Whisky Nine One, Sierra Bravo Two Zero did you copy?'

19:38:17 'Two Zero copied.'

19:38:21 'Mike Whisky Nine One roger.'

The road had occasional places where it broadened slightly to allow wide vehicles to pass. The Golf slowed as it approached one of these, pulled in, then came to a standstill.

19:38:35 'Mike Whisky Seven Six, vehicle stopped. One person on board. No details and I can't see the plate from here. Last three letters were obscured by black tape. Stand by, I'll get back to you with details.'
19:38:50 'Seven Six, roger. Do you want the other units to keep travelling?'
19:38:56 'Seven Six, just to be in the area please. I'm not a hundred percent sure which lane I'm on now.'
19:39:05 'Mike Whisky Seven Six, roger. Watch your back mate.'
19:39:11 'Seven Six, will do. Standby...'

I thought the other side had surrendered rather meekly; in the forest and the back lanes most of the idiots reckoned they had a fighting chance of shaking us off. No matter; I undid my seat belt, then got out and went forward to speak to the driver, who appeared to be the sole occupant. As I approached, the driver's door of the other car opened and a guy got out. I assumed it was a 'he'; most of the idiots causing death and mayhem on the highways generally were. He was taller than me, about six foot or so, dressed in a camouflaged army jacket and jeans. His head was masked by a balaclava, the type favoured by blaggers and the IRA; holes for eyes and mouth and that's it. It wasn't a reassuring image.

What scared me shitless was the shotgun he brought out of the car, swung round and pointed at me. I don't just mean in my general direction either, I was looking down both sodding barrels. Ironically I'd run through this sort of scenario in my mind countless times before, and indeed something similar had been sprung on me in a firearms training exercise once. This time, though, it was for real. I went cold and my spine chilled. I thought for a split second that he just wanted to frighten me, and it worked. But scaring me was certainly not the only thing he had in mind. All I saw was a bright flash, heard the

7

explosion of the shotgun and felt something like a truck hitting me full in the chest at the same time, the force slamming me back against my own vehicle. I felt no pain, but just confusion as the world spun around me and nothing made sense for a couple of seconds.

I came round to find myself slumped on the ground looking up at the world and, more specifically, at the gunman standing over me. He didn't seem worried about being recognised because he lifted the balaclava away from his face. I recognised him immediately as Lee Patrick bloody Summers, scumbag of this parish and one of our local criminals. Summers was never one for exchanging pleasantries with ourselves and this occasion was no different. 'Fuck off, copper' was the last thing I heard before he fired the second barrel.

I was momentarily stunned again but this time my mind cleared more quickly and I found myself up on my feet, looking down at my recumbent figure. I was a mess, I have to say. The body that used to be mine was lying on its back with a gaping hole in the chest, dark red blood oozing through the wreckage of my high visibility jacket. I wasn't moving anymore and my eyes were open, staring up at where Summers had until recently been. Summers, seemingly satisfied with what he presumably thought was a useful day's work, was getting back in the Golf. I automatically looked at the registration number, still obscured by that damned tape and, through habit, reached for my notebook and pen. I didn't seem to have them on me.

Summers drove away. He hadn't even switched off the engine so he just floored it and sped off. I glanced back at myself but I was just lying there uselessly. Bizarrely I felt annoyed that I hadn't bothered to put my hat on as I got out of the car.

'What the fuck happened?' My first words when it all settled down, were uttered to no one in particular. I saw myself lying on the ground and the thought struck me that I must be having some sort of out-of-body experience. Looking at the damage to my body, I wondered if I was dying. I had read and heard plenty of stories of supposed near-death experience so it didn't take me long to draw the obvious conclusion. It occurred to me that I needed to pull myself together and get on with trying to recover my wits and get help for myself. Try as I might though, I couldn't put myself back in my body, but just stood there getting increasingly frustrated and concerned. It was, I noticed, becoming misty; either that or my eyesight was failing. And then I can only think that I fell asleep.

19:43:20 'Mike Whisky Seven Six from control.'

19:43:52 'Mike Whisky Seven Six status update please.'

19:44:07 'Mike Whisky Seven Six, no signal.'

19:45:12 'Mike Whisky Seven Six, is everything OK?'

19:45:53 'Mike Whisky Seven Six, this is Force Control Supervisor. Nothing received. Please confirm receipt of this message.'

19:46:16 'Mike Whisky Nine One from Control, what's your location?'

19:46:23 'Nine One, we're about two miles out of Stambridge. Have you got a more precise location?'

19:46:35 'Mike Whisky Nine One, Seven Six said it was possibly the road up to Stoney Fold. It's about half a mile north west of Parker's Farm, are you anywhere near? We need a welfare check on Seven Six please.'

19:46:50 'Nine One, we are about three miles from that locus. We will expedite if you like.'

19:46:47 'Nine One from Control, this is, strictly speaking, a welfare check so it's at your discretion. Mike Whisky Seven Six, are you receiving anything?'

19:46:58 'Nine One understood.'

19:47:20 'Mike Whisky Seven Six, if you can hear this message, we are not getting anything from you. Nine One is attending to assist if required. Confirm if you receive this transmission please.'

19:47:48 'Mike Whisky Seven Six, nothing received. Mike Whisky Nine One please expedite. Seven Six last contact was immediately prior to him stopping a suspicious vehicle in a remote location. Please proceed with due caution.'

19:48:12 'Nine One, all received.'

19:51:07 (Emergency transmitter button activated by PC6204 in MW91): 'Control from Nine One urgent assistance required this location. Officer down, one officer, serious injuries, we need an ambulance and back up urgently. No other vehicle or persons at scene.'

19:51:21: 'Nine One roger, what sort of injuries to the officer and is he conscious?'

19:51:29: 'He's got really bad injuries, honest to God, he looks like he's been shot, no response to us. He needs an ambulance ASAP, he doesn't look clever. Can we have supervision and SOCO up here too? It looks likely to prove fatal. I think we've lost him.'

CHAPTER TWO

When I woke up I was sitting in what appeared to be some sort of waiting room. The walls were a sort of marble-effect in grey-blue. It was clean, cold and clinical. The floor was polished in dark grey. It was quite light, with skylights but no windows. I couldn't see out. I had no sense of time though; suddenly a door opened and a woman walked in. Being a member of the old school, I stood up. About five foot four, she was reasonably slim, and wearing a green tunic with loose-fitting trousers. Her hair was a mid-blonde, shoulder length, the tips curling inwards. Her light blue eyes held my gaze. Her age was slightly less than mine; if I had to guess, I would have put her about forty. Her voice was soft and caring as she addressed me. 'Hello, Nick, how are you feeling?'

I wondered for a moment how she knew my name.

'I'm a bit confused. I don't remember coming here. For that matter I don't know where I am.'

'Would you like to sit down?' This was delivered gently but in a way that suggested that I would need to, so I did, back on the chair I had just vacated. 'Nick, I'm afraid I've got some important news for you. You need to know that you're dead. There's no easy way for me to tell you that.'

She was delivering a death message then, something I had had to do countless times. The family sees you walk up to the front door, in uniform, wearing your hat. Your face is expressionless. They open the door, you look them in the eye and ask to come in, firmly but softly. They start to pick up the vibes from your body language and your tone. You don't faff around with flowery language; that gets in the way of the message you have to give them. They need to understand with absolute clarity. 'Dead'. Not 'fatally injured', not 'passed away', not 'didn't make it'; you have to tell them straight. Just as this lady was telling me, but right now this wasn't about my wife, my child, a member of my family taken from me. It was about me, taken from my family, such as it was.

We've all got to go some time. We tell ourselves that every day of our earthly lives. 'It'll be sometime but I'll be alright today' we reassure ourselves. It's comforting in a way and saves us from lying awake at night, tearing ourselves apart at the thought of one day shuffling off that mortal coil, the one I'd not so much shuffled off as been blown away from.

It wasn't quite what I'd expected though. There were no heavenly harps twanging away, no kindly bearded St. Peter offering to take my ticket and allow me through the pearly turnstile, as opposed, I'd always hoped, to him saying 'Sorry mate, the lift to the fiery basement is over there. You won't be needing your coat'.

She must be used to this, because she didn't look at all surprised by what I imagine was a confused look on my face. I just had that feeling you get when someone has told you something that knocks the stuffing out of you. It took a few seconds while I went over the events of the past, how long? Minutes? Hours? Did time have any meaning now I was supposedly staring eternity in the face? Then the penny dropped.

Shit.

This was real.

I wasn't going home tonight. Or ever.

I wasn't going to my brother's birthday party next month.

It suddenly didn't matter whether my football team got promoted at the end of the season, because whatever they did, they'd be doing it without me. My blood, what there was left of it after Summers had finished his work, suddenly ran very cold. No wonder she had urged me to sit down.

Everything, absolutely everything, had changed in an instant. My plans, however trivial for my daily life, my hopes, dreams and aspirations, had simply vaporised. I sat there for a while, my head resting in my hands as I tried to conquer the overwhelming feeling of panic. It's hard to describe the totality of the sensation. When I had lost close friends, which had happened a couple of times in the course of my career, it had been so hard to focus on getting on with normal day-to-day routine, but I knew I had to go to work, get to the shops, and keep things ticking over. No shock, no sudden bereavement or intense grieving, can possibly compare with the realisation that your own life on Earth has come to an end. Sitting there, stunned, I felt the warmth and light pressure of an arm around the top of my back, a hand resting on my shoulder. It was immensely comforting and reassuring; after a while, I found myself drawn back to what now passed for reality.

'What's your name, if you don't mind me asking?' Hardly the slickest of lines, but my mind was still trying to maintain its very tenuous grip on the situation. I knew nothing about my companion, I realised; I presumed she was some sort of functionary in this place in which I found myself.

'I'm Chris, or Christine, whichever you prefer.'

'Hi Chris. Are you here to welcome me?'

'Yes, we knew you were on your way and I was told to grab you before anyone else did.' I hadn't got the faintest idea what she was on about right then, of course, but it all became clear later. However, her matter-of-fact demeanour helped me get my head together, and begin to assess what on earth (or perhaps elsewhere) was going on.

'I really am dead? This isn't some kind of a sick wind-up by my mates and I'm in hospital or something? If it is, fair play, I'll admit you've taken me in and I can laugh about it. I can dish out the wind-ups but I can take them as well.' Last chance, please, Chris, I thought, to tell me it was all a joke and we could all have a really good laugh at my expense. It wouldn't be the first time I'd fallen for an elaborate stunt; they'd once been a rite of passage in our job till the politically-correct commissars abolished humour in the police.

'Nick, I promise you it's for real. There's no walking out of the shower like in Dallas, writing the entire thing off as a dream, I'm afraid. This is the Afterlife, or whatever you choose to call it. For now, try to simply accept the fact. Before, remember, you used to take it for granted that you belonged there, that everything was real. Maybe it was, maybe it wasn't, but in your mind everything was right, wasn't it?'

'Is this Heaven?' I'd not been a church-goer since I was a child, though I'd always had a sneaking feeling that I would be well-advised to hedge my bets.

'It's complicated, is probably the fairest answer I can give you at the moment,' Chris told me. I got the impression that would have to do for the time being. 'You'll probably need some time now to get your head together. I've taken the liberty of arranging somewhere for you to stay while you're settling in. You can be alone or in company as you see fit. I'll show you where we've put you and you can talk some more, or just chill out if you like.' At that, she got up and went to the door. 'Come on, Nick. Let's get you sorted.'

The door opened onto a corridor. There were no stairs; everything seemed to be on one level. Chris opened another door and daylight streamed in. We stepped outside into bright sunlight. A path ran alongside the building from which we had just emerged. Externally, it was dark brown brick with tinted windows. The single storey structure had a dark grey slate roof with numerous skylights like those I had seen in the room when I had first arrived. The building itself was not what you might call an architectural masterpiece; in fact it looked like a health centre or other retreat for public servants to lurk in as they fervently plot ways in which to avoid serving the public.

The building was surrounded by what appeared to be extensive parkland. This was not the usual scruffy and semi-derelict mixture of grass and play areas that pass for parks in the sort of areas where I had previously worked, but more like the sort of carefully nurtured landscape found surrounding stately homes and exclusive golf courses. Here, though, there were no fairways or greens to spoil the inspiring blue and green vista. It was, quite simply, the most stunningly beautiful landscape I had ever seen. Lush, vivid green grass covered gently undulating slopes, the building standing in a slight natural hollow. The slopes were populated by white-barked trees, like eucalypts but without the messy peeling. Their leaves were olive green in stark contrast to the trunks and branches. There were a series of low valleys, most with paths winding through them, and a series of streams of crystal-clear water, with occasional pools. The area was spotless, and appeared to be an oasis of calm.

There were people scattered around, some alone, others in pairs or small groups. From a distance, some of the forms were amorphous, elongated forms of the generic human shape, whilst others were clearly identifiable as individuals. It was still totally unreal to me, but the feeling that I would wake up any minute and find it had all been a dream suggested to me that it was anything but. After all, how often in a dream do you feel actually think you are dreaming. I asked Chris about the less substantial figures.

'They haven't yet picked up on your spiritual signal, so they don't reach out in return. If you focus on them and want to connect, they will see you and decide if they want to accept you. If they do, you will see them become more distinct.'

'How do I make myself visible to them?'

'It's a similar process. Just imagine that you are on patrol in uniform. You want to be seen; it's a similar mind-set. And if you don't want to be seen, just think of working undercover. That's where we've got an advantage over most of the rest.'

'You mean it's a bit like becoming a friend on Facebook?' I offered.

'I can't really say as I'm not familiar with that particular phenomenon,' Chris replied. 'I died before it was invented.'

I couldn't think of a sensible reply to that; it was obviously going to take me some time to adjust to life in a new dimension, so I just looked at a particular figure that was drifting slowly towards us, about twenty yards away. I willed myself to see them as a person and, after a few seconds, it took on the form of a middle-aged man, dark-skinned and about my height. The guy looked at me, smiled and walked past.

The park was my idea of heaven, tranquil but not a wilderness. Although I enjoyed adventure holidays I was no Crocodile Dundee and some civilised greenery with nice fresh water was just what the doctor would have ordered. Except the last time, when I really needed a doctor, there were none around of course.

Chris led me to another modern building, still in the park. Light yellow brick, with tinted windows, it looked like a student hall of residence. Fortunately, though, it lacked the air of untidiness and anarchy so often found on those premises.

The entrance lobby was surprisingly light and spacious. The central feature was a fountain, clear water splashing onto large smooth polished rocks with fronds of greenery surrounding it. There obviously wasn't a hosepipe ban in the

Afterlife, which either meant it rained a lot or the Angel of Municipal Engineering was more efficient than his or her earthly counterparts. Easy chairs also seemed to be in abundance as there were a number of these placed neatly around the fountain. Best of all, there was no TV screen endlessly cheering us up with rolling news coverage, though I could envisage the coverage of misery and disaster providing useful prior warning of an influx of new arrivals.

An open plan staircase took us up to a landing with corridors leading away in different directions. Chris strode purposefully along one of these, eventually pausing by one of the numerous doors.

'This is your room, Nick,' she informed me, opening it and ushering me inside.

'I'm impressed, you've got it all very well organised. You must have been busy. Did sort all this out yourself?'

'Good grief, no. We have admin people who do all that. Remember all those bureaucrats working tirelessly away in their offices back where you came from? It seems for many of them, that's their idea of heaven. It keeps them happy and fulfilled here too, and means we don't have to worry about tasks that for anyone else would be tediously routine. Of course, they've had all their endless bloody forms taken off them otherwise they would just make our lives more frustrating which would defeat the object, of being here, but they seem to cope. If you want something, just ring them.'

'Don't tell me they've got a Help Desk...'

'No, there's always someone who answers it in person and deals with your problem themselves. We do have the automated answering machines that I understand are now all the rage in Help Desks and Call Centres back there. Those are used in the Redevelopment Units to inflict a purgatorive experience on the inmates.'

'Redevelopment Units? What are they, dare I ask?' There was so much to take in; it was like my first day as a cop all over again.

'The RUs are where the bad people go when they arrive here. You'll get to see them when you bring in a recalcitrant soul. You know, a scumbag, or someone who hasn't made any effort to live a reasonably decent life. We've been getting a lot of politicians recently, for some reason.'

'I couldn't imagine why that might be,' I muttered, thinking of the recent scandals involving what appeared to be a large proportion of our political elite. For all I knew, it might have been a worldwide phenomenon, not just confined to our septic isle.

'Right, Nick, get yourself settled, freshen up and then if you fancy socialising in a bit, give me a knock and we'll go to the bar. If you prefer you can just chill out for now. My pad is just across the corridor if there's anything else you need.'

'No, I could use a stiff drink after what I've been through. I'll see you in a bit, Chris. Oh, by the way, is there a key?'

'You don't need one. There's no crime here; you can get anything you want free of charge so no point in thieving. Also, we're a very select bunch!'

I looked around the main room which was a spacious lounge. A picture window with blinds formed the far wall, the view being the parkland we'd walked through earlier. Night was starting to draw in by now and the daylight was fading. A black leather settee rested against one wall, a coffee table languishing in front of it. A couple of reclining armchairs took up more of the floor space. To the left were two interior doors. A quick exploration revealed that one of the doors led to a small but adequate kitchen and the other to the bedroom. A double bed dominated the latter, with cupboards and an en-suite. I had a quick look round but decided I would explore more thoroughly later on.

Chris went to a sideboard and took a glass from inside. From her pocket she removed a small bottle, filling the glass with the contents. A dark and red liquid, it looked like a good claret. 'Trust me and drink this, it will help you relax,' she told me. 'Then I would recommend you have a lie down and rest for a bit. You'll be fine Nick. The hard bit's behind you now.' Then she left the room.

I followed her advice, swallowed the drink which was a light and fresh fluid with a slight sweetness to it, then walked into the bedroom, the door closing itself softly behind me. I sat on the bed which, spookily, was just as firm as I like beds to be. I lay back, kicked my shoes off, swung my feet onto the bed and fell deeply asleep.

CHAPTER THREE

Waking up in a strange bed is disorientating enough at the best of times. It takes me a good few seconds to remember where I am and what I'm doing there. Just imagine coming round from a deep slumber and confronting the reality that in fact you really are dead. Lying on the bed I reviewed the events earlier on and, eventually, found I could accept the fact once I confronted it in my mind.

I could see daylight easing its way round the blinds covering the bedroom window and I figured that I had probably slept straight through the night. I swung my legs off the bed and wandered through to the en-suite bathroom. A power shower over the bath looked like an attractive option. Getting out of my rather crumpled clothes, I turned on the shower and stepped under it. Having found myself in idyllic surroundings as I had walked with Chris over to the accommodation earlier, and then having slept in a bed that was just right too, I was not surprised to find that the water temperature was perfect. Everything, it seemed to me, was pretty much to my taste. It was like playing a starring role in Goldilocks, just without the trial and error of eliminating the porridge that was too hot or too cold. I assumed that was so that there was nothing to annoy me unduly. Maybe getting totally pissed off with stuff was part of our development in the last life and, having come through all that, it was no longer considered necessary to wind us up. I decided I could probably get used to that.

My perfect shower over, I got dry with the absolutely wonderful towel that I found neatly folded over the rail. Then I wondered what I was going to do for clothes. My uniform, discarded on the bathroom floor, was probably surplus to requirements. I picked my shirt up and examined it. Miraculously it was no longer blood-stained, which seemed a bit bizarre. Neither did it have a big hole in it, but then again, nor did I. That was good news; at least I wasn't messing the place up and Chris hadn't mentioned anything about me leaking from a gaping wound. I supposed I'd left all that behind as well, which was probably for the best.

Inspired by the notion that they'd thought of everything, I strolled back into the bedroom and started poking about in the cupboards. Naturally enough, they contained a variety of clothes, all of which I liked and all of which seemed to be my size. This no longer surprised me. I selected a blue polo shirt and denim jeans. No doubt someone would tell me if I was under-dressed. I stuck with my black leather combat boots, at least for the time being. They were both comfortable and comforting. I thought of the old Western saying 'Bury me with my boots on', and laughed inwardly.

There was a light knock on the door. I opened it to find Chris, resplendent today in a white blouse and light green knee-length skirt.

'Sorry I didn't make it to the bar last night, I went out like a light,' I greeted her.

'Most people want a good sleep when they get here, so we've learnt from that. You went through an adjustment period. It wasn't last night, I have to confess; you've been out of it for four days.'

'I've never slept four days in my life...' I began, before realising how pointless my comment seemed. 'Is that normal?'

'It varies from person to person. Your soul, which is by now your entire being, has largely adjusted to the change and you will find that you start to accept everything naturally, just as you did when you were born back there.' She smiled. 'The drink helped too, I expect. I came to take you to breakfast. Don't worry, I won't be hounding you for ever, but you still need to know where everything is.'

I thought that being hounded by Chris might not be the worst fate that could have befallen me. I'd not paid a huge amount of attention to her the previous day, as my mind had been on other matters. Now, though, I looked at her anew. Slim faced, her hair curled where it met her shoulders, her eyes were a deep blue and her slim lips a natural pink. Without an apparent trace of makeup she still managed to look attractive without overdoing it.

She smiled at me, eyes crinkling slightly. Her round, seemingly firm, breasts were accentuated by her blouse. I had to remind myself that trying to chat her up was probably not the most sensible course of action at that precise moment, but I was pleasantly surprised to find myself tempted.

'Am I OK dressed like this?' I thought I had better check while I still had chance to change. 'I mean, what do we wear to go out around here?'

'Whatever you like, Nick. As you are probably beginning to work out there are no unnecessary rules or etiquette here. It's all about being yourself, the real you, not worrying about putting on appearances. You could wear a three-piece suit, Speedos or a bed sheet as a toga for all anyone else would be bothered. I think you'll look fine as you are but the choice is yours.'

'I forgot to pack my swimming trunks, so the Speedos aren't an option I'm afraid.' Such a refreshing approach saved me faffing around trying to make a decision as well.

'You look fine, whatever you're happy with. You can chill out, you know. We really are very relaxed about things. Come on, then, I could eat a scabby horse.'

I would, by now, have felt somewhat let down if the menu did indeed feature *Cheval Scabieuses* as the Chef's Special as it wasn't one of my own particular favourites. However I didn't actually think it was all that likely that this place would be that desperate for food. I thought I was just about managing to cling on to some semblance of reality though at the back of my mind still lurked the possibility that I was at risk of losing the plot entirely. I followed Chris back along the corridor and down the stairs.

She led me into a large canteen, liberally equipped with tables and chairs. A number of other people sat, sprawled or loafed around, many of them with plates of food. I felt instantly at home. It was just like a police canteen. There was even the obligatory pool table. I'm rubbish at games like that but the thought crossed my mind that if I was to be here for anything resembling eternity, at least I'd have the chance to learn.

We joined a fairly short queue in the serving area. A full English breakfast for me; bacon, two fried eggs, mushrooms, tomatoes, beans and chips. A nice big mug of coffee to go with it, and some toast and butter. Cholesterol was no longer a worry, I reminded myself. Chris had a bowl of Grape Nuts, some toast and a cup of tea. Each to their own; I was hungry though. It certainly tasted good as I demolished the plateful. As I tucked in I picked up our previous conversation where we had left it before my long sleep.

'Is there no St. Peter after all? No elderly relatives queuing up at the end of the tunnel of light to greet me?'

'No, Nick. That was all made up by people with a vivid imagination and a hidden agenda, whether that might be to con grieving relatives out of a few quid, sell some books or subjugate entire populations by threatening them with hell-fire and damnation unless they do what they're told.'

'I suppose that means religion is complete shite.'

'Well I wouldn't exactly put it that way. Faith is individual and something everyone needs to work out for themselves. A lot of harm was done in the name of religion by some people for their purposes though, I will give you that. How could any of them know the truth from their perspective back there? They all made it up, every one of them. They're all in for a shock though. Can you imagine haranguing people for years about how they are going to roast for all eternity because they don't see things your way, then you get here and find them all quite happily carrying on regardless with not a pitchfork or demon in sight? They'd never let you hear the end of it.'

'Do I get to find out the ultimate truth? What it's all about, and all that?'

'Well there's no rush, is there? You're going to be here quite a while and there's plenty to take in. And this is just another level of consciousness, and there will doubtless be more beyond this one. We know more here than where we've all just come from, but nothing like the whole truth. If you think I can tell you what it's all about, why we are here, or there, or wherever, I can't I'm afraid. But the main thing is this time round that at least I know that I don't know. You know that too so I wouldn't get away with fobbing you off with any old rubbish that I've made up to control you.'

'Loads of times I'd go to a sudden death, and I'd look at the body and think that at least they now knew the truth about life after death. Was I wrong because in fact they didn't?'

'Well we know a lot more now than we did before. The biggest difference is that we know there are at least two levels of existence, because we are fully aware of what went before, and we know there is this one. If you think about it, you spent your last life wondering where you came from and where you'd be going, didn't you?'

'Yeah, I did. Every bloody day, in some way I suppose. After I'd shaken off all the religious dogma I got thrust down my throat, I figured that reincarnation was probably the most likely thing to happen to us after death. You die and then immediately get reborn as someone else. I never bought into the 'coming back as a cockroach' thing if you were bad, but I sort of presumed there'd be some cosmic payback going on. I had a string of lousy relationships including three marriages, till I finally stopped bothering trying to find a woman I really loved and wanted to be with all my life. I just presumed I'd been really bad to some poor lass in a previous life so it was karma.' I thought this was getting a bit deep for a breakfast-time conversation so I decided to move swiftly on.

'Chris, you said when we first met that you'd wanted to grab me before anyone else did. What on earth...what did you mean exactly? Have you saved me from a fate worse than death or something?'

'You're the sort of person we like to look out for. You were a police officer, you did the job for the right reasons, to deal with difficult things, try and sort right from wrong, you weren't just in it for the kudos, or the money...'

'I always used to say I joined the job because I liked uniforms and was bullied at school,' I joked.

'Well, you always knew deep down that was just your sense of humour, Nick, wasn't it? I think your motives ran deeper than that, otherwise you would have got fed up with the job a long time ago.'

'Yeah, you're probably right. I can't hide anything from you can I?'

'No you can't, so don't even try!' At least that drew a smile from her, and a lovely, even radiant, smile it was too. Chris might not have had wings and a halo but just then she managed to look pretty angelic.

'OK then, what is it you want to rope me into? If I'm going to be around here for a bit, I suppose I might as well do something useful.'

'Your arrival here is very well-timed, believe it or not. We are recruiting what you might call soul collectors. Our bosses prefer to call us Soul Retrieval Officers as it sounds less judgmental, or something. The job has actually had many titles down through the ages. At the moment the department is styled the 'Overdue Souls Retrieval Unit', though it was previously 'The Office of the Angel of Death', till some bright spark decided that we don't actually do death; our being here is supposedly some sort of proof that it doesn't exist. We're not allowed to call ourselves angels either, as that might offend the sensibilities of those who didn't subscribe to a belief in the afterlife while they were alive, and would have trouble coming to terms with having got it badly wrong. So the title was wrong on just about all counts.'

'Are you offering me a job?'

'We thought you might like to join us, now you're here. You'd be a collector, which basically means going back there and giving a helping hand to those whose time has come but are too stubborn to let it happen. We'll explain everything, and you get a bit of training. Having been a cop, you'll be used to taking on board new ideas, acquiring new skills and then just cracking on with the task. The boss has been getting some grief recently because his soul count isn't what it might be. You'll be aware that life expectancy is going up back there but that gives a few people the chance to slip through the net. We can't be everywhere. If you've got the average cop's sense of humour, you'll have the time of your life, if you excuse the rather insensitive expression. 'Life begins at death' was how one of my colleagues jovially summed it up when I started.'

This was, I thought, totally bizarre. Such a short time since that scumbag Summers had blown me away and now it seemed I was being sounded out about a job acting as some sort of celestial assassin. Talk about swept along, I hadn't even had time to grieve for myself, but maybe that's why they hit you so fast with something to take your mind off being dead.

'I'd certainly like to hear more about it, Chris. I suppose I might as well do something halfway useful with my time. There's nothing to lose really, is there?'

'You're not under any obligation; this is what passes for Paradise after all, but I think that people like us might find the prospect of eternity without any action a trifle dull.' I could see that; I hadn't got round to planning for my retirement as I'd been enjoying my job and hadn't been too excited about the thought of pruning roses. At least I'd saved myself some mental exercise dreaming up ways of filling my retirement as I hadn't managed to survive that long. The thought flitted across my mind that I might as well not have bothered about paying into the police pension scheme either. Still, the Government would probably be happy that I had selflessly ceased to be a burden on the tax payer.

We were sitting at one of the tables in the centre of the room. The other cops, as I assumed they were, appeared to be a complete mixture of backgrounds. I remembered that my colleagues were recruited, if that is the right term, from all over the place so this was not really a surprise. Chris looked towards a guy who sat by himself a couple of tables away.

'Danny, care to join us?' Danny looked over, got up and ambled across. A tall, strongly-built African-Caribbean, he was in his early forties, I guessed. His head was shaven and his muscular appearance suggested that he liked the inside of a gym. Pulling back a chair that scarcely seemed adequate to hold him, he sat down.

'This is Nick, Danny. I mentioned him last night, thought you might like to team up while he learns the ropes.'

'Hi, Nick.' Danny shook my hand with a grip that suggested significantly more power than it presently exerted. 'Welcome to the machine, mate.'

'Cheers, Danny. Good to meet you.' I still wasn't entirely sure whether we were expected to be pleased to be here but a bit of courtesy never hurts.

'Danny's one of the boss's favourite operators though I keep telling him that makes him the Reaper's Pet,' Chris added helpfully.

'Yeah, right.' Danny grinned, and then turned to me. 'Have you met him yet?'

'Not that I'm aware of,' I told him, glancing at Chris in case she suddenly pointed out that I'd already met the Chief Harbinger of Doom without actually realising it.

'I'll fix that up as soon as we've finished here. He's in his office just now, doubtless plotting the downfall of a significant proportion of the human race.' Put like that, it didn't sound the most enticing of appointments, but I had occasionally had dealings with senior bosses in my earlier existence and had the knack of bowing and scraping to rank down to a fine art. In a disciplined organisation, I had long since realised, rank demands respect. Individuals, on the other hand, have to earn it.

'When's your next job, Danny? You must be due to go out on one aren't you? Nick can see what's involved.' Chris finished her tea and looked into the cup as if willing it to refill by itself. From what I'd experienced so far, I wouldn't have been at all surprised if it had.

'I've got one sorted now. Should be straightforward enough, just an old dear who has somehow made it to one hundred and six despite being bedridden for the last forty years. Want to come along, Nick?'

'I might as well start somewhere.' I told him. I drained my own mug of coffee and noted that mine didn't miraculously replenish itself either. There was a limit to perfection after all.

Chris stood up. 'Come on then, Nick. I'll introduce you to what passes for our Lord and Master round here.'

CHAPTER FOUR

I followed Chris out of the room and into a long corridor, featureless apart from a number of doors leading off it. The general colour scheme was monochrome, graphite floor flecked with metallic silver whilst the walls were mid-grey. Considerable effort had clearly been made to ensure that everything was barely noticeable. No pictures or photographs adorned the sides of the corridor, which appeared to end at a blank wall fifty feet or so away. In keeping with the bland neutrality, the temperature was just right, neither warm nor cool. Strikingly there were none of the other items you would expect to see, radiators, pipes, even fire extinguishers. I suppose there's little need to consider Health and Safety when you're already dead, or maybe some enterprising soul had half-inched them all to sell to those unlucky enough to be queuing up to stoke the infernal flames, if indeed that was one of the options. I made a mental note to ask Chris about that one; I was sure she'd have a view on it.

Chris stopped by the third door down on the right. There was an engraved plastic plate on it which read 'Director of Soul Retrieval'. She opened the door, stepped through it and held it for me, which I took as an indication to follow. I don't know what I'd expected but a small office with a single desk with chair, along with three other easy chairs, would have seemed slightly mundane under the circumstances. I was beginning to think that the Afterlife wasn't all it was cracked up to be. There didn't seem to be a Director of anything sitting in there, unless he or she was shy and had taken to hiding under the table. However, before I could make any offhand comments to Chris along those lines, she indicated one of the easy chairs, upholstered in a nice shade of royal blue. 'Take a seat; I'll see if he's free.'

I sat down as invited and noticed another door which had

been hidden from my view on the way in. Chris knocked, then opened the door and leaned in. 'The gentleman formerly known as PC Nick Kerridge is here now. I thought you'd like to meet him.' There was some barely-distinct muttering from within, something to the effect that my new boss was up to his bloody eyes at the moment and this new bloke would have to wait till he'd finished his call, after all he's not in any rush. Chris acknowledged him a couple of times, with an 'Okay', then closed the door and turned back to me. 'He won't be a minute, Nick, he says he'll be with you as soon as he can.' She then surprised me somewhat by sitting down behind the desk and opening a folder, and then the penny dropped that this might, in fact, be her own office.

'Where do you fit in then, Chris?' I just had to know. A lifetime of professional curiosity was hard to shake off, but I'd always held the view that a good cop was a nosey cop.

'I'm the Director's Staff Officer,' she told me. 'That's a posh title for dogsbody, or gofer, or however you like to put it. It's supposed to be useful career development for me and it makes a change from going back out there dealing with the great undead.' It was an interesting phrase, at which I must have visibly raised an eyebrow. 'It's a term of endearment for our clients,' she explained. 'They aren't dead yet but they've overstayed their welcome back there, so we have to give them some encouragement. They don't count as living because they are illegals.'

It was an interesting concept, I supposed. Of course, I'd never given it much thought previously. I'd come across any number of people who survived accidents or illness by some apparent miracle, usually something that was widely celebrated. On the other hand there were plenty of scumbags who seemed to have nine lives. The ones who really got my goat were the idiot drivers who walked away from the carnage they had caused, often at the cost of the life of some poor innocent sod who happened to get in their way. I'd always thought there was no justice in such cases, but now I was just starting to get the faintest inkling that payback was possible.

So many questions were starting to accumulate in my mind, but notwithstanding my four day lie-down and Chris' assurance that that had helped me acclimatise, I was still trying to get my head round how I could remain interested and focused when I should still be in shock. I asked Chris about this. She glanced up from her file. 'We all cope differently, Nick. Your time had come and subconsciously you knew it. That's why you didn't try to run or hide when it happened. You didn't hesitate when getting out there and trying to deal with your killer. If it hadn't been your time, you wouldn't have found yourself in that situation in the first place. You'd have been off sick that day, or made some decision that put you somewhere else. Because your time was up, now you're here, you won't grieve for what you've lost. You now know that you'll see your family and friends again sometime, and there's no point in tormenting yourself.'

'Is it always that easy? I thought that all those ghosts were tormented spirits that couldn't accept they had passed on.'

'There are a few who don't buy into their new reality,' Chris conceded. 'They won't take it in and just wander round the place moaning and sobbing. Usually they think it's all someone else's fault of course. But then again there are plenty of people for whom that was a way of life in any case. But if you think about it, if most of us didn't accept what happened and we all decided to hang around haunting places, then you wouldn't be able to move for disembodied spirits clanking chains and wailing all hours of the day and night.'

'What if I died before my time, though? Wouldn't that be a bit awkward?'

'Of course, but fortunately it doesn't happen very often. If it does, it's due to someone stuffing up with the paperwork and getting the wrong date. That's all handled by a massive department, in any case. What we always used to see as fate is really the working of some bureaucrat who works out who dies when, then engineers some means of seeing them off. Fate Planning, they call it, probably just because it's such an evocative word. I'm not really sure how they do it but it seems to be effective, most of the time. When it goes wrong and someone escapes their destiny, that's where it causes work for us. But you're right. It does result in some souls being not just tormented but totally pissed off. They need to be carefully and sensitively managed otherwise they go a bit postal and start trashing the place. Usually we manage to get people to put it

28

down to poltergeists but in reality it's not good for the corporate reputation.'

I was glad we cleared up a few more points. I could have made a fortune with all this knowledge back there. But then again, there was probably a very good reason why all this was not common knowledge in the earthly domain. I changed the subject. 'Am I allowed to ask what happened to you then, Chris?'

'Of course. It's not exactly a taboo subject. Most people are quite happy to chat about how they died, after all it's what we've all got in common. We all had to go sometime.' She seemed quite chilled about it all; I wondered if she used to be a cop too. She provided an answer straight away. 'I was in the job, not a brilliant officer but I loved it. In my case, it was nights that did for me. I fell asleep driving home, simple as that. I don't even know what I hit. One moment I was thinking about winding the window down to wake myself up, the next I was in that waiting room where I met you.'

'How did you feel about that?' A career spent trying to sound sincere meant I now had a habit of speaking like a police trainer when someone told me of their own personal hardships.

'Surprised at first, but as it was my time, I accepted it. I had a couple of kids, but was separated from their dad. He would have had to look after them and I've no doubt he did a good job, and the woman I thought of as his floozy was a good step mum, I have no doubt. Like I said, before; if you accept it, it's so much easier. Plus I know I'll see the kids again sometime. They'll probably have kids of their own of course. It's those who can't adapt who are really unhappy, forever trying to go back and keep in contact, or wander round the places they used to love. Haunting places must be miserable. Soul-destroying, you might say.'

'OK thanks for that Chris. At least now I'm not worrying about breaking down inconsolably.' A thought occurred to me. 'Can I go to my own funeral, by the way?'

'If you want, but I wouldn't recommend it. I went to mine and I'd never been more miserable in my life. Seeing my family in bits, whilst I fully accepted that I'd gone, was really difficult. The funeral's for them, not for us. You can't communicate with them because even if they can be sensitive

29

to us, their brains are too overloaded right then. And miserable people singing is just dire.' At least she was honest. 'After an experience like that I can see why some people go for this celebration type of funeral.'

'OK, sounds reasonable, though I think it's a shame really; I'd thought it would be a laugh watching the bosses all saying how much they valued us when to them we were literally just numbers most of the time. Maybe that's a cynical view, but I'm sure you can relate to it.'

'Yes, but you'll soon realise that, in the scheme of things, it doesn't really matter anymore. But it's up to you.'

'No, it's OK, honest. I'll give it a miss.' I moved on. 'Do tell me about our glorious leader, Chris. Who is he, the Grim Reaper?'

'You could say that. You remember I said we used to be called The Office of the Angel of Death?'

'Yes, but I keep wondering if you're winding me up.'

Chris smiled again, her teeth showing white through her lips, so more of a grin. 'No, I was deadly serious. That's who you work for now, if you want to.'

I was starting to get intrigued now, though I was understandably a bit nervous about meeting such an iconic and, I had previously thought, mythical figure as the Reaper, as I still thought of him. Just then, Chris' phone rang. She picked it up. 'Hello. Hi Paul, yes, that's great. I'll bring him in.'

Paul? What kind of name was that for the single most feared figure humanity had ever conjured up?

Chris stood up and went to the door to Grim Paul's office. 'Come on then, Nick. I might not be able to help you meet your Maker, but Paul's the next best thing.'

I followed her into the office. I must admit, I'd expected something a bit more Gothic, black drapes, candles perhaps, stone walls. A cloaked figure standing on a platform commanding me to prostrate myself before him would just complete the picture. The reality was rather mundane. Rosewood office furniture graced the office, along with a nice beige carpet and modern blinds. The Grim Reaper was standing in the middle of his office, holding a golf putter with which he addressed a golf ball, stroking it just wide of the mouth of a waste bin lying on the floor. God help Tiger Woods if the boss decided he needed expert tuition then. He turned to me, smiled and held out his hand to shake mine. 'Hello Nick, old chap. I'm Paul. Glad to have you with us,' he boomed.

Paul was about five foot nine, stout with unkempt hair and a beard that would have suited an Old Testament prophet. He looked just about the least scary person I could remember encountering, especially as he was wearing jeans and a red and blue striped polo shirt. With his stentorian voice he could have earned a living as a Brian Blessed impersonator, should anyone have needed to hire one. The homely image of the office was enhanced by a coat stand in the corner from which hung an anorak and, bizarrely, a sombrero. This caused me to smirk, another failing of mine, as I couldn't take this scene totally seriously. Paul saw this, checked my line of vision and explained loudly. 'Ahh, the sombrero, yes. Nice conversation piece that and just something I like to put on to cheer the staff up when they need a laugh. We're long enough dead so we might as well enjoy ourselves.' He guffawed heartily. This was a refreshing attitude to the hereafter, I thought.

'You're not quite what I expected, if you don't mind me saying so, Paul.'

'What were you expecting? I'm desk-bound most of the time and don't get out anything like as much as I used to. Sometimes when it's quiet I can pop along with you to keep my hand in. But don't see it as me looking over your shoulder.'

'What will I be doing, dare I ask?'

'I don't know if Chris explained to you, though I expect she'll have made a start. Most people, when their time is up, come along with us without kicking up too much of a fuss. Sometimes, though, the number-crunchers in Life Expiry overlook the fact that they are due to turn up their toes so they go overdue. Other times, whoever is tasked with bringing them over to this side is half-asleep and they have a miraculous escape. That's a pain in the backside as well.'

'And then there are all those bloody sanctimonious, meddling do-gooders and busy-bodies who think they were put on Earth to save lives', Paul continued. 'You know, the medical people, even the blasted Samaritans. They just can't leave well alone, can they? Play havoc with my bloody figures, they do. Every life they claim to save is an overstayer we have to go and fetch back', he went on. I wondered if his intention had been to welcome or simply harangue me.

'In any case, the system gets cluttered up because the renegades shouldn't still be there and it upsets the proper order of things. It can have a knock-on effect as well because they still interact with those who are legitimately alive when really they shouldn't be there. So we get a notification and have to intervene. That's where you and your colleagues come in. You'll go and fetch them. You need to escort them because otherwise they have a tendency to wander off as, by their very nature, they're somewhat reluctant to give up the ghost. You do your research, see how they can be despatched, then bring them through to the reception point. How you despatch them is up to you, but it is a question of making it look convincing. If it's something really off the wall it makes people wonder what's going on, then they start to worry. Nice and unobtrusive, that's how I like us to work. We absolutely mustn't give the game away. Keep 'em guessing, that kind of thing.'

'Do I get the hooded cloak and big long scythe thing? My hands look normal, not nearly bony enough.'

'Don't worry, we've moved with the times. You wear what you're comfortable with. Unless you choose otherwise, none of your clients will see you until they've come through to this side, with your help of course. They'll be surprised enough as it is, without you pointing at them and scowling from some bloody great big black hoodie. It's casual dress here the whole time. You can even wear a football shirt if you like. If that's your thing, though, I'd prefer it if you didn't wear a United strip. I hate them; they're in league with Satan which is why they've won so much recently. I'm biased though, as I used to support Arsenal. Not what most people would associate with the Grim Reaper of course. I used to think about turning up at Old Trafford some time when Man United played Arsenal, just to stand on the touchline in something like the gear you described, pointing at their manager. That would've given the moaning old git something to complain about.'

'That sounds reasonable enough. So why does death get such a bad press? I mean, why spend all that time and effort scaring us all witless? Wouldn't everybody be happier if they knew the next life really was something to look forward to?'

'There are a couple of reasons, Nick. We don't do a lot of interaction with the living, so most of the noise comes from all those religions. Basically they get off on manipulating people and it helps them enormously if they can frighten them into compliance. They're all a bunch of control freaks when it comes down to it. The other thing is that we really have to encourage people to stay alive till it's their right time. If they knew it was so good over here the suicide rate would go through the roof and nobody would stay there a moment longer than they had to. That's why most of the methods of transition are so unpalatable. No one ever dies of anything nice, because we need to close death off as an attractive option. For the same reason we don't want the living to know there really is life afterwards, as a lot would put up with the nasty stuff involved in transition just to get here early as well. Anyway, forget about all the negative imagery from before. It serves a purpose. You're probably finding that being dead isn't exactly what you expected either.' I thought that was something of an understatement.

'Do we go through all that rigmarole back there for a reason?' I had to admit I was finding this conversation fascinating.

'Yes. It was a start. You were there to learn and develop, same as why you are here, but with a lot of constraints. You needed to learn about boundaries, physical as well as moral. What some people called The Seven Deadly Sins were about learning ethical limits. Some learned better and faster than others. Those who didn't make the grade in their allotted time go to the Redevelopment Units until they can show the necessary respect for others. In some cases even that isn't sufficient and they have to be back-classed. Reincarnation, you'll know it as...' Paul tailed off, and went to his desk, picking up a manilla folder. 'You did OK, according to your file. You acted sensibly and responsibly, most of the time anyway.'

'I did a few things I'm ashamed off, especially now it's too late to do anything about it.' I considered I might at least be honest, as Paul doubtless knew all about me in any case.

33

'You've hit the nail on the head there, old son. No one's perfect and mistakes are expected. How can you learn otherwise? The main thing is you felt remorse when you stuffed up; that's what it was all about.'

Something else just dawned on me. 'Everything here seems so real. I can feel stuff, I thought I'd pass right through it. And we shook hands too.'

'It's because we are in the same dimension. Go back there, and you will be doing soon, and you'll be invisible, able to pass through material stuff, and all that. Unless of course there's a need to interact but we'll introduce you to that in good time.'

'Oh right. Incidentally, why me? Aren't there thousands of us arriving here every day?'

'You were a cop, Nick. You can handle this line of work; you're disciplined, professional and you're not squeamish. We like cops and that kind of person, ideally those who came to us before they got too jaded. Not the bad apples, obviously, though there aren't too many of those, despite what the papers would have you believe. Most of the collectors were still working immediately before they came over. You've still got a hunger for the work, so I'm sure you'll do us a good job.'

'I hadn't planned on retiring just yet, and this career move was something of a surprise. Were we all killed in the line of duty? I hadn't realised the job was so bloody dangerous!'

'It wasn't always necessarily in the line of duty, Nick, no. You'll have spoken to Chris so you'll know she had an accident. Then there's illness as well. Plus you have to bear in mind we recruit from all over the place. You can imagine that in some parts of the world your life expectancy as a cop isn't great. But on that note, you'll mostly be working in areas you are familiar with; we find it's best that way.'

'How many of us are there?'

'Not as many as you might think. We don't need to provide 24/7 cover, and you're only called in to deal with the really stubborn cases. Chris will show you to the main office. You work from there. It's easy going. You pick up your files, talk it through with whoever you're teamed up with, go and sort it all out, bring the client back to the Reception Unit, and the job's sorted. Then you go home. Or to the bar if you prefer.'

'Does that mean we have a duty roster?'

'Good grief, no. There's no need. There's no pressure on you to be here at any particular time as you don't get paid.' That was something that hadn't even occurred to me. Paul continued. 'We don't deal in money here. You'll find that your reasonable needs are all met, and if what you think you want isn't reasonable, you probably don't actually need it anyway.'

Paul leafed through the folder, which had my name in felt tip on the cover. 'No major issues, I see.' Forty-eight years of my life on Earth were summed up in five words. He moved on. 'All I expect is that you do what I ask and stick to the rules. Remember they are there for a purpose. In return, you get a nice existence here and we also support you with your spiritual development, which is why we're all here. There's no rank structure, unlike in your previous service. You answer to me, and Chris looks after all the admin. Any questions?'

'If I'm just allowed to ask as I go along, that would suit me fine. I presume there's no particular rush? Plus I would imagine you are quite busy.'

'There's plenty of time Nick, and if you feel like asking anything when I'm not around then I'm sure Chris will talk you even further beyond death if you give her half a chance. As for being busy, yes, I've usually got plenty to keep me occupied. Picking up these death-shy overstayers takes a bit of organising. These things don't arrange themselves you know. And as you can imagine I have to attend endless bloody meetings too. Four of them I had yesterday! I mean what is the bloody point of all these meetings if you spend your entire time sitting around talking instead of doing anything half way useful.' The volume had gone up again as Paul's sudden rant against pointless meetings got into full flow. I wondered if his hitherto calm and amenable manner concealed anger management issues or even a propensity for excited delirium. He wouldn't be the first senior manager suffer from those, in my experience.

'Sounds like where I used to work,' I told him. 'Our bosses were never out of them. They changed things just for the sake of something to do, I used to think.'

'Well I'm trying to change things,' Paul went on, loudly. 'Some of these committees and reviews are necessary I grant you. The population of Earth keeps rising exponentially and the average human lifespan, whilst it is increasing, does so at nothing like the same rate. So we've got a hell of a lot more souls to bring in each year. At the same time the old levellers like disease and, to a lesser extent, famine, have been rendered less effective. So that's two of the Four Horsemen of the Apocalypse who won't be gracing the winners' enclosure.

That's what comes of allowing people to explore and experiment back there. They learn a lot and build on that, so they learn even more. They start off solving a lot of the more pressing issues, like starving to death every winter if you don't learn to produce and starve food. Before you know where you are, they've worked out a structure for the atom and a structure for the universe. They don't actually know that either of them exist, but they've built some fairly convincing models of what they think they are like. The thing is, they believe they know how everything happens, but no one still has the faintest idea why. And we're certainly not going to tell them! Even war, which was spectacularly successful for keeping the flow going, especially in the Twentieth Century, is far more limited now. So we've continually got to innovate.

'The Termination Processes Committee has its work cut out finding ways of bringing new technology into the equation. Humanity comes up with some great breakthrough, like nuclear power, and we have to see how we can use it. We've been running a small pilot project with nuclear power stations to see if they can bring in manageable numbers. Nuclear weapons were a good laugh but if we started using them the numbers generated would overwhelm us as all sides would get in on the act. It's all a question of capacity.'

'Does that mean there are limits?'

'Yes of course. The current population of earth is about seven billion, give or take a few million. And let's assume for the sake of argument that the average lifespan of a human, as set down in the Bible, is seventy years. That gives us one hundred million souls a year to process. You might have thought illegal immigration was a contentious issue. Just think what we've got to deal with. We can predict our souls' arrivals with a reasonable degree of certainty, but if we suddenly had a nuclear holocaust we'd easily double that and it would take forever and a day to sort it out. So the Inbound Souls Resourcing Committee is yet another one for me to attend.'

'Where do you fit everybody? The place is hardly overcrowded from what I've seen.'

'You're no longer in a physical dimension, don't forget. We're all ethereal now. Remember that old philosophical question about how many angels could dance on the head of a pin? You're in that territory now.' Paul stood up. 'I could bang on about that for ages but I'd better press on. If you're interested I'll tell you more about it later. I've not even mentioned the Post-Mortem Inspectorate Board yet. The bane of my life, they are. At least they would be if I was alive.'

I shook the Grim Reaper's hand again and left him to his putting.

Chris had evidently left the room at some point during my meeting with Paul, and was sitting at her desk. She looked up and smiled. 'OK, Nick? Not so bad for everybody's worst nightmare, is he?'

'Is he always like that or does he have a dark side?'

'No, he's fine, though a bit loud sometimes. I've heard that speech no end of times. If you really piss him off then he'll let you know. It's his singing that's really difficult to stand.' I have to say that I would put pissing off the Angel of Death pretty far down my list of 'Things I Would Like to Try', though, of course, already being dead would put me at less of a disadvantage at the outset. Chris went on. 'Anyway, Danny will be picking you up in a couple of minutes. You can go on a retrieval with him. It'll be good for you.'

CHAPTER FIVE

'Come on then, Nick, we'll get started.' Danny towered over me as I slouched in an easy chair opposite Chris' desk. An inch short of six feet tall, thick set and finely-honed from the gym, if such a thing existed here, my new colleague was an imposing character. Leaving Chris to get on with her day job in peace, I followed him out of the office. He led me along another bland and featureless corridor. I was beginning to think there might be a bright future awaiting me as an interior designer as no one else seemed to be bothered about making the buildings remotely interesting or distinctive.

Opening an otherwise unremarkable door, Danny ushered me into a large office. Like the canteen, it was instantly familiar to me, as I think it would be to any cop. Tables were arranged in double lines, with computers and phones cluttering their tops. A number of trees had selflessly given their lives, either this existence or from last time round, in order to provide the necessary quantity of paper to keep the place topped up. I could have been in any police station I'd ever visited.

One wall was dominated by a line of pin-boards, which were now providing a home for much of the paperwork. Memos, I suspected; it was not necessary to read them to verify this; a header, two or three paragraphs and a scrawled signature marked various pieces of paper out as bearing edicts from on high. How many, I wondered, were about work and how many about the Golf Section, given the Grim Reaper's enthusiasm for the sport? I made a mental note to glance at them later. I was sure they'd still be there when I got back.

Of significantly greater interest was the display of mug shots arranged in an apparent hierarchy on the boards in the central area of the wall. Marked 'Priority Targets', many of these faces were eerily familiar. I was momentarily taken aback at the individuals concerned, until I reminded myself that I was no longer working from a divisional traffic office. This place easily outstripped even New Scotland Yard as a nerve centre for operations involving the most verminous members of the human race. Robert Mugabe and a clutch of other despots and mass-murderers all featured prominently. Pride of place went, perhaps unsurprisingly, to Osama bin Laden, though I was somewhat amused to see that someone had marked a thick 'X' in red marker pen across his features. A date with ballpoint pen comments '*Neil and Raj were here*' in one hand and '*Jammy bastards*' as an alternative viewpoint, indicated a degree of local pride and rivalry along with the suggestion that his demise might not have been down to US Special Forces after all. Big League stuff indeed.

For now, I had stopped asking too many questions. Just accept it all, I thought. There would be plenty of time to satisfy my curiosity later, I was quite sure. No one else in the office seemed particularly star-struck so in all likelihood this became normal business. Danny sat down at one particular desk, told me to grab another chair and bring it over. Sitting next to him, I wondered if he was going to fire up the computer but he just opened his top drawer and pulled out yet another manilla folder. 'Elizabeth Roberts', in the ubiquitous black marker, suggested that this would tell us all we needed to know.

Danny handed the folder to me. 'Have a quick look, mate, and tell me what this means to you.' Opening the covers revealed a sheaf of papers, the title page bearing a colour photograph of an extremely elderly female. She was much older than even the most geriatric wrongdoer I had previously encountered, but then again, at the age of one hundred and six, she would take some beating. I reminded myself that she was not a criminal, at least in the conventional sense, but she was wanted by us nonetheless.

Along with her name, last known address and date of birth, was another entry marked '*Scheduled transfer date*', this being 28th May 1991. Becoming more aware of the euphemisms endemic in this organisation, I deduced that this referred to the date of Liz's original intended appointment with Paul the Grim Golfer. Somehow she had managed to buck the system for more than twenty years, which was quite impressive to my mind.

The bulk of the paperwork was a running log and like most such police documents, you had to start at the back and read forward.

Initially, it appeared that no one was too exercised about Elizabeth's impromptu spell of overtime, as most of the early entries were simply notes stating '*Missed Transfer date – to be monitored*' and similar such bureaucratic comments. Eventually, after monitoring her extra time gallivanting for fifteen years or so, someone appeared to wake up to her situation. '*This soul is well overdue. I know she's not causing anybody any harm but she shouldn't be allowed to get away with it,*' read one acerbic entry. It appeared that even avenging angels could get out of bed on the wrong side. This impression was reinforced a couple of pages later by another comment. '*She's reached her century, what are you waiting for? Paul says (loudly) get a bloody grip*'.

The latter comment, invoking the name of our leader, appeared to have stirred up a flurry of back-covering and blame reassignment. Entry after entry explained why it was not possible for the writer at that particular time to locate this woman, go back to fetch her, fit her into the Reception Unit's busy schedule and so on. The usual myriad reasons for doing nothing when it would probably have been quicker to go and get the job sorted. I was only surprised that no one had claimed that Elizabeth was believed to be dead. That excuse wouldn't wash here.

The upshot of this litany of woeful inaction was that eventually the job wound up with Danny. 'They just can't be bothered a lot of the time. There's always a rush when it's a juicy shout but an old biddy just doesn't get them excited,' he told me when I queried why it had been so difficult to track down a bedridden centenarian.

I worked my way through the file, eventually reaching the front. We appeared to be institutionally incapable of implementing procedures with even the faintest suggestion of common sense, and this was so deeply ingrained that it extended through to the Afterlife. For the life of me, I could not see how this particular collection could be so difficult.

'It says here she's been in a nursing home for twelve years, it's got the address here, room number and everything. I

40

presume we can get in there OK?' I commented.

Danny grinned. 'Piece of cake, mate. We can be in and out before you know it. Let's go to the Reception Unit, then we can fetch her in.' Standing up, he took the front sheet and ran off a photocopy which he folded and put in his shirt pocket. Collecting the folder, he walked to the door, with me following a few paces behind, feeling like the Sorcerer's Apprentice.

The Reception Unit was a large room, bare of furniture except for a large fixed counter, its top about chest height. Other, smaller, rooms led off from the main area.

Behind the desk stood a thickset man with short grey hair and a moustache, who had the bearing and manner of a supervisor. He was addressing a dishevelled man, scrawny and with straggly unkempt hair to his collar, who stood in front of the desk with his head bowed staring at the floor. Probably in his late thirties although he could easily have been a few years either way, the scruffy bloke looked as if he had been living rough for a while. His shirt and trousers had seen much better days which must have been some time in the past.

Two other men were also present. One lounged against a blue metal door, as if to stop their companion turning round and legging it, whilst the other was leaning with his arms folded, on the desk. Danny greeted them in passing as we found a place to stand unobtrusively. 'William and Pete, they've just collected this bloke and are booking him in,' he explained. The scene had all the hallmarks of a custody office with a scumbag being produced to the sergeant.

'You're five months overdue, son,' the Reception officer (or whatever title he enjoyed) was telling the scruffy bloke. 'You were supposed to catch pneumonia, it says here, and because you were living on the streets it should have done for you.'

'Not my fault,' mumbled the recently-deceased tramp. 'I felt like death warmed up and took myself off to the hospital. I think they got fed up with me when I decided to camp out in their boiler house so they found me a bed.'

'Well, you'll be pleased to know that your dossing days are over now. There's no homelessness here. We've got a nice warm cell for you till we get you sorted. These two helpful chaps will have a chat with you and then we'll see where we go from there.'

'Am I really dead? That's what these two told me but I reckon they're having a laugh.'

'You certainly are, mate' the supervisor said. 'You are as dead as the proverbial dodo. Welcome to the next world.' He addressed the collector across the desk. 'Cell five, Pete, then you can get him interviewed.' Pete escorted his detainee away.

The main room now being clear, Danny introduced the supervisor as Nigel. Despite being the supervisor, Nigel wore no uniform, favouring a tropical shirt and khaki shorts, detracting from what might otherwise have been a more formal appearance.

Danny gave Nigel the details, helpfully leaving him a photocopy of Elizabeth's file front sheet. There was some discussion about how she might have avoided her transfer for so long, then Nigel appeared satisfied.

'Better get out there and don't come back without her. I'll look forward to the introduction when you fetch her in,' he told Danny.

I was wondering, idly, how we would get back to the old place. Would we, I speculated, beam down like the Archangel Gabriel in some idealised Christmas film? The answer was far more prosaic. Danny went to the blue metal door previously leant against by William, at which Nigel pressed a button. I followed Danny through it into a holding cell, which had another metal door, dirty grey this time against a side wall. The internal door clanged shut and I heard a faint buzz at which Danny pushed the outer door. It led to the outside world and we walked back into the old world.

The door, bare metal on the outside and covered in graffiti, opened into a narrow alleyway, about six feet wide, with a very high stone wall topped by dense foliage. As we exited we nearly collided with a couple strolling arm in arm along the alley, engrossed in each other until we nearly knocked them flying. Danny apologised profusely, to which they smiled an acknowledgment and continued on their way.

'Good job I had switched to being visible otherwise they'd have been really confused by a door opening entirely by itself.' Danny commented. 'Useful tip number one for travelling back here. They'll think no more of it.'

'I'd better do the same then, otherwise folks will think you're talking to yourself.' I thought hard about being on foot patrol and was gratified whenever a pedestrian made eye contact and walked around me. They could obviously see me so the system worked.

'Where are we going?' I enquired, almost as an afterthought.

'The Penarth Grange Nursing Home, if this file is to be believed.' Danny glanced inside briefly.

'According to Chris, we can catch a number 89A or B bus on the hour from Customhouse Street.' He paused to consult his map. 'Which is about quarter of a mile this way. We're in Cardiff, if you were wondering. Queen Street station is just up there, about two hundred yards, in case you want to catch a train instead.'

I had indeed wondered where we were going. 'Cardiff? I thought when you died you went to Heaven, not bloody Cardiff. An eternity of wind and sodding rain? Stuffing great.'

'Yeah, maybe not what you were anticipating. Most of my work is in the South West UK Transference Region as it's now known. SWUKTR, pronounced 'Swuckter' by those in the know. Anyway, Paul prefers us to work where we know if possible. It saves a lot of messing around, getting lost, that kind of thing. Although of course, being the boss, he could post us anywhere he chooses. If he had taken a dislike to you, you'd have wound up somewhere hot, fetid and so full of stiffs-in-waiting you wouldn't know what day it was. He used to favour Baghdad as a punishment posting though lately Syria seems to be the destination of choice for anyone who he thinks is a bit above themselves.'

I hadn't visited Cardiff for a while, but the old place hadn't changed much. The thought passed through my mind that I'd once told someone I wouldn't be seen dead there after I left. I certainly got that one wrong.

We strolled through Cardiff, skirting the city centre itself as we headed in the general direction of the main railway station. Finding the appropriate bus stop, we stood apart from the rest of the short queue for the 89A which was due next.

'What do we do about bus fare? Aren't we cash-free or

something? Or did Paul issue you with a debit card? I can't somehow see him going for the flexible friend approach.'

'You are forgetting one thing, my friend.' Danny was grinning now, delighted to have all the aces in this particular game, so new to me. 'Think invisible. We just stroll onto the bus. If you're invisible you can walk through the doors if you want to, if they're closed that is. It's amazing what the mind can accomplish when it's unfettered by physical constraints. You can walk through the door but still sit on the bus seat and not fall through the floor. No, I don't know how it works either, before you ask, which I know you want to.'

'One thing at a time,' I responded. 'I'm still trying to get the hang of the 'Now you see me, now you don't' stuff without making a pillock of myself by walking into a bloody door in front of a busload of punters.'

'Fair enough, but it really won't take you that long, mate.' I was glad Danny was confident about this. It was still hard to remind myself that, as far as I was aware, I'd only been dead for a few days. Until, that was, I saw an old copy of the Daily Mail apparently discarded by another passenger. '*In Cold Blood*' the headline would doubtless have screamed had it had the gift of speech. A sub-heading added '*Police officer shot dead by mystery gunman. Police admit to being 'baffled'.*' That my colleagues were indeed baffled was glaringly obvious to me but, even though I had actually been there, I was hardly in a position to shed light on the identity of the 'mystery gunman'.

The force Press Office had kindly provided my official mug shot, the same one that was on my warrant card, and a brief biography. '*PC Nick Kerridge, 48, was a member of Western Division Roads Policing Unit with twenty-two years' service. His divisional commander, Chief Superintendent Alan Bridgford, described PC Kerridge as 'a highly competent and well-regarded officer who will be sadly missed by all his colleagues in Western Division.'* That was nice then, though I'd personally not had too many dealings with the aforementioned Mr. Bridgford. However, I imagined that he would have been briefed by my line management and at least he'd made an effort.

The article added that my ex-wife, Helen, was being

consoled by family and friends. I should think that 'consoled' was a massive overstatement given the acrimonious divorce she had dragged me through, and that if she was distraught about anything, it was that the two years' salary my nearest and dearest were entitled to as death-in-service benefit would now go to my brother rather than her. I was sufficiently cynical to know that Helen would play an Oscar-winning part of the grieving widow, notwithstanding the fact that we couldn't stand the sight of each other. Thankfully we had never had any children, something I had always regretted but now, at least, there were none to be bereft at the loss of their loving father.

I was focusing mostly on the personal aspect of the Mail's front page article, but took the time to skim-read the rest of the piece, such as it was. Early days yet, naturally enough, and there was no sign of the afore-mentioned mystery gunman or his car, which, I had anticipated, would by now have been found burnt out a few miles away, smouldering on a patch of open land. I wondered if I would ever find out if this particular murder-mystery would be solved.

My musing was terminated by the appearance of the bus, a couple of minutes after its scheduled time of eleven o'clock. Following Danny's advice, I thought invisible and the driver didn't give us so much as a glance as we slipped onto his bus at the end of the queue.

A bus ride is a bus ride, whether you are alive or dead, and the twenty-five minute run to the centre of Penarth, five miles or so outside Cardiff, was as mundane now as I was sure it would have been in my previous life. At least I had the opportunity to come back, though, and I did wonder how the majority of souls coped, those who I realised probably had no opportunity to return to turn their old haunts into new ones.

Penarth Grange Nursing Home, it turned out, was a large house in North Park Road. Handy for the town centre and the seafront, neither of which I suspected Lizzie had visited in recent years, the building looked like it had previously been two semi-detached dwellings. Light grey stone in construction, with white UPVC window frames, possibly a 'buy one, get one free' deal from a double-glazing company, the house sat in small but adequate grounds behind a neatly-clipped hedge which shielded the ground floor from the tree-lined road. Danny led the way as we walked up the very narrow tarmac drive. Turning right and passing some large windows we came to the front door, made of weather-stained wood with a coach lamp on either side of the door-frame. A venerable doorbell waited hopefully for a visitor to press it. In our case it waited in vain, as Danny had no intention of announcing our arrival.

'Time you learnt to walk through what you have previously thought of as solid objects,' he told me. 'It's very straightforward. Think invisible and just imagine an empty space behind the door, or wall, or whatever. Then walk into that space. Trust me, it works. Observe the master...' With that he seemed to be absorbed by the door vanishing, as it were, into thin air. A momentary pause and he reappeared just as suddenly, walking through the wood.

'Your turn now, Nick. Just visualise what you think is behind it. If it helps, it's an entrance hall with some stairs on the right hand side. There's no one watching so if you bang into the door you won't look a prat. Except to me,' he added encouragingly.

I fixed in my mind the image Danny had suggested, ignoring the big brown door between me and my imagined destination. Three steps and I was inside, as simple as that. The fact that the entrance hall was completely different from how I'd thought seemed to have made no difference. Turning round, I thought of the front garden, took a couple of steps forward and I was on the doorstep looking at Danny's grinning face.

'Simple isn't it?' he said. 'Now you're an expert. Let's go inside and have a ratch around, see if we can find Elizabeth.'

I followed Danny through the door, literally, and stepped back into the entrance hall. I could hear voices from a room leading off the main passageway so went forward to the doorway. By sidling up to an open door, very quickly putting your head round it and immediately withdrawing it again you could gain a good idea of what was in the room before anyone inside could react. Called a 'head flash' in the trade, it was an invaluable technique they taught on the Basic Authorised Firearms Officer Course, at least when I'd been on mine. This time, the head flash revealed a large lounge occupied by six or seven elderly people sitting in armchairs and a sofa. There was a coffee table in the centre of the room, and a television which was switched off. No one had noticed me, and then it dawned on me that I was still invisible so could have wandered in and stood on the coffee table without attracting attention.

'Remind me what she looks like,' I said to Danny, who handed me the file front sheet with our girl's photograph. It was clear that she had not been in the front room as the occupants all looked at least twenty years younger. Then again, at one hundred and six years old she probably felt that she was entitled to a lie in. I mentioned this to Danny, who took the sheet back and had another look.

'We need to check which room she's in now. The file says it's number eight but we'd better confirm that or else, knowing our luck, we'll get the wrong person and Paul will probably not see the funny side this time round.' There was no register to be seen in the entrance hall, but then people wouldn't tend to book themselves in and out of the establishment with any degree of regularity.

I walked further along the passageway, past the lounge with its residents who were still oblivious to our presence. A telephone rang behind one closed door so I walked straight through. This was turning out to be a very handy trick, I thought. I was in a small office, looking at a desk and chair. Sitting on the latter was a middle-aged woman, by now engaged in an earnest telephone conversation. She did not look up as I stood insubstantially in front of her. Behind the desk was a whiteboard with a list of room numbers, printed in permanent marker. A name was written alongside each number; I noted that a dry-wipe pen had been used for these suggesting that this was not seen as a permanent arrangement. There was no Elizabeth Roberts, though there was a Lizzie, and she was in Room Six. I strolled through the wall this time, just to see if my new-found skill only applied to doors. It worked fine. 'Smartarse,' was Danny's response when I materialised in the passageway.

'Good job we checked. She's in Room Six,' I told him.

'All we need to do now is find out where that is,' Danny replied.

'Well it's no use asking me, I'm new here myself.' I'd

always been prone to sarcasm but if I thought Danny would take offence I was reassured by his broad grin.

'You and me both, mate. We'll find it. Upstairs might be a good place to start.'

We climbed the stairs to find another corridor running the length of the house. Corridors, I thought, were becoming something of a regular feature of my new existence. We were more or less in the middle. It didn't take long to find Room Six. Once again the door was closed but I was getting used to this by now. The room was small, and in a domestic house it would have been adequate for a child. A window overlooked the back garden whilst in the room was a single bed, armchair, small wardrobe and a sink. Elizabeth, and she certainly looked like our lady, lay in the bed, dozing in the warm sunshine that streamed through the window.

'Are you happy this is her?' I didn't want to stuff up on my first job. Danny was looking at some medical notes he had found on a clipboard lying on the armchair.

'These notes have got her name on them, the room is allocated to her and she looks like the photo. Good enough for me.' Danny sounded convinced. 'She's asleep by the looks of it; our collections don't get much more straightforward than this.'

'What do you do now?' I was feeling a sense of dread. My career had been spent saving lives and dealing with the traumatic aftermath when I wasn't been successful. There are times when you have to carry out unpleasant tasks, I had experienced those. But the prospect of taking life appalled me, especially from a very vulnerable and seemingly innocent old lady. I wondered if I was actually cut out for my new role.

'Watch and learn, my eager apprentice. We can use any number of techniques but there's no need to go over the top this time. The lady deserves some sensitivity and respect.' Danny walked to the side of the bed and gently placed his hand over her mouth whilst pinching her nostrils with his thumb and forefinger. It didn't take long as she had little strength with which to put up a fight. She stirred briefly as if having a bad dream then, after a minute or so, went limp. When Danny removed his hand from her mouth she lay still, her mouth open.

A much younger woman climbed off the bed having, it seemed, occupied the same space as the old lady in the bed. Dressed in a white full-length nightdress, she was about five feet six tall, slim and had long chestnut hair. She appeared to be in the first flush of adulthood, early twenties or thereabouts.

'Who are you?' She seemed only mildly taken aback to find two strange blokes standing by her bed.

'I'm Danny, this is Nick. We've come to fetch you, Elizabeth. You're a bit late.'

'Late for what? And please don't call me Elizabeth, I always prefer Lizzie.'

'You are late for the next world, Lizzie. Which is where we are taking you. You've just passed on, or however you would like us to phrase it.'

'Am I dead or am I dreaming?'

'Look at the bed, Lizzie. That's the old you. The real you is the one standing in front of us.'

Lizzie turned round and gasped. 'My god!' She turned back to us, her face crumpled and she started to cry. 'I don't want to be dead, I've been terrified of this all my life. What's going to happen now?'

Danny could be surprisingly compassionate. He put a hand on each of her shoulders and looked into her eyes. 'We've all been through this, Lizzie, and it's nowhere near as bad as you might think.'

Lizzie sniffed, wiped her eyes, and looked back at Danny. 'Who are you two, by the way?'

'We came to get you, and take you to where you were supposed to be twenty years ago,' he told her. 'I mentioned you were late. Now we have to make sure you don't wander off. We can't have you traipsing round Penarth for all eternity like a lost soul, can we? That's literally what you would be, in fact. Now relax, close your eyes, hold on to my arm and follow me.'

Danny led Lizzie straight through the door. It occurred to me that a door opening and closing might have attracted unwanted attention. 'Come on folks, let's get our taxi.'

'Taxi?' I muttered to him. 'What's that all about?'

'When did you last take a prisoner into custody on the bus? It's like calling up a van for transport. I shouted it up while

49

you were faffing around mingling with the masonry. It'll be outside.'

We walked invisibly back along the corridor, down the stairs and out through the closed door. The chatter from the lounge continued unabated. How long, I wondered, would it be before anyone went to check on Lizzie?

There was a black Ford Galaxy parked outside the gate. It definitely hadn't been there when we went in. Danny opened the rear door and ushered Lizzie inside, following her. In the absence of specific instructions I got into the front.

'Alright, Danny?' I recognised the driver as William who had presumably left the late and probably unlamented tramp I'd seen earlier to the tender mercies of Pete.

'Yeah, no problems mate. Lizzie's as good as gold, aren't you, love?'

Lizzie had, up till now, been very quiet since the initial shock of dying. 'I try not to cause any fuss.' She spoke softly in response to Danny's somewhat rhetorical question. Having been in the same situation so recently, I felt a degree of empathy with her, though in my case I hadn't had a reception committee, or indeed a taxi laid on for me.

Lizzie seemed to blossom as she gradually came to terms with what had happened and she was soon bending Danny's ear. In response, Danny was turning on the charm so I left them to it. Danny had an easy manner that, on this occasion, helped to keep Lizzie relaxed. It was different to being sarcastic and winding up prisoners, which used to be so enjoyable when taking them into custody before. I left them to it, choosing instead to look out of the window and enjoy the sights of the Cardiff suburbs.

'How're you finding things?' William interrupted my thoughts.

'OK mate, you know what it's like. There's plenty to get used to, such as being here in the first place. It was all rather sudden.'

'Think of it as a new posting. You'll be used to those, I expect. You miss your old mates of course but if you think positive you soon fit into your new team.'

'Yeah, good analogy. The leaving do was pretty shite though in my case.'

William laughed. 'It's so often the way, particularly with those of us here. What happened to you?'

'Some bastard with a sawn-off took a dislike to me. God knows why, we'd met a few times before but I didn't think I'd ever given him cause to dislike me that much. I just wanted a chat with him about what he was up to.'

'I'd always expected something like that,' William grinned. 'Eight years on a firearms team, sieges, spontaneous and pre-planned jobs. I even got a commendation for disarming a psycho with a machete while I was unarmed. I thought I was immortal. Till I got run over on my fucking day off. It just goes to show, you never know the moment, do you?'

'I bet that pissed you off!'

'Oh, it did, big style. Serves me right though. I was texting my girlfriend while I crossed the road. They never put that in the bloody Green Cross Code.'

'Maybe your relatives can sue the Department for Transport for that particular oversight,' I suggested.

'I'm sure they'll have tried. My ex was into all that 'Where there's a blame, there's a claim' crap. I'd changed my will a few months earlier, so my girlfriend got my life insurance and I'd told work she was my beneficiary.' William laughed. 'My ex-missus wouldn't have been best pleased to put it mildly so I should think she'd have sued anything that moved. Tough shit.'

Another successful police marriage, I thought. At least I wasn't alone in that regard.

William changed the subject as we drove through the city centre. 'Are you joining our team? Danny says you're fairly local.'

'No one's said yet. The boss mentioned something about working where you know, and Chris stuck me with Danny so I could learn the ropes. I'm not fussed. I worked in the South West so I know South Wales and Bristol of old, which is one thing I suppose. At the end of the day I'll go where I'm told. You know how it is.'

William grunted something incoherent that I imagined signified his agreement. We made our way past Cardiff International Arena then turned into a fenced car park. Getting out of the car, I recognised the alleyway so knew we were near the door to the Afterlife. We walked up to the graffiti-covered door. Danny knocked rhythmically, then a buzzer sounded faintly and he pulled the door towards us. He ushered Lizzie in, almost casually blocking any last-minute escape route with his heavily-muscled arm. William and I followed, the door closing softly by itself. Nigel was still in situ behind his desk, evidently preoccupied with some document or other. Some sort of celestial custody record, I imagined. Having encountered numerous custody sergeants in my previous incarnation, it wouldn't have surprised me if he'd been completing a crossword, writing a letter or filing a tax return from some lucrative spare-time activity. In my experience it was always extremely rare for a custody sergeant to be ready when you arrived, eager to get another misguided client booked into the judicial process. As if on cue, he glanced up. 'I'll be with you in a couple of minutes,' he told us, before losing himself once again in his task.

Lizzie was, by now, a lot happier than she had been earlier and was chatting away to Danny who, to give him credit, was bearing the aural onslaught with admirable fortitude. Arms folded she was leaning back against the wall, her white nightgown making her look almost virginal. Possibly that was why Danny was paying her close attention. He had, up till now, largely kept his own counsel so I knew very little about him. Maybe I should make a bit of an effort to get to know my colleagues, I decided.

'Over here now, love.' Eventually through with whatever had been keeping him from us, Nigel looked at Lizzie. His manner was professional, if such an attribute was appropriate in this dimension, but also gentle. 'Who have you brought me today, Danny?'

Stepping up to the desk, Lizzie looked nervous again, her carefree demeanour disappearing as suddenly as it had materialised. Danny handed his folder to Nigel. 'Elizabeth Roberts, though in fact she prefers to be called Lizzie. Twenty years overdue though I have to say she's been good as gold with us. I'll cancel her on the Late List as soon as we're done here.'

'OK, thanks, Danny. Right, Lizzie, I'll get you booked in and then these nice gentlemen will have a quick chat and we'll see where we go from there.'

The booking-in procedure was straightforward, pretty similar to custody in fact, though with a few twists. 'Date of death' would have made our blood run cold back on earth, especially in the context of the custody suite, but here it replaced the more familiar date of birth. It was far more relevant of course. There was no need, apparently, to search the new arrivals either. The old saying 'You can't take it with you' was absolutely correct, so no one had to go through the rigmarole of detailing the personal detritus of the usual earthly criminal detainee, the coins pulled from grubby tracksuit pockets, the battered mobile phone, the credit cards, often in someone else's name suggesting that they'd been unlawfully obtained.

Lizzie stood there in her white nightshirt, no possessions to hand over. She had nothing material to show for her hundred and six years of mortal existence. I wondered how the formerly rich and powerful coped with suddenly being penniless when they were brought in. All the trappings of wealth and riches gone in an instant. I bet they were gutted.

Danny took his file back from Nigel. 'Any particular interview room, Nige?'

'Any one you like, Danny boy, they're all free mate.'

Lizzie and I followed Danny as he ambled towards a room off the main office. A table and four chairs filled most of the available space. There was, I noticed, no tape recorder. I mentioned this to Danny. 'Forget what happened before. We just want an account from them. We've got no way of proving or disproving what they tell us anyway. And they're not under caution either.' He grinned. 'If we do think they are lying to us then we just mention to them how close they are to the fire and brimstone. That concentrates the mind wonderfully, I find.'

'What happens to them after that? I hope CPS don't have a stranglehold here as well.'

'No chance. Nothing would ever get done, would it? If we had to consult them here I think we'd know we'd gone to Hell.'

The Crown Prosecution Service had been the bane of the working life of all of us working as cops, deciding what, if any, charges would be laid against the offenders. Known to many as the Criminal Protection Service, it had a reputation for being reluctant to take any but the most cast-iron of cases to court.

Danny continued. 'We talk to the lady, then have a chat to Nigel. He's got a lot of power. He decides whether we let her straight through, after a bit of advice, or put in for a bit of spiritual development. If she's in for the latter, it's not too painful. It's better than being sent back again like the people who've been really evil.'

'Paul wasn't joking then, when he told me about reincarnation being reserved for the hard cases?'

'It's only used in extreme circumstances. There's always the danger that they won't have had their memories properly wiped. You can remember everything about your previous life and so could they, unless we wipe it all out. Usually if it goes wrong, they get slightly altered recollection, which most of them interpret as meaning they used to be Napoleon or Cleopatra. Just occasionally, it gets completely stuffed up, and they have quite clear and lucid recollection, usually when they are still children next time round. We mostly send back serial killers, sadists, child-killers and war criminals, plus those sociopaths who never actually managed to kill anyone but never achieved any degree of spiritual link up. That's how it was explained to me anyway. Anyway, enough of that for now. We need to get you sorted, young lady.' Lizzie's earlier look of apprehension had returned, and I wasn't sure that Danny's casual discussion of the facts of afterlife had made things any easier.

Danny switched seamlessly into police officer mode, sitting opposite Lizzie with his folder in front of him.

'Can you confirm for me your name, that is the name you were born with, and your date of birth?' She did so, to Danny's apparent satisfaction.

'According to our records, you were supposed to come over here twenty years ago. Thinking back Lizzie, can you remember anything around that time that happened to you that might have been relevant?'

'How do you mean, relevant?'

'It's an unusual concept, I accept that, but twenty years ago did you think you were going to die?'

Lizzie pondered this question for a few seconds. I felt sure she'd have noticed a near-death experience.

'I've had a few times when I thought my time was up, mainly when I've been ill. My health went right downhill after I got mugged and that would have been about that time I suppose.'

Danny turned over a few pages in the folder, eventually seeming to find what he was looking for. 'Ah yes, you were attacked in the street, weren't you? There was a passing ambulance so they intervened and prevented you coming over. Or saved your life, as they saw it.'

'That's right. I remember lying on the pavement and I was suddenly all calm and warm. I thought well this isn't too bad, then next thing I was in hospital with all bright lights and beeping noises. I was angry then with the person who'd attacked me, and thought well I'll show you. That seemed to help me pull through. I don't know if they ever caught him though, horrible man'

Thinking about this snippet briefly, Danny turned over another page or two, found what seemed to be an interesting bit and read it. 'You'll be interested to know that he's been over on this side a while now. He got stabbed to death in a fight over drugs money. What goes around, comes around.'

'I hope I won't bump into him again. I wouldn't want to renew our acquaintanceship.'

'You'd probably never know. It was nothing personal, for what that's worth. His destiny included sending you over when your time came. Except he stuffed up, as he was actually a fairly inadequate individual who didn't have the strength or determination to carry his attack through. He was also doomed to live a miserable life and die horribly, if that's any consolation.'

Lizzie was silent for a few seconds while she took that in, looking past us as if deep in reflection. Then she came back to us, more positive and relaxed. 'Funnily enough, now you've told me he didn't actually choose to harm me, however you might phrase it, I feel a lot better about him.'

'OK Lizzie, we'll try and wrap this up. After you were attacked, how did you feel about your life? I see your health went downhill, as we were trying to get you over here.'

'In other words, you were trying to kill me off!' Lizzie

actually laughed now and it was clear that she was accepting what had happened to her. I felt sure now that she'd be alright. She continued. 'I was never the same after that really, and had a couple of heart attacks and a bout of pneumonia. I kept thinking that I'd survived being mugged so I wasn't going to be let down by my own body till I was good and ready. I just never felt the time was right. If I'd known I was getting my younger self back and that I'd be in such good company, I'd have let things take their course.' Addressing the last part specifically to Danny, it seemed she had taken a real shine to him. From his own beaming grin, he was lapping it up.

'Right, that seems to clear it all up, Lizzie. Stay here a minute and we'll go and see where we go from here.' He stood up and left the room. Responding to the 'we', I followed him over to the desk where Nigel was once again engrossed in the celestial racing pages or whatever it was that took up his time.

'Go on then, what excuse did she come up with?' Nigel raised his eyebrows expectantly as he awaited Danny's answer.

'Her nemesis stuffed the job up, for which she was truly grateful at the time. So grateful, in fact, that it gave her the determination to resist our subsequent attempts to bring her over, as a result of which she gained herself twenty years extra time. She understands the score now and there's no suggestion of anything untoward.'

'I'll write it off as 'Advice given' in that case. I'll arrange for a Greeter to collect her and get her settled in. Want to take her through to Reception?'

'Will do, mate. See you later.'

Turning to me, Danny asked me to collect Lizzie from the interview room. We led her from the suite and after a short walk, Danny ushered us into the featureless room I had arrived in only a few days before. 'We have to leave you now, Lizzie, but someone will be along for you in a sec. Don't mention to them that you were late, that's all done and dusted now. I hope we'll be seeing you around. Take care, love.'

And that was it, for now at least. We left Lizzie to the tender mercies of her Greeter. I asked Danny if we should have waited but he told me 'No, we don't let the Greeters see us. We don't want them to know that Lizzie overstayed in case they start getting all judgmental. She won't tell them, I'm quite sure.'

'What's next?'

'That's us done for the day. Freshen up then come and socialise with us if you like. I expect you could use a drink by now.'

'Too bloody right I could. Lead on, mate.'

CHAPTER SIX

'How long have you been dead, Danny, if you don't mind me asking?' Having showered and changed, I was now sitting in the bar of our accommodation block with William and Danny. Glass and chrome was very much in vogue, with black leather seating. Whilst Danny's imposing frame was occupying a suitably spacious armchair, I had the luxury of a two-seat settee to myself. A tinted glass coffee table served as base for our glasses as we periodically drank from them.

'I don't really see myself as dead. I feel every bit as alive as I did before, and that's always surprised me when I stop to think about it. But in terms of when I came over here, that's hard to say as well.'

As Danny settled back in his seat, I asked 'Does time pass here at the same rate as before?' It was something I had been pondering for some reason. William took up the theme. 'It seems to, which certainly helps with our planning when we go back on jobs. Like Danny mentioned before, no one but us here uses calendars, at least not openly. Time is constant but dates aren't relevant to most people and certainly it would make adjusting so much more difficult if you kept thinking about the relevance of what day it was in your previous life.'

'Do we operate on a 'Need to Know' basis?'

William nodded. 'Certainly, it's another hangover from before, so that should help you feel right at home. We aren't actually supposed to tell anyone else what the date there is. It's sensitive information.'

'Does that mean calendars and diaries are restricted documents?' I asked, having a mental image of new residents being forcibly searched on arrival in case they were trying to smuggle in a wall planner.

'It's not expressed quite like that but they don't help the cause,' William conceded.

'I suppose if we're looking at Eternity then months and years are meaningless,' I speculated.

Danny sipped his drink some more then put it back on the table. 'Yeah. What I do know is that after a short while I stopped thinking about what day it was. But to answer your question, and sorry about being so pedantic, I would guess about ten years from the dates I've noticed when I've gone back there on jobs.'

'I take it you were in the job, mate. You've got 'cop' stamped all over you.'

'I'd got twenty two years in. I joined in my early twenties, at a time when attitudes towards black officers weren't quite as welcoming as they became later on. It was a bit trying, to put it mildly.'

'Where did you wind up?'

'I did a few years on patrol then went into CID. There were some snide remarks about tokenism but I think I proved myself several times over. Then I got talked into undercover work. I'd split up from my girlfriend though, which made things a bit easier as I'd hate to have had her worrying about me all that time I was away.'

'That's a job that would have taken guts. Where were you, South West like you are now?'

'West of England Constabulary, though we got sent out of force for the UC work. In a lot of ways it made things easier for me, if I was working in the West Midlands or London, as the cops there were used to black colleagues so it was nothing new. And certainly having a black face was an asset when getting under the surface of the drugs business there. I used to wind up working the door on some right bloody dives. For some reason I looked the part. I can't imagine why anyone would think that.' Danny grinned at me as he reminisced.

Reaching for my glass, I took a mouthful of my drink. It was unlike anything I'd come across before. I thought it was a cross between fruit juice and a crisp white wine. Alcoholic, I was delighted to note, but with an almost indescribably beautiful taste. The Ancient Greeks believed the Gods had their ambrosia and I thought this might have been what they had in mind. It was, of course, free and no one had yet mentioned that it was ever in short supply. We simply helped ourselves from a dispenser, of which there seemed to be several lined up on the counter. I wondered if they were different flavours. I decided I would work my way through the lot, just to see. Whatever it was did not appear to have a name and was just offered to me as 'a drink'.

William stood up. 'Gotta go, guys,' he told us. 'I think I'm on a promise.' Without telling us more about what was doubtless an enticing prospect, he left the bar. I turned back to Danny, keen to learn more of his personal story.

'What happened to you in the end, Danny?' I'd been curious about Danny's story and it was good to hear him relax and talk. Without wanting to appear too nosey, I was curious about my new colleague and wondered what lay behind his reserved exterior.

'One UC job too many. I'd been working my way to the heart of a crime group, though my bosses back at the department were getting a bit twitchy. I'd talked my way into a job as driver and minder for some bloke who had the cocaine franchise for a large part of South Wales. He set up a meeting with a trafficker who said he could bring the gear through Avonmouth Docks, in containers of bananas. Part of your five portions a day I suppose.'

'Your old stamping ground?'

'Yeah. I'd not actually worked in Avonmouth itself but the meeting was at a hotel in Bristol. It was actually called The Bristol Hotel, like it was the only one there. Anyhow we showed up there, had our meeting, and then the guy I was supposedly working for and the trafficker decided to go on a pub crawl to celebrate their deal. I was a bit cagey, to put it mildly.'

'I bet you were. I'd have been crapping myself.' I'd never worked undercover but a few of my colleagues had and I had the utmost respect for them. To be out and about on your own turf was fraught with danger.

'I couldn't get out of it either as to all intents and purposes I was miles from home. It must've been about the third or fourth pub, the Red Lion, in Clifton, just a small place on a street off Whiteladies Road, and we were in there. I'd been sent to the bar and was just taking the beers back to the table for them, when one of my old shift came in to do a licensing visit. I didn't think we still did pub visits but for some reason this lad was. Anyway he said to me 'Hello Danny, I've not seen you around for a while. Where are you working now?' I managed to shut him up and he left.'

'Did the bad guy hear?'

'I didn't know if I'd been compromised at the time as he didn't say anything. I should've left but I was so close to a major result that I thought I'd chance it. Bad move as it happened.'

'They took you out?'

'Yeah, he must've done some asking around. Anyway a couple of days later he wanted me to take him to another meeting, this time in an old warehouse in Swansea. As soon as I got there a couple of his heavies appeared and pulled shooters on me. He told me I was a fucking scumbag, filth, all that kind of stuff. You think if it ever happens that you'll just turn and leg it, but there's nowhere to go. No way you can outrun a bullet, my friend. I thought I could talk my way out of it but they'd put me on my knees. One of the goons stuck his handgun against my head and next thing I knew I woke up in the waiting room, you know, where we dropped Lizzie off.'

'Did Chris meet you, like she did me?'

'No, it was Nige funnily enough. He's been here for about fifty years I think, and does a bit of recruitment every so often. He got run over by a trolleybus in Hull while he was on a shift night out. Or it might have been a tram, you'll have to ask him!'

'No, it was definitely a trolleybus, guys. That's another story I've heard countless times.' Chris had wandered in, grabbed a drink and come over. 'Mind if I join your gang?'

'Be my guest, there's plenty of space on my settee.' I stopped slouching and made room for her. 'How was your day?'

'I was going to ask you exactly that.' Chris smiled as she raised her glass to her lips. Her deep blue eyes gazed deep into mine for a second, and I felt a pleasurable buzz run through me as we connected. I hadn't noticed earlier how fine her hair was and now, backlit by the sunlight still streaming through the window, it seemed almost to glow. It curled under her jaw line and chin, framing her face and emphasising her fine features. I felt myself drawn to her almost hypnotically.

'I think for once the word 'interesting' might sum it up.' I returned reluctantly to what now passed for reality, having been lost for a micro-eternity in the pools of her eyes. 'It seemed so normal just going back there, yet at the same the ground rules had changed. All this walking through walls stuff, and the woman's transformation from old lady to young girl, made it seem more like a dream.'

'You'll get used to it, same as you got used to your existence last time round. It's like being reborn, but as an adult, so you don't have to spend years learning all the basics.'

'Being a child wasn't so bad, as I remember. It was being a teenager that was tortuous.' I grimaced at the memory of how vile I was as an adolescent.

'Well this time you avoid all that hormonal terrorism.' Another smile, another eye contact. Chris took another sip from her glass. 'What do you think of our local brew?'

'I could get used to it. Does it come back to haunt you in the morning though?'

'I've never had a hangover with it so far. It's funny really. Because it's unlimited, and free, no one is ever in a rush to overdo it. You'll find you drink at your own pace and you'll just achieve that nice warm friendly feeling you get after the first couple of glasses of the evening. It sustains you at that level and that's generally sufficient.'

Free booze, no hangovers. I wondered if the Afterlife Marketing Board had considered capitalising on the idea. Church attendances would rocket if they used that slogan. Then again, so would the suicide rate, I thought. Paul had a point when he mentioned that.

Chris turned slightly, not wanting to exclude Danny from the conversation. 'How did Nick manage on his first mission?'

'Yeah, he did alright.' That was good to hear. In fact, apart from being invisible and walking through solid objects, it had been very similar to my previous job. Except that in my old life I'd never actually killed anyone as far as I knew.

'I'm sorry, I shouldn't talk shop in here but I bear glad tidings from our Glorious Leader. He's got another job for you both.'

'Oh? When's that?' Might as well keep busy I suppose.

'Tomorrow. And you'll be delighted to know he's coming with you.'

For some reason, the words 'He's coming with you...' hung heavy in the air. I glanced over at Danny, who had gone into some kind of instant mega-sulk. As someone who had spent his career judging people's character, I could tell that something irked him. 'What's the problem, Danny? You don't look best pleased.'

'It's just that Paul hates to come back empty-handed, which can be a real pain in the backside,' he explained to me. 'Sometimes you have to work really hard to get people sorted out but still some of them really won't take a hint. But Paul always wants us to bring them back with us, come what may. He keeps going on about performance indicators based on how many souls we get hold of, so he needs to get as many as possible.'

'It looks like there's no escape from the performance culture. I thought I'd have left all that behind.'

'I dunno, mate, on the other hand maybe he's just a raving psychopath. We're not supposed to bring back those whose time isn't up but mistakes do happen and inevitably there's a load of explaining to do and a bloody stack of paperwork. Fate Planning will usually have all sorts of clever stuff mapped out and the person we actually bring in then turns out to have been pencilled in for some key action further down the line. When we bring them in too early, it throws out all Fate's plans and they get pretty pissed off about it. I suppose the classic example would be asking what would have happened if Lee Harvey Oswald had leaned a little too far out of that Book Depository window, and fallen off the ledge? Kennedy would've lived, at least a bit longer, and the rest of the Twentieth Century would've gone off on a different tack entirely. I had a chat to an old mate of mine who works there now, and she said they've got contingency plans for the key players, all the politicians and that, but they can't cater for everything. Even if it's only Joe Soap who gets taken out early, there can still be a knock-on effect.'

'Oh, right, and there was me thinking it might be out of consideration for all the needlessly-bereaved relatives, when actually it's because it upsets some desk jockey's Friday afternoon. What do they do if we bring one in too early?'

'They have to change another person's actions, ideally without spoiling anything else. In reality it's like they are working out duty rosters. If one person's not available they have to bring someone else in, that kind of thing. It's possible to sort it out but takes some reworking and they all moan like hell.'

I could relate to that, having had a career's worth of dealing with roster clerks. I always imagined that there was a special place in the hereafter reserved for police planners and now it seemed I'd been right all along. 'How come Paul can get away with it, though? Rank hath its privileges here as well?'

'In a way, I suppose.' Danny took another drink and stared thoughtfully into his glass. Was I to expect a true pearl of wisdom, I wondered, as he looked up? 'But in reality, it's not so much that he is allowed to get away with it, it's more like he knows we'll pick up the pieces with Fate. They don't like having a go at him personally, because of who he is I suppose. Whether that's because of his status, or because his girlfriend is Head of Fate Planning, I'm not sure. Maybe it's because, although he can't actually do them any harm, they think he'll pop back there and sort out their descendants.'

Deference to rank and organisational hierarchy obviously weren't the preserve of mere mortals, it would seem. I wasn't sure, from the brief interaction I'd had with Paul, that petty vindictiveness was something he would trifle with, but maybe you didn't get to be the Angel of Death by being Mr. Nice Guy.

'All I'm saying is watch out when he goes back there with you.' Danny was warming to his theme. 'Last time he came out with me it was when my target was going on holiday. It wasn't particularly well-timed but we were busy and these things do happen. When we got to the target's house, he had already left with his family and they were on their way to the airport. Paul wanted me to bring down the plane they were travelling on just to make sure we got him. He was actually quite excited about that as he'd got some new gadget to deal with these computerised control systems. He's always being talked into trying out something a bit innovative and his enthusiasm can get the better of his common sense sometimes. Mind you he's not the first. One of his predecessors got a bit

64

carried away when he went back early last century and saw a poster advertising the Titanic as being unsinkable.'

'He didn't like them tempting fate, you mean?'

'More like boys with their toys. He'd had a bet on with someone in Human Technical Development that whatever science came up with, nature could get the better of it, so he thought he'd try to prove a point with an iceberg. The rest, you might say, is history,' Danny added laconically.

'I caused you to digress.' Not that Danny had needed much encouragement but he went on 'Trashing a whole plane load of innocent victims just to get one bloke who'd outstayed his welcome seemed a bit harsh so I persuaded him we should join the target on the trip. That was a laugh in itself because we can just waltz through security without anyone batting an eyelid, and yet we regularly cause more mayhem than any amount of terrorists. Still, the authorities back there haven't managed to come up with a way of stopping us despite countless millions spent on Health and Safety. But I'm digressing again. Anyway we got on the plane and stood quietly at the back with Paul taking the piss out of the cabin crew during the safety drill. I just wish he'd had the Grim Reaper outfit on but if he'd accidentally made himself visible the chaos would've been out of this world. So I managed to keep his hands off the controls and we made it there without actually killing anyone. We followed the target and his family to his hotel, then on the first night we got him drunk and did him in the swimming pool. At least we got a weekend in Benidorm out of it. Mind you if ever there was a target-rich environment then that was it.'

'Tempted to do some overtime?'

'Yeah, well it was off-season and the place was full of coffin-dodgers so I figured the odds of some of them having overstayed must be pretty good. Anyhow we had to bring matey-boy back to Reception with us and as soon as we got back, another job came in. It was rather mundane and supposed to look like an unfortunate accident. The guy was quite well-balanced so we couldn't really get away with staging a suicide. As you'll remember, cops are loathe to take topping yourself at face value, and any hint of an anomaly will stick to the case for ever and a day. Remember those cases a few years back when various scientists and other officials started getting up the nose of the British Government? A couple of those happened to be overstayers and we had a new team working. They thought that staging suicides would be the thing to do, but didn't get them quite right and the stench and insinuations of Establishment foul play still haven't died down from what I can see. Anyhow, strangely enough Paul was suddenly busy for that one and I wound up taking a cop from some far flung and arid backwater with me. I like to work cleanly and get the job sorted, but he just wanted to try and plug the target into the mains and batter him about the soft fleshy parts with any blunt instrument he could lay his hands on.'

'You've digressed a bit too much there, Danny. What was the point?' I wondered, having lost the drift of what he was saying about our leader.

'Paul will usually say he's coming with us if he's desperate to boost the soul count, irrespective of their overdue status. So be prepared for slaughter on an impressive scale if he says he's coming along. That's my point, but I have to say that the trip with Salim is one I've never forgotten,' he added helpfully.

'You are a bit squeamish sometimes, though, Danny, you have to admit,' Chris chipped in. 'Salim probably just thought that was the most effective way to make sure the target came with you.'

'Yeah well, trying to get the guy to stick his fingers inside a toaster was always going to be a bit hit and miss,' Danny replied, raising his eyebrows. 'It was over the top really, when I'd already arranged for him to take a tumble down the cellar steps. It was just showing off. Salim, you'll meet him in due course, wittered on and on about how good short, sharp shocks could be, especially as he didn't think the cellar steps were far enough. 'Thirty feet, that's what you need Danny, trust me. Anything less and there's a chance they'll just lie there with a broken leg making a lot of noise,' was what he told me. In the end I gave in, anything for a quiet life, and we sat around waiting for the target to run a bath then we found his wife's hair drier had a really long flex so Salim plugged it in, switched it on and dropped it in the bath.'

'That went well then, I suppose?' I just had to ask out of professional curiosity.

'Oh yes. Bit of a bang when the fuse blew but the damage was done by then. It's a good accident to fake, too, as it could happen to anyone. Unfortunately this guy was as bald as a coot which no doubt led to a lot of questions as to why he would need a hair drier in the first place. I have confess that I hadn't thought of that either, in the heat of the moment. Luckily no one here went back to check our work on that occasion.'

'Does someone usually check up on us?' I hadn't anticipated a rigorous and intrusive inspection regime.

Chris had that one covered. 'We do get quality control checks once in a while, but usually Paul sorts them out. Initially you'll be working with someone else, usually Danny, perhaps even Paul, so you don't tend to get audited then. You will get the occasional check, like when you were a probationer, but if you do the job competently you'll get left in peace.'

'Is he coming out to see how I do? As well as reducing the population himself, I mean.' I addressed this to Chris in the hope of a more objective assessment of the boss's motives than I would expect from Danny.

'It's probably a bit early for that, as you've only been on one retrieval so far. He usually leaves it a bit longer. It could be he just wants an excuse to get out of the office for a while or, more likely, there's some meeting he needs an excuse to miss. Saying he's the Senior Retrieval Officer for a case is never questioned by those upstairs as they don't tend to get involved in the messy side of the business.' Then with a grin she added 'As I mentioned before, it might be because Danny is the boss's favourite!'

'Fat chance of that,' came Danny's retort. 'Last time he told me I needed to stop getting involved in the rights and wrongs and focus on bringing them in. He said not to bother if I got someone too early, Fate Planning have stuff all else to do and need to get off their backsides and do some work. Easy enough for him, I suppose. He just has to scowl at them or ask after their family in that rather menacing tone he favours when he thinks he's not getting his own way.'

'Want me to sort something out Danny?' Chris asked.

'All I'm saying is that I've got a couple of reasonably straightforward jobs and I could do without Captain Carnage sticking his oar in and messing it all up. Right, anyone for another drink? My round.' Without bothering to wait for a reply, Danny ambled over to the bar.

'What are you going to do about Paul?' For all his welcoming and light-hearted, if somewhat loud, demeanour, it sounded from Danny as if the boss was not lacking in energy or determination, so I was curious to know if he might be deflected.

'Don't forget I control his diary,' Chris replied with a smile. 'Ways and means, Nick. I happen to know that some of his mates are meeting up with a visiting delegation from Valhalla. Paul is well into all that fallen warrior culture. I'll sort him an invitation and that'll be him out of Danny's hair, or what there is of it anyway!'

Danny was still at the bar, seemingly deep in conversation with a couple of youngish-looking women. Fair play to the guy, he seemed to have a natural charm and maybe chemistry worked over this side as well. I thought I might be waiting a while for my refill if he really got stuck in. I looked back at Chris. 'What passes for entertainment here? I mean it's alright in here but is there a wide range of activity?'

'Typical cop! The chance to spend eternity in a nice bar, free booze and no hangovers and still you find something to complain about!' This was, I had to accept, a fairly accurate appraisal but at least it was accompanied by a smile.

'You were a cop too, don't forget,' I grinned at her. 'You never lose it, so they say. You're not in denial are you?'

'Oh, I can find plenty to whinge about, don't you worry. It is force of habit, you're not wrong there. We were never content at work unless we were in everything, were we?'

'True enough. I did find, though, that I even used to get annoyed by other people complaining. I think my pet peeve was the first sunny day we'd have, which usually was it for the Summer, some old duffer would start going on about 'Oh I can't be doing with this heat' when you just knew that the previous day they were probably banging on about how crap the weather was.'

Danny returned with our drinks but not, I noticed, his own. 'I've bumped into a couple of the women from my old team so thought I'd have a catch up with them. So if it's OK with you, Nick, I'll leave you and Chris to chat and see you both later.' Danny himself clearly felt this was OK as, without another word, he left the glasses on the table and wandered back to his newly-acquired harem.

'Don't mind us Danny,' muttered Chris. 'You OK for a bit, Nick? It's a bit early to turn in!'

'Yeah, I'm fine thanks. Just getting into my stride here. You know, they did away with our police station bars a few years back so it's good to find they've not been abolished here too.'

'A few late cops have said the same thing. It surprised me when I first heard it as I always thought they were part of the scenery. No one would've envisaged getting rid of them back then. Good grief, we'd have had to go and drink with the public!'

'They always told us it was because of the shortage of space, or the cost of running them, but I think that was a load of bollocks personally. The killjoys at the Home Office were just hell-bent on eradicating police culture. When pressed, the bosses were always able to point to some incident where someone had gone over the top and caused some embarrassment. We never do help ourselves, do we?' I took another long swig of my drink. It was a taste I was quickly acquiring. 'You must have come over a bit back, Chris, if you missed the purging of all that was fun in our workplace.'

'1988 it was, the fifth of October. It's funny now, it's the day you die but you see it as your birthday here, though we don't count the years.'

'Just to be really intrusive, how old were you at the time?' I always was a smooth talker.

'Forty three,' Chris replied. 'And before you point it out, I know what the calendar says back there. I'd be sixty eight now and old enough to be your mum. But I'm not that old in any meaningful sense.'

'You don't look it.' That much was certainly true. She definitely looked good in a baggy beige jumper and jeans. I stole a glance at her face, a few lines indicating a gentle maturity but it was a young one for all that, lighting up when she smiled. It was framed by her corn blonde hair, worn loose. Every so often, and quite unconsciously, she would gently draw it back behind her ear, from where it would inevitably free itself once more, to hang over her cheek when she leant forward to reach for her glass. I decided that I was starting to enjoy being dead.

CHAPTER SEVEN

It was what I used to know as Boxing Day. The three months or so since I'd arrived had soon passed as I settled in, both socially and in my new role as one of the Grim Reaper's henchmen. Our latest retrieval had been straightforward, if a little poignant, because of the time of year. Danny and I had let ourselves in whilst our target, who rejoiced in the name of Dilbert Simpson, enjoyed what was to be his final mince pie. After expiring on the kitchen floor Dilbert joined us in our dimension, having lost a good few stones weight in the process. It was amazing what sudden death could do to the figure and, having been on a number of trips by now, I was no longer surprised when the object of our attentions morphed into a spiritual form that bore only a limited resemblance to how they had looked before. Most of them looked much better for it and this was certainly the case with Dilbert. I wondered if he would use the opportunity afforded by this involuntary makeover to choose a different name. On the other hand, maybe he was rather attached to it. I thought better of asking him right now as he was still coming to terms with having this Christmas, and all his subsequent ones, cancelled.

Danny summoned our lift, which arrived shortly thereafter. Dilbert was, not unnaturally, very quiet as he tried to get his head around what had happened to him. His widow still snored away in the front room. We helped Dilbert get into the vehicle, then made our way back through Bristol towards the motorway.

'What's he up to, I wonder?' Danny speculated as we looked out of the van window at a solitary figure under the street lights, peering over the side of the bridge we were driving over. 'Thinking of ending it all, perhaps?' I ventured. The figure, who was wearing a shabby duffle-coat, looked to be about five foot ten, proportionate build and in late middle age. I surmised that he was a male, this impression being due not just to his build but also because, gracing his ruddy complexion he had a beard that even Paul would have been impressed with.

Dilbert was sitting in the rear next to Danny while I sat up front with today's driver, a young lad named Gordon. William being on a day off, we had been collected by Gordon who was a cheerful enthusiastic young man in his very early twenties. In keeping with what was rapidly turning into face-fungus day, our chauffeur sported a fine handlebar moustache. Gordon had been over on this side for a while, having been a bomber pilot in the 'Big Show', as he referred to World War Two. His flying career came to a sudden and very sticky end when his Lancaster fell prey to a night-fighter in the vicinity of Frankfurt. Gordon did the decent thing, struggling with the controls of his blazing and increasingly wayward aircraft which did at least enable the rest of his crew to bail out. It was too late for Gordon, however, who managed, with the help of his nose-diving Lancaster, to excavate a rather deep crater in a cabbage field, much to his eventual satisfaction. 'Hopefully a few of the blighters went without tea.' he rejoiced. Gordon had, it transpired, wanted to be a police constable before the war intervened, and the Afterlife had, somewhat ironically, given him the chance. I had warmed to the lad straight away.

'One of the other teams told me about him. They call him 'Don't Jump Derek', apparently,' Gordon offered. 'He keeps coming back to this bridge, looking over the edge and a lot of people think he's going to jump, but he hasn't, at least not yet.' 'This bridge' was the Clifton Suspension Bridge, a magnificent Victorian edifice which was a prominent landmark in Bristol. Gordon went on. 'I wonder if that makes him an overstayer. I mean, if the chap hasn't actually tried and failed, he might not count, but if he's supposed to have jumped, but hasn't, then surely he would be.'

'If you think too much, you'll only fry your own brains in this job,' muttered Danny wearily. My colleague had been in a grouchy mood all day, having been tasked with today's retrieval when he had other plans. However, Chris had been quite persistent and, as usual, had persuaded Danny to go along with the plan. Once again, she had stressed that Paul was getting grief from his own bosses to get stuck into the overstayer backlog or face a short sharp bout of departmental restructuring.

I pondered Gordon's point. 'Has anyone bothered to check him out?' I asked.

'I don't think so; we've never had cause to intervene and I don't recognise him from the wanted list,' he replied. 'That's not to say he's tickety-boo, but he's not one of our priority bods.' I was also becoming used to a much wider variety of speech patterns which differed not just according to cultural and geographical origin but also through time. Gordon, having transferred across in 1943, used some words and phrases which, to my ear, sounded wonderfully archaic. Goodness knew what he made of the way I spoke.

'Well there's no harm in having a look when we get back,' I surmised. 'While Danny and I check in our friend here, would you mind having a quick look in the files? Is he actually called Derek or is that just a nickname?'

'I think it is his name,' Gordon told me, adding 'My chum Pete told me that they had the window down and heard some chap shouting 'Oi, Derek, don't jump!' and Derek waved and said something back. Pete got the distinct impression that it was his name anyway, so after that whenever they saw him, they would shout 'Don't jump, Derek' as they went past. Not that Derek could hear them of course but it gave them a jolly good laugh. I'll have a shufti when I've dropped you off. Be a wizard show if he is an overstayer. The Chop Wallah will be most impressed.'

The Chop Wallah; I liked that. I mentally filed it in my ever-growing list of nicknames for our glorious leader; I was sure Paul would revel in it.

Leaving Bristol and crossing the Severn into Wales took us a little time but we had plenty of that. As far as I was able to deduce, in this part of the world, the Afterlife was only accessible from Cardiff, a view that was no doubt a source of considerable amusement to recently-departed Welsh people. Given the choice, many of them would happily have gone even further and manned the barricades to prevent any of their English neighbours getting in.

After booking the subject into Reception, Danny and I

grabbed a coffee, then I said I would go and see what Gordon had managed to find out about Don't Jump Derek, if indeed he was identifiable as such. 'Oh bloody hell, do you have to?' was Danny's grumpy response. 'We'll only have to go back and get him and I did rather have plans.'

'Even if he is wanted, I don't actually intend to go and get him now. Tomorrow will do fine,' I retorted. 'No one else need know just yet and I'm sure Derek will be in no rush to join us otherwise he would've taken the great leap a long time back.'

Leaving Danny to his self-induced strop I drained my brew and wandered off in search of Gordon, who I eventually tracked down in the intelligence office. He had a pile of several dozen brown folders on a desk and was trawling through them. 'What you'll find is that the records are filed by the subject's last known location, original due date and then surname, so it's no use looking under 'D' for Derek. You can help yourself to a few if you like.'

There was an adjacent desk that was not presently occupied, so I took half the remaining pile and sat down. 'I used my powers of deduction and assumed that Derek lives within a short walk of the bridge, a couple of miles maybe, as he seems to go there quite often. I don't think it is the sort of thing you'd do if you had to make a major effort and take the bus, or drive there. The parking charges would be enough to drive you over the edge, what?' He'd obviously made an effort to keep up with current affairs, it seemed, as I doubted that car park charges were too extortionate in the forties, if they even existed at all. Gordon was evidently showing promise as a detective, I thought, then realised that he might actually have been doing the job for seventy years in Earth time, several decades more than I had managed. It was a sobering thought.

Oblivious to my mental musings, Gordon continued to explain his rationale. 'I've started with the most recent as I've just got a hunch that he's maybe not a lot overdue, just there or thereabouts. Most overstayers are deliberately trying to avoid what's coming rather than contemplating the next move. So I think he's very marginal' he conceded. 'Of course, there's always the possibility that he isn't actually due and when he is he'll take a dive. Just hope I'm not wasting your time, old boy.'

'We'll never know if we don't look,' I encouraged Gordon,

as I started to leaf through the first folder on my pile. 'Are all these overdue, Gordon?' I wanted to know. 'There seems to be quite a number.'

'They're all on the list,' he confirmed. 'You'd be surprised how many there are. I think that's why the top brass are in high dudgeon about it. We can't bally well be everywhere. Don't forget it's usually only the serious cases we deal with.'

'Is there a limit on who we can take on? I sort of assumed that we would have some element of discretion but could take any transgressors, no matter how short they overstayed, a bit like how we dealt with traffic tickets.' As I said it, I wondered whether Gordon had ever received a ticket for driving offences, deciding it was unlikely as his personal contribution to Germany's sauerkraut shortage had occurred some time before fixed penalty notices were thought of.

'No, we can quite legitimately bring in anyone who has overstayed, but most of the time we just go and look for those who are taking the piss. There are enough of them to be going on with as it is.'

It didn't take us long to find Don't Jump Derek. His beard helped us narrow down the likely suspects to two, one whom was then discounted as he had moved to Bristol from Barbados a number of years earlier so did not share our chap's rather red-in-the-face appearance. He was indeed called Derek, his surname being Bissett, fifty six years old and recently added to the overstayer list. His was rather a sad case; his wife had left him a few years earlier for our side of the divide, the couple being childless. Derek was still bereft and had been totally unable to come to terms with losing her. His joyless existence had been made even more miserable when he was made redundant after thirty years loyal service to his sole employer. In Derek's position I thought I would probably have topped myself a lot sooner.

Despite all his woes and apparent fascination with long drops, Derek's time had only expired a couple of months previously. All those trips to the bridge when it wasn't quite his time had become a habit, I reasoned, now it seemed that he did not actually realise that things had moved on a bit and he should go ahead and take the plunge.

'What do you reckon, Gordon, should we go and do the

decent thing, give him a helping hand so to speak?' I had decided by now that Danny might best be left to wallow in his current miasma of discontent, whatever its cause. I was, by now, qualified to act on my own and I thought it might be interesting to see how another colleague worked.

'I'm up for it,' Gordon confirmed with what appeared to be his trademark enthusiasm. 'We should get it cleared first. I'll give Fate a ring and make sure they've not got anything last minute planned that they've omitted to put on his file. It does happen occasionally. Back in five.' He took the file out of the room, and I presumed he meant minutes rather than any longer units of time.

That gave me time to wander down the corridor where I thought I might pester Chris for a minute or two. We'd not exactly been living in each other's pocket though we had been socialising whenever possible and I was definitely feeling a growing attraction, something I hadn't experienced for a little while before I departed my last life. She was ensconced in her office, enduring a prolonged bout of deranged caterwauling that emanated from Paul's inner sanctum. The victim of today's cultural slaughter was of '*Nessun Dorma*'. I wondered if Paul had been tapping up Luciano Pavarotti for lessons since his arrival this side, but it didn't sound like it.

'What a bloody racket,' I mouthed, putting my hands theatrically over my ears. 'You can't say I didn't warn you,' Chris whispered, managing a smile as she spoke. 'It was worse when he went through his punk phase, though, for what it's worth. He particularly enjoyed belting out songs by the Sex Pistols. '*I am an Antichrist*' had him rolling around in stitches for some reason. He even went out of his way to meet up with Sid Vicious when he came over, but in the event it was all a bit of a let-down. The real Sid was actually a nice young lad who was completely disorientated, so Paul never achieved his dream of singing '*My Way*' as a party duet with him. It was probably just as well as they'd have cleared the room. Anyway, young man, what can I do for you?'

'You can come out for dinner with me if you're at a loose end later on,' I suggested optimistically. 'That is, if you've nothing more exciting planned.'

'I'm staying on tonight for His Grimness but tomorrow

76

night I'm free if you're paying,' she told me. I took it as the read that the reference to payment was just a quasi-ironic figure of speech given that everything we needed was in abundant supply and free of charge. On that basis there was no harm in agreeing. 'I'm thinking of doing a spontaneous retrieval tomorrow, Chris, just a slight overstay we came across this morning. I'll do it with Gordon; you'll know him I presume.'

'The lad who was a bomber pilot? Yes, nice chap, unless the subject is a German. You'd think he'd have got that out of his system but these things take time. To paraphrase Basil Fawlty, *'Don't mention the war...'*'

'Is the boss OK with us sorting out our own jobs?' I continued. 'Up till now I've just dealt with the files I've been given.'

'At the moment with the backlog, anyone you can bring in will help his figures so I'm sure you'll find he'll be at least slightly grateful. He's been out there himself quite a bit recently causing his usual mayhem, naturally enough.' Chris' phone started to ring which I took as my cue to leave. 'See you tomorrow. I'll give you a shout when we are back and sorted.'

'I'll hold you to that,' Chris smiled sweetly as she reached for the handset.

I went back down to the intelligence office, but Gordon had not yet returned so I had a look round. The paperwork was stored neatly in manilla folders, placed on shelves in some semblance of order. This was how we used to work, I thought, before the advent of computers meant that the system was thrown into total chaos. There were hundreds, if not thousands, of such files on metal racks and the whole place had the dry musty smell of an old library.

I pulled out the odd file here and there to see the scale of Paul's backlog. It was as Gordon had told me, with the folders arranged geographically, then in order of when their subject was supposed to have snuffed it. Some went back a number of decades, and many of these were supposed to have died young. I did some quick mental arithmetic and at least their chronological age now was still realistic. One or two would have been slightly older even than Lizzie had been when we got to her, which was certainly going some. It was rather poignant looking at some of those files, especially those for children and for young military personnel. I secretly hoped that not too much effort had been made to track them down; many of the files bore little evidence of an enthusiastic and robust investigation. The absence of any latter-day Methuselahs suggested to me that at least their files were weeded when they succumbed to the inevitable.

The subjects were spread far and wide, indeed throughout the world. None, I noted, related to anywhere other than Earth. Maybe we had truly been alone in the Universe, at least in that particular dimension.

Interestingly, for an intelligence office, there was no one else there. I found that unusual. Such places, in my own experience, had more than their fair share of desk jockeys loafing around drinking coffee and complaining about how busy they would have been had they not been dossing about doing sod all. They didn't express it in precisely those terms but I never seemed to meet a Field Intelligence Officer who claimed to be under-tasked; neither did I ever seem to meet any who were actually running around doing something about their workload.

My reverie of such happy times was ended by the return of Gordon, who confirmed that the actual demise of Don't Jump Derek wouldn't inconvenience anybody, with the sole exception of Derek of course. 'Ops are on in the morning,' I thought of commenting to my war hero buddy, but I didn't want him to think I was taking the proverbial. I decided enough was enough for the day, so wandered down to the bar in search of somebody else to bother.

CHAPTER EIGHT

Exiting the following morning through the usual portal to the dank and rather nondescript alleyway in Cardiff, we mingled invisibly with the small scattering of passengers waiting for the Bristol train. I asked Gordon why we couldn't just take a car as we would need to call one up to collect us all after the deed was done. 'Not really sure on that one, old boy,' he replied. 'I just imagine it's to save resources if we don't get a result. It's probably an incentive scheme. Remove an overstayer; win a car, something along those lines.' That would make a really catchy slogan in some of the more reactionary newspapers, I decided, and spent the next few minutes deciding which rag would have been most likely to stick it on their front page. The *Daily Mail* or *The Sun*, I concluded.

The thought of the British media reminded me about my own recent mentions in its pages. Being two days after Christmas itself the populace was not exactly over-exerting itself but the country hadn't actually ground to a complete halt, as it would have done over the previous couple of days. We'd definitely have had to go by car then as the UK came to its traditional festive period shut-down. There wouldn't have been any papers either but today a few people were browsing through tomorrow's chip wrappers.

'I want to have a look at the paper, to see if they've made any progress with my case,' I told Gordon. He gave the matter some thought; it's not an easy matter when you are both ethereal and invisible so he suggested I alter both of those states. 'I think they might notice if a newspaper started reading itself,' was his considered opinion. However, I could hardly materialise in front of the other passengers as this would cause an even greater degree of consternation on their part, unless I could somehow persuade them that we were filming an episode of Star Trek, which seemed unlikely.

'I'll have to nip out of sight and then saunter back round here like nothing's out of the ordinary,' I concluded, suggesting that he should join me. 'You need to be visible too otherwise they'll think I'm some nutter mumbling to myself and I'll get kicked off the train.'

Gordon agreed with my line of thinking, but then further complicated things by pointing out that if we were visible, we'd need tickets and as we didn't have any money that was a problem. 'Can you contain your curiosity till we get to Bristol, old boy?' he asked. 'We might have a bit of time to kill before Derek shows up, assuming he comes back today, and being seen then shouldn't cause any particular problems.'

I couldn't argue with that so we mingled amongst our mortal companions until the train arrived. It still seemed wrong, somehow, to travel without paying, but that wasn't exactly by choice. On the other hand, by sitting on the luggage rack we weren't exactly depriving fare-paying punters of a seat.

The train dropped us in the city centre, so it was a bit of a stroll out to Clifton and the bridge. En route I did manage to find a couple of discarded newspapers in readable condition and, having substantiated ourselves, I took these with me. After we had found a handy bench with a view of the approach to the bridge from Derek's favoured direction, I settled down to browse through them while Gordon sauntered over to the bridge itself, to check that our chap hadn't already arrived and despatched himself.

After all the agonising I'd gone through about reading the papers, it didn't take me long to establish that there was not a single mention of me in either of them. This was, of course, somewhat annoying but I shouldn't really have been surprised, as it was nearly three months since my murder. I couldn't expect to be in the news every day, I realised, and the world was moving on without me. At least I now knew that I couldn't rely on the press to keep me up to date on the progress of the investigation. Momentarily it crossed my mind to engage someone in conversation and ask them if they knew if an arrest had yet been made.

Fortunately, before I set off along that particular path, Gordon returned to disrupt my pre-occupation. I told him there was nothing in the paper and that I was considering direct contact, wondering if that was permitted. Gordon, however, was quite adamant on the point. 'Don't even think of it old son,' he advised. 'You might just zero in on someone who had been following the case and then what would happen if they recognised you? First, they'd run away shouting and second, they would go straight to the press to sell their story. You'd be in the bloody news then, but for all the wrong reasons. *'I chatted to cop's ghost about his murder.'* You can just imagine the headlines and the Chop Wallah would go off his trolley with you. He goes doolally whenever someone on a trip back gets photographed as he's convinced it will put the cat amongst the pigeons.' So that was a 'no' then, I thought ruefully, which meant I needed another plan.

'Fair point,' I conceded. 'I'll shut up about it for now, but I still need to know. Any sign of Drop Dead Derek, or whatever he is about to become?'

'Not as yet but it's early days,' Gordon said. 'I think he generally shows up in the afternoon, like he did yesterday, but it was still a good idea coming here before lunch just in case. Who knows, he might have had plans for later in case he couldn't go through with it.'

Although mid-winter, our bench was sheltered by a rocky outcrop behind us, and the weak sunshine wasn't blocked by leaves at this time of year, so our wait was quite pleasant. We were sitting about sixty yards or so from the toll booths and I whiled away the time spotting dodgy motors, drivers using their mobile phones and sundry other moving traffic offences occurring around me, things I could no longer do anything about, of course. When I got bored with that, and having made absolutely sure I was invisible and insubstantial, I amused myself by crossing the road directly in front of oncoming vehicles and their oblivious drivers. Inspired by my childish antics, Gordon decided to go one better, executing an impressive swan dive off the bridge. He was, of course, totally unscathed and simply swam ashore and climbed up to the road surface again. So then I had to have a go, which took some mental fortitude as all my natural impulses were screaming at me not to be so bloody stupid. However, following various squawking noises from Gordon suggesting that I was a chicken, I launched myself into the void. It didn't hurt and, what's more, I didn't even get cold and wet. The effect on Derek would, naturally enough, be radically different.

Bored at last with flying and swimming, we lounged around and Gordon regaled me with his war stories. Unlike those of the average cop, his actually involved considerable quantities of high explosive, not to mention bullets, cannon shells and other assorted technical nastiness. I knew that Gordon was far from alone in having failed to survive the conflict; listening to his detailed and harrowing account of his service I was astounded that anyone had managed to get through it at all.

Eventually, around mid-afternoon, we saw a bearded figure in a duffle-coat ambling along the pavement on the other side of the road. He was totally unaware that we were watching him, as we had already decided that it was for the best if we remained invisible, especially since I'd finished the newspaper. It wasn't a matter of saving the toll, as it appeared that they had chosen not to charge pedestrians. It simply made matters easier if Derek thought no one was watching. We shadowed our target, as I now saw him, about half way across the bridge. The water, nearly three hundred feet beneath us, looked no more enticing than it had when I was dithering about leaping into it earlier on. I shouldn't think it seemed particularly inviting to Derek either.

He'd stopped now, and was staring silently into the distance. The city lay some way in the distance, with the genteel white buildings of Clifton itself atop the hillside to our left. Between Derek and the precipitous drop was a substantial metal fence, topped by five strands of wire, fiendishly designed to deter anyone from climbing over them. Was this, I wondered, the reason for Derek's apparent indecision? Slightly more than head height, it would take a determined effort for the average self-harmer to clamber over the barrier and do away with themselves. Far easier, I considered, for them to go to nearest railway line and dive under a train, however rough that might be on the engine driver.

Derek stayed there for some time; I didn't have a watch that day so it was hard to say exactly but as the sun moved round I estimated he was there the best part of an hour. Looking at him, I could see tears welling in his eyes and trickling slowly down his cheeks. He seemed to be a soul in torment, though what I knew now made me fairly certain that he would make a startling recovery once free of the existence to which he was currently bound. The more I watched Derek endure his misery, the more convinced I became that it was because he couldn't climb over the fence.

'What do you reckon, Gordon, should we just pick him up and lob him over? We should be able to manage with the two of us if we're quick.' I had been back enough times by now to know that we could exert the necessary force whilst still remaining out of sight.

'Now might not be the best of times to kill someone, old son. It's the rozzers.' Gordon was looking along the bridge towards the toll booth near our bench. I followed his gaze and saw the once-familiar sight of a police car cruising slowly towards us. I thought for a moment that it was just a coincidence; the car would just continue past us on its merry way. I'd clocked the CCTV cameras dotted around the bridge, another anti-suicide measure I presumed, but if Derek was well-enough known to have passers-by entreating him not to jump then, I deduced, the local plods would be used to him by now so probably wouldn't have bothered. They wouldn't have where I used to work, anyhow. On this occasion, as so often, I was wrong and the patrol car drew to a halt. The passenger side window wound itself down, by the miracle of electric control, and the driver, alone in the car leant across. A young female bobby, probably early twenties I guessed, greeted Derek warmly. 'Alright my love,' she offered. It was not politically correct though it was in an exceptionally pleasant tone. She ignored Gordon and me, presumably because she couldn't see the pair of us, which was a relief under the circumstances. 'Hello, miss.' Derek sounded rather morose and it dawned on me that despite an hour or so monitoring him we hadn't had a peep out of him until now.

'A couple of drivers called us because they were a bit worried about you. Is everything OK?' She did look genuinely concerned. She also looked extremely well turned out, which made a pleasant change from many of my erstwhile colleagues who usually managed to look like they'd been dragged through a hedge in the course of their duties.

'Are you new here?' Derek wanted to know. 'You'd know me by now otherwise and I haven't seen you before.'

'I started going out on my own last week,' the PC told him, her West Country accent quite pronounced. 'I'm still new to the area and getting to know who's who. So what do they call you then?'

'I'm Derek Bissett, and I've lived in Clifton for all my fifty six years,' he told her helpfully. 'I just don't really want to live here much longer.' We didn't want him to hang around much longer either, but with the plodette paying close attention, it didn't seem we could do much about it.

'Why's that, Derek?' she asked sweetly. 'It's a lovely place. Where would you rather live than round here?'

'I don't want to live anywhere else. I'm just fed up with living full stop.' Derek turned back and stared forlornly into the distance, lost in his own world for a few seconds. The car door clunked as our unwitting colleague got out and came round to our side of her vehicle.

'Mind if I join you?' she asked, somewhat rhetorically in my opinion.

'Let's all have a party, why not?' muttered Gordon under his breath, which was rather pointless; as we were insubstantial he could have bellowed it through a megaphone and she couldn't have heard us. Without waiting for an answer, the PC climbed delicately over the metal girder that separated the roadway from the pavement and stood next to Derek. Things were not going to happen anytime soon at this rate. Maybe, I thought, she was going to arrest Derek under the Mental Health Act and get him sectioned.

'I'm Rachel,' the PC told him. At least she didn't add 'Hi there' or 'How can I be of assistance?' either of which would have been options in today's pink and fluffy policing world. The introduction had little effect on Derek, who was still staring into space. So Rachel, fresh from Training School, or wherever probationers got sent in the local force, kept on trying. Bless her, she didn't give up easily and before too long Derek was grudgingly responding and gradually the stilted interview became a full-blown conversation. We could only listen while all this went on, so I perched on the car bonnet.

Gordon, fearless as ever, stood on its roof to get a better view, though of what I couldn't be quite certain as the scenery from our lofty vantage point was quite spectacular already. Maybe he just liked heights and missed being at twenty thousand feet with flak bursts and searchlights for company. 'Attention seeker', I thought, but then again he was invisible to everyone but me.

I have to say, Rachel was doing a sterling job, having teased from Derek his life story and all its woes. So compelling was his story, and effective her efforts to get him to see life in more positive vein, that I began to empathise with her, and mentally cheer her on. She'd spoken to her control room, explained that she was counselling a potential suicide and, betraying the blind faith that is drummed into you, however temporarily, at Training School, she'd asked for a trained negotiator. If they'd sent one, I'd have given up the ghost, but she was out of luck. When the controller had presumably stopped rolling around the floor in fits of laughter at this outlandish request, Rachel had been told that none were available just now and there would be a costly call-out involved if she really needed one.

With the confidence of relative youth, Rachel evidently considered that things were going swimmingly, and not in the way that Gordon and I had in mind. She told control that she would keep talking to Derek and let them know the outcome. It was agonisingly clear that she expected to talk Derek round and help him get the support he needed to rebuild his life.

It dawned on me that the lass had seriously bought into the notion that she was going to succeed in saving Derek, which would be an immeasurable boost to her professional confidence. I pondered the consequences to her self-esteem if she failed, as was our intention and concluded that she would really take it to heart. In fact, it was quite possible that she'd be absolutely gutted, decide that she wasn't cut out for the job, and quit in favour of a less tormenting way of earning a crust. This would be a crying shame as she seemed to be an officer with potential; at least that was what her communi-cation skills suggested. I found myself coming round to her way of thinking; maybe Derek deserved some happiness, if only till our bureaucrats noticed that he was missing. He was only a couple of months overdue when all was said and done, and it was simply by chance that we'd noticed him, rather than someone having identified him to us as a priority target. I concluded that there would be no harm in leaving him be and getting home. No one need be any the wiser, we could come up with a convincing reason for not completing our task, and in any case I had what might turn out to be a hot date with Chris to look forward to that evening. This course of action seemed even more sensible given that it didn't look like we'd get much chance to bring Derek back with us, the way things were going with Rachel's skilled negotiating.

I voiced my opinion to Gordon, who didn't agree. His view was that Derek was due to come with us, and he was expressing this quite forcibly. He had moved on to stating that we should get on with the bally job like we were supposed to, when a vehicle horn sounded right behind us. Rachel and Derek jumped visibly, so it was probably a shame that Derek wasn't actually perched on the parapet at the time, as that would have accomplished the task for us. A Ford Transit van had somehow squeezed through the barrier on to the bridge and, with Rachel's patrol car being slightly away from the kerb, the driver wasn't too confident about getting past without removing the constabulary's wing mirror. 'I'd better just move my car, but do you promise not to do anything drastic and I'll come back to you?' she asked Derek, who swore blind that he was feeling a whole lot more positive. He'd be inviting her round to his place for tea next, the way this was panning out, I thought, as Rachel waved an apology to the van driver, got into her car and drove off along the roadway.

'Sod this,' said Gordon to me, 'Now's our chance so just get your bloody finger out and give me a hand, there's a good chap.' His latent leadership qualities, doubtless honed under fire, came to the fore and I reluctantly realised that resistance was useless. 'Grab his legs, vertical lift and tip and his momentum should carry him over.' Suffice it to say that this smash-and-grab approach worked a treat. We rushed Derek who was probably quite surprised to suddenly find himself airborne, and about four seconds later even more stunned to find that he wasn't airborne any longer, but was dead instead.

Yelling 'Follow me,' Gordon then leapt into the void so I went too.

86

CHAPTER NINE

'Golden Gordon, the Boss calls him.' Chris took another forkful of paella from her plate and, having imparted that particular gem, savoured the taste of her meal. 'He's almost as driven as Paul when it comes to bringing souls back. Don't let his pseudo-naïve 'Can I have a go?' demeanour fool you. Gordon is a dab hand at all this.'

The golden boy and I had recovered Derek's immortal soul from the side of the River Avon, having left the soggy bits of his corporeal presence to whichever poor sod was unlucky enough to fish them out of the water. He'd been disorientated, which was normal under the circumstances, but we had our 'Welcome to the Afterlife' chat with him, and he'd soon come round. Despite the sincere ministrations of PC Rachel, who was by now probably wondering with an increasing sense of foreboding where Derek had gone, he was genuinely relieved to have made the move. His main concern was being reunited with his late wife, which was understandable. 'Don't worry about that, old son,' Gordon reassured him. 'When we've got you booked in, Reception will give you a Greeter and put the word out to your missus that you're here. She'll probably wonder what kept you; that's what they normally ask.'

The post-retrieval interview was a formality as Derek's reticence had been short-term and due solely to the difficulty of getting round the anti-suicide measures on the bridge, which were there for good reason. I took advantage of the opportunity to introduce myself and ask Derek if he'd seen any updates about my case. 'There was quite a bit about you at first,' he told me. 'But then it all went quiet. I've not seen much recently, now you mention it.'

'Has no one been locked up?' I was disappointed, to say the least. Derek confirmed the inconvenient truth that, indeed, no one had been but was unable to pad out his answer any further. Having finished with him after that, we packed him off to share eternity with the love of his past life.

Thanking Gordon for his enthusiastic endeavours, I made my excuses and left him to his evening. He'd received word when we got back that the final member of his old bomber crew had finally made it over after ninety years on Earth, so they were all holding a reunion of their own. They would all, I imagined, have reverted to being the exuberant youths they were during their earlier time together, so their evening promised to be lively. Now I was aware of his long-borne grudge against his former foes, I just hoped that he didn't get it into his head to take his mates back to Germany to round up a few souls that they'd missed liberating in the war.

I returned to my perfectly adequate apartment and had a long soak under the shower. As I relaxed under the warm spray I thought back over the events of the day. I have to say I was still a bit bothered about the brutality of what we had done, and this played on my mind. I wasn't convinced that Derek had actually wanted, deep down, to end it all. If he had, I reasoned to myself, he'd have found a way. Rachel, the fair cop, had done a great job in making him see things in a more positive light and I was also concerned how she would cope when she eventually found out the reason why he wasn't where she'd left him when she got back. The poor lass could have been traumatised for life; I'd seen it happen to more experienced colleagues than her. Added to that, Derek was a lot less overdue than many others, and certainly would not have been tasked out to us for quite a while, so his demise was wholly down to me. I'd been the one to encourage Gordon to track him down and come with me. If the truth be told, I was also a bit embarrassed that I'd tried to back down in front of Gordon, and wondered if he now thought I lacked bottle.

Having towelled down, I donned some clean jeans and a casual shirt, found a new pair of unsurprisingly comfortable trainers in the cupboard, then gave Chris' door a quick knock. I heard footsteps padding softly across the carpet and she opened the door. There was what appeared to be a genuine smile of greeting for me. 'Are we still on for some-thing to eat?' I asked her, trying to sound suitably chilled.

'Don't worry, I hadn't forgotten,' she assured me. 'I'd have given you a shout if you hadn't beaten me to it. Give me ten minutes or so and I'll be ready. You are very welcome to come in and wait while I sort myself out,' she offered. 'That way there's no chance of any of your colleagues calling by and hijacking you to go to the bar, just for a quick one. I know what you lot are like.'

'That's a sweeping generalisation!' I protested.

'True though, isn't it?' she countered, as she moved from the door into the main room of her apartment. I couldn't argue with that, so didn't. Instead, I followed her inside. It was very light, with predominantly white furniture and walls subtly illuminated by wall-mounted lamps. A matching white shag-pile carpet was contrasted by a large black rug in the same material. Through the full-length picture windows, the gradually-diminishing daylight still played its part in lighting the room.

Unlike in the real world, as I still thought of it, the balance between natural light and dark outside seemed to remain constant, in a ratio of about two to one, which was just as I liked it of course. I wondered if everybody liked the same amount, or perhaps what I saw was just what I wanted to see. I was starting to have a sneaking feeling that all of this other world existed in my imagination then concluded that, for all I knew, the same might have been the case in my previous life. If the apparent world chose to revolve around the machinations of my mind, who was I to argue?

Inviting me to sit down, Chris then left for the privacy of her bedroom which, I assumed, had a similar en-suite to my own. Indeed shortly after, I heard the rush of water as she had a shower herself. I considered offering to scrub her back but thought better of the idea at this time. I seemed to have landed on my feet, even if they had momentarily grown a little cold at the implications of my work. I didn't want to spoil the amenable working and social arrangements that came with it by coming on too strong with Chris. If I picked up vibes of mutual sexual chemistry, then that would be another matter. The early signs of warmth from Chris were still apparent but she hadn't gone out of her way to drag me into her boudoir and ravish me, so I thought it better to progress with a degree of caution.

None of my physical self-control prevented my mind from imagining her in the shower, water glistening as it cascaded onto her shoulders and upper body, streaming over her breasts before making its way past her most intimate parts and thence down her legs to the basin of the shower. Lucky old water, I thought wistfully. Then the thought occurred to me that, given the perfection of everything around me, perhaps all I had to do was go with my idea of a perfect evening, and it could happen. When I was being honest with myself in the previous life, which did happen occasionally, I had never known a satisfactory long-term relationship that started with rampant bedroom gymnastics on the first date. So I knew deep down that such passionate antics were not likely to be on the menu tonight, and that was something with which I was actually very comfortable, with a possible view to the future.

I was disturbed from my quasi-pornographic reverie by Chris emerging from her bedroom in a light blue bath robe, her hair wrapped in a cream towel. As she walked, the fabric of her robe shifted slightly under the influence of her breasts which were I was quite sure, unrestrained for now.

'How rude of me,' my hostess commented. 'The sun's well over the yard arm and I forgot to offer you a drink. What would you have had before?' In my past life, I assumed she meant. 'A vodka and tonic would have been a nice start to the evening,' I informed the vision of damp loveliness standing before me. Chris made her way to the kitchen and emerged shortly after with my tipple of choice. Top lass, she'd even thought of adding ice and a slice. Her own glass contained a lightly-hued pink liquid which might simply be wine. Seeing my enquiring glance, she confirmed that it was indeed a very fine rose, adding 'Get that down your neck' for good measure.

She disappeared back into the bedroom, from where I heard the strangely mundane whirring of a hair dryer. I decided to stop trying to find a rational explanation for everything and just accept things as they were. Somehow, though, I doubted that I would be able to contain my curiosity; it was such an inherent facet of my character that it wouldn't be easy to keep it satisfied indefinitely.

Chris' bedroom door was ajar which enabled us maintain a run of small talk as she got ready. From my seat of the large and sumptuous L-shaped sofa I caught an occasional glimpse of her as she moved round the room. I liked what I saw, not least because she was, at least temporarily, clad only in a black lacy bra and panties, quite skimpy and very fetching. It was as much as I could do not to choke on my vodka and tonic. Her skin, although not that of a twenty-year-old, had certainly avoided, or maybe in its passing over had shed, the inevitable enhancement in terms of fullness or stretch marks that her earthly age might have led me to expect. It was certainly a pity that the absence of such imperfections could not be communicated to women in the mortal realm; it would certainly cheer them all up and give them something to look forward to. I wondered if I would get the chance to check any more closely, but reminded myself it was my choice not to rush. Despite my self-imposed embargo on questioning everything, I briefly wondered if sex did actually happen in the Afterlife.

Within the promised ten minutes, Chris had emerged from her room fully clothed, which was probably just as well for my slavering and lustful imagination. She had chosen a lilac blouse with a delicate floral pattern, worn loose over the top of a knee-length plain white skirt which was cut generously, giving the appearance of being light and summery whilst emphasising the light tan of her calves. It seemed that tights and stockings weren't strictly necessary in these parts. Her hair was also worn loose, having gained some further body from the wash and blow dry to which it had just been subjected. I couldn't see any visible make up but, perhaps inevitably, her face showed no sign of needing any artificial help to look absolutely gorgeous. Eschewing anything more than low heels on her shoes, Chris was a good four inches or so shorter than me and I instantly felt a rush of protectiveness towards my date for the evening.

'Where are you taking me, gorgeous?' I enquired of her. I was surprised that she hadn't found it necessary to suggest that I stop standing around with my tongue out, gawping. That was certainly how I felt as I tried to maintain a sensible conversation and avoid giving the impression that I just wanted to drag her into the bedroom and get to know her a lot better, and soon.

'There are any number of places you won't have been too yet, unless you've been gallivanting around without me hearing about it,' she smiled. 'It all depends on what you fancy,' she went on and smiled. 'For your dinner, I mean,' she added helpfully. That was me well sussed then, which served to remind me to try and behave. Like most blokes, I seemed to flag up any dishonourable intentions well in advance so I shouldn't have been surprised that Chris could read me like a well-thumbed novel.

'What would you recommend?' I asked in an attempt to appear sensible, avoiding the temptation to add anything potentially laden with innuendo. Suddenly it felt like an eon since I had last gone through the motions of flirting and chatting-up that were integral to the process of a first date. I'd approached the idea of asking Chris out as just a friendly and sociable gesture, even though I had long since recognised that, being honest, I fancied her immensely. Now we were here, I felt as tongue-tied and gauche as a teenager.

Fortunately, Chris was so easy to get on with that, once I got over my unexpected bout of first date nerves, the conversation really started to flow in earnest. Rather than stick to the tried and tested subject of anything related to work, we each opened up on our lives, loves and backgrounds. It did seem somewhat bizarre, talking to someone who was so close to me in apparent age but whose life experiences stemmed from a time some twenty years earlier. It had been a bit different chatting with Gordon about his service in Bomber Command which, although fascinating, was a living history lesson rather than a possible prelude to a closer personal relationship. I was sure Gordon would forgive me for making that distinction.

We left the accommodation block and strolled into the last rays of the evening sunshine. The park was bathed in a soft golden light that toned down the normally vibrant colours of the foliage. There was a path leading through the woods which brought us to a lake; it then followed the shoreline towards a group of buildings about half a mile distance. Although I had done some exploring since arriving, I hadn't previously followed this route and certainly wasn't aware of the lake or our destination. The vista was stunning; trees lined the lake which looked crystal clear. On the horizon, the amber light of the setting sun reflected off snow-capped mountains. Around the lake shore were pines as well as the eucalypts, their combined scents being a heady mix. You couldn't make it up, as they say.

Still chatting, Chris slipped her arm through mine as we strolled along the lake shore. There was birdsong too, as if many of the songbirds that had disappeared from the gardens and countryside back there had made it into the Afterlife. Maybe they had, and I hoped that there were no cats here. If there were, maybe the moggies had turned vegetarian. The Afterlife was all the better for their presence, whatever the reason.

Soon enough we arrived at a single storey white Mediterranean-style building with a terracotta-tiled roof. It was, not unnaturally, a pleasantly warm evening and the lake shore was not plagued by flying insects, which was very considerate of them. This made the option of a seat on the terrace particularly attractive. It goes without saying that a table for two was immediately available. I was beginning to wonder where would be the first challenge to this all-pervading perfection; I saw fit not to mention this to Chris as I didn't want her think I was whinging again. Perfection, I could put up with and I would hate to spoil a lovely evening.

We were shown to our table by an attentive and courteous waitress. Years of diversity training made my 'gender-specific term' radar ping when she introduced herself by that title, adding for good measure that she was called Irina and she hoped we would have a pleasant evening. I wondered what some of the humourless politically-correct types would think should they get this far and find that they had been wasting their efforts and that labels didn't matter so much here. On the other hand, maybe they went to a Redevelopment Unit when they arrived to deprogram their miserable control freak tendencies. I certainly hoped so and made a mental note to see if I could visit an RU. If nothing else, I was curious to see how many defence briefs and senior police officers were getting their comeuppance at long last.

Irina fussed around us, offering us some mineral water and breadsticks to tide us over while we considered the menu and wine list. Her name and accent suggested an Eastern European origin; when, inevitably, I asked her she told me she was from Transylvania adding by way of reassurance that, no, she wasn't a vampire. I expect it wasn't the first time she'd been asked if she was a member of Count Dracula's family. An eternity fielding the same pithy question might wear a bit thin, in my opinion, but so far she'd retained her sense of humour.

The terrace afforded us a magnificent view of the landscape as the sun set, the sky darkening gradually to a deep azure. We ordered wine, a carafe of white to start with. Due to logistical difficulties, it was not possible to order specific labels, so we went for the house offering, confident that it would be almost annoyingly wonderful. It was. The food similarly gave me little to complain about. All this perfection was beginning to grate a little; after all, when everything is absolutely spot-on, what is there to aspire to? This did make me feel ungrateful and then the penny dropped; if everything appeared to be exactly to my liking, perhaps if I lowered my expectations, then my perceived reality might bring itself down to my new standards. I decided to try this, only not just yet. The thought 'Be careful what you wish for' sprang to mind. I was happy for this evening to be perfect in every way.

After a garlic-enriched starter dish of mussels we chose to share a suitably large bowl of paella. I'd asked Chris shortly after arriving in the Afterlife who did all the various tasks and this applied just as much at the restaurant as it did at work. It transpired, and indeed was obvious when I thought about it, that for certain people their job was more of a vocation. This would, I considered, apply especially in areas involving creativity such as creating and serving a culinary masterpiece. For a chef to run a kitchen with an unlimited variety of high quality ingredients, with capable and willing staff serving grateful and discerning customers must be heaven indeed.

I'd been bringing Chris up to speed with the events of the day, on the basis of what they had meant to me, rather than as a dreary account of work undertaken. She knew that we'd brought Derek in; there seemed to be a hotline from Reception to the Grim Reaper's office, presumably so that he could dispense words of wisdom and generally micro-manage if he was anything like the senior bosses to whom I had previously been accustomed. The Chop Wallah, as I now liked to think of him, was very impressed with our bit of proactive retrieving and had waxed lyrical to Chris about it. This resulted in me telling her about the change of heart I had whilst sitting on the bridge waiting to chuck Derek off it. To Chris, at least, this was understandable but she also saw the other side of the argument. Putting up with Paul's constant moaning about performance didn't really give her much excuse I supposed. 'He wants to record his gratitude to both of you too,' she told me. 'He just loves dishing out awards and commendations for work over and above, and all that.'

'It was all down to Gordon, not me,' I stressed. 'I would feel like a fraud if I bigged up my role. He pointed Derek out, did the initial research and got a grip when I was all for giving it up as a bad job.'

Chris imparted the fact that Gordon was already held in high esteem, adding that it would do me no harm to join him on his lofty perch in the Grim estimation. In the end we decided that Chris would emphasise Golden Gordon's excellent work and tell the boss that I had just gone along to give him, and Derek, a helping hand. That way, everybody would be happy.

The evening had gone well, I thought, although I didn't want to push things too far, too fast. The stars were out in the clear sky and I was intrigued to notice that although there were discernible clusters of stars, none of them were familiar as constellations. The ancient pharaohs would have been gutted, I thought, when they got here and found no sign of Orion. They needn't have bothered building all those pyramids after all. On the other hand, without Orion, they might still be out there, wandering around, trying to find the place.

Our wine having been finished, there was no immediate sign of Irina our non-vampiric waitress, so I told Chris I would go to the bar and ask for another carafe. The restaurant inside consisted of a single large room with numerous wooden pillars and beams forming large and small areas. This would suit parties as well as more intimate surroundings. It took a few moments for my eyes to adjust, but when they did and I glanced round, they were drawn to a secluded corner. At a table for two table, and totally engrossed in their own company, sat Danny and PC Rachel.

Rachel was no longer in uniform, favouring a pink tee-shirt and blue jeans. With her hair loose, she actually looked more mature than the young-and-eager cop she had seemed earlier that day. As they saw me, their faces both broke into broad grins. 'Don't jump down my throat, Nick,' said Danny, which Rachel seemed to find unbelievably funny for some reason. 'You've already met Rachel, I understand.'

'Yes, in the line of duty, so to speak.' I was trying to work out where she might fit in to the scheme of things. 'Go on then, what the hell was all that about with Derek?' I asked them.

'That's what you might call a bit of a blue on blue,' Rachel replied, still smirking. 'Danny told me that you'd got the bit between your teeth over Don't Jump Derek, and had fixed up with Gordon to go back and fetch him, so we thought we'd wind you up a bit by making it a bit more of a challenge.'

'You certainly did that. I was on the point of giving up on him but Gordon was having none of it. I suppose you know about that now Danny!'

'Oh yes,' my esteemed colleague confirmed. 'I've had a full run-down from Rachel, you can rest assured about that.' The wink, aimed at Rachel, and the beaming grin which was clearly for broader consumption, suggested that there would be plenty of mileage in this gem of information.

'I presume you were fully aware of us then, Rachel. You do a good line in deadpan acting in that case.'

'I saw and heard it all,' she said, still clearly amused. 'At one point I was sorely tempted to tell you to get off my nice clean police car, especially when Biggles was messing about on the roof. I'd love to have done it just to see your reaction, but it would've given the game away and confused poor old Derek no end.'

'How come Gordon didn't recognise you?' I assumed they'd met before.

'He did. Gordon was in on it too. He thought the idea was 'A jolly good wheeze', as he put it.' Typical; I'd been well and truly stitched up. It was a good effort, I told them.

'How long were you intending to carry it on for?' I asked Rachel.

'Oh, there was no rush. I was wondering who would get

bored and go home first, you two or Derek, but then of course that blasted Transit tried to squeeze through so I had to move the car. When I returned you'd all gone so I came back here.'

'Anyhow,' Danny chipped in. 'What brings you to this fine hostelry? I thought you tended to just lurk around the bar of an evening.'

'Yeah, well I got a bit bored of my own company so thought I'd try a whole new experience.'

'Don't tell me; let me guess...you've persuaded Chris to join you?' Danny's grin was as broad as ever. 'That poor lass must be at a seriously loose end if she agreed to that!'

'Oh I'm sure she was. But she's borne my company with admirable fortitude. Anyway, why did you think that?'

'I might be daft but I'm not bloody stupid,' laughed Danny. 'I've seen the way the two of you have been besotted with each other ever since you got here. It's about time you got your acts together.'

'Well now we're no longer secret, why don't you two come outside and join us. It's a lovely evening out there.'

Danny looked at Rachel. 'What do you reckon, sweetheart?'

'We'll come out and say hello but we wouldn't want to cramp your style!'

'I've not much style to cramp, if the truth be known,' I retorted. 'As we're all here in one place we might as well enjoy it. I'd better get two carafes of wine. Red, white or rose?'

'Mmm, I'm happy with anything vaguely liquid.' Rachel looked at Danny. 'You sticking on red?'

'Yep. If you get one red and one white, we could always try mixing them and get a rose,' Danny suggested, helpfully. Innovative thinking but I could imagine many a connoisseur turning in their grave over this sacrilege. However it seemed to be a reasonable compromise.

Having at long last obtained the promised carafe I was delighted to find that my companion was still at the table where I had left her. 'If I'd thought on I'd have mentioned to you we were coming down here. We could've made a foursome right from the start.' Chris's greeting to Danny and Rachel indicated a total lack of surprise at seeing them together.

I wasn't initially sure whether or not Danny and Rachel were an item, so I let that one ride; I assumed that this would become clear in the fullness of time, if indeed it was any of my business.

Perhaps inevitably, we spent the rest of the evening as a group, which I didn't really mind. It was good to see Danny in a good humour, and Rachel proved to be lively company. Chris didn't seem to resent their intrusion on our evening though neither, I was pleased to see, did she seem to consider their appearance to be a form of rescue from an otherwise dull occasion.

Finishing our meal the four of us slowly made our way along the lake shore, Chris slowly causing us to fall further behind. Danny and Rachel were hand in hand, and it seemed that Chris wanted to allow them their space. I figured this wouldn't be too much of a problem for them once they reached whosever accommodation they had in mind for the night, but I didn't insist on hurrying up. We came to a turn in the path that gave us a magnificent view of the lake. She stopped, and a pull on my hand ensured that I turned towards her. Without a pause, she put her arms round my neck, pulling my face down towards hers. Kissing her seemed the most natural thing in the world right then, so I did. We didn't see Danny and Rachel again that night.

CHAPTER TEN

Lee Patrick Summers was a worried man. He hated coppers, always had done; but he'd never actually contemplated killing one. His thirty years on the planet had not, it has to be noted, noticeably helped the advancement of civilisation, nor had he contributed to the nation's wealth by paying any tax other than that levied on his occasional winnings at the betting shop. There were those, Guardian readers for the most part, who, had they been called on to defend Summers, would have pointed out that he grew up in squalor and deprivation, despite having been born in a relatively wealthy country, certainly in comparison with the developing world. Summers was the unintended consequence of his mother's predilection for unprotected sex with casual acquaintances as a form of evening entertainment.

His poor start in life was exacerbated by his mother's addiction to cheap alcohol and increasingly costly cigarettes, rather than her devotion to her son. Left to his own devices, Summers had never realised the advantage of paying attention at school. His occasional attempts to pass an interview for work, when lent on by the Department for Work and Pensions, were hampered by an apparent inability to communicate by anything more sophisticated than a Neanderthal grunt, along with an insistence on constantly picking his nose. Honest toil having mysteriously eluded Summers, he felt compelled to turn to a life of crime.

His thick-set brow and small piggy eyes, small protruding ears and shaven head were unlikely ever to see Summers winning a beauty contest, though he might have looked the part had he chosen a career as a top-flight footballer. Sadly he lacked the ability and motivation to practice any sport so that particular path to celebrity and greatness was also denied.

Petty theft became sneak-in burglaries as Summers entered

his teenage years. Some of these, though, were a little too close to home and, whilst his fellow estate-dwellers were somewhat reticent when it came to helping the police tackle criminals in the area, Summers soon learnt that a short sharp kicking would ensue if he burgled houses linked to what passed for the local crime families in Stambridge. Not being particularly valiant, Summers had taken the hint and thrown in his lot with the Flynns, who considered that they ran the local area.

There is, according to the back of a matchbox I once read, a Japanese saying: 'The dog thinks he is part of the family, but to the family he is just the dog.' So it was with Summers and the Flynns. Maybe not the brightest, but he could be relied upon to carry out mundane and undemanding tasks, even those that slightly greater intellects than Summers would have realised carried an obvious degree of risk. No stranger himself to the application of unlawful violence, Summers was soon tasked with collecting debts for the Flynns.

He enjoyed the variety; the challenge of enforcing drugs debts from the numerous users and low-level dealers on the sink estates around the city was alleviated by the simpler task of leaning on those hard-up residents who had felt compelled to borrow money at exorbitant interest rates from the loan-sharking arm of the Flynn business empire. Paid what he considered to be a fair rate for his strong-arm efforts, it then dawned on Summers that he might do even better if he could set up and run operations under the family's sleazy franchise. To that end, the family patriarch, Joseph Flynn, decided it would be quite amusing to see how a complete numpty like Summers would prosper if given a bit more rope.

Not wishing to put at risk any of his existing enterprises, Flynn looked around for an expansion opportunity. Word soon reached him that an uncharacteristically effective police operation had taken out a ring of suppliers covering the Welsh valleys, leaving the consumers trembling, sweating and desperate for someone to meet their insatiable demands.

Summers' choice of subordinate dealers, those who would push out smack, weed, amphetamine or even, occasionally, cocaine, was necessarily limited and not of the highest quality. There were those who, without fail, would pay up promptly whilst others were more grudging. Slowly but surely,

Summers found that his debtors' list was growing and, whilst he was just about able to keep his head above water, his new work was by no means lucrative. Fortunately, his prior experience in collecting drugs debts stood him in good stead as a punch in the mouth of a reluctant payer was bound to concentrate their mind wonderfully. However, Summers still found that he had, at any one time, substantial amounts owed to him, so whilst his personal balance sheet, had it been written down, would have looked healthy on paper, in actual cash terms his money was still in the pockets of other people.

When Flynn offered him the opportunity to buy heroin in bulk, and on credit, Summers saw only the possible gains and not the risk. He would, he decided, offer this to his dealers for a discount, but only for cash up front. What, he thought, could possibly go wrong?

The threads of Summers' worthless existence started to unravel, as they are wont to do, in a small way. After sheltering in his shoebox of a bedsit for much of what had been a wet and windy day, Summers decided to collect the promised kilo of heroin from Flynn, who was ensconced rather more comfortably in his executive dwelling on the outskirts of Stambridge. Having thrived from his criminal enterprise, Joseph (never 'Joe') Flynn was determined to enjoy the fruits of his illicit labours. He was equally determined not to allow the likes of Summers across the doorstep; the scruffy oik was likely to trample mud and God knew what else all over the carpets which his Doreen prized above all else, the way she went on about it. When Summers rang, Flynn instructed him to call in on number one son, Joseph Junior (who was always known as 'Joe' to avoid confusion). Joe was at one of the family's many lock ups, a shed behind an old house which was in the process of being renovated, albeit at a snail's pace. So Summers dragged himself from his pit and made his way through the wind and the rain, meeting Joe at the lock up as darkness fell.

Summers knew Joe of old and had always been envious of the heir apparent to the Flynn millions, as he was sure was the case. Joe, for his part, saw Summers as one of the staff, simply local cannon fodder who helped the wheels of the Flynn crime machine keep turning. However amenable and magnanimous

Joe might appear outwardly, he didn't mince his words when he held an opinion.

'I told my dad he must be fucking mental giving you a kilo of smack', Joe told Summers by way of greeting. 'If you fucking shonk him, you're going to be trundling around on one of them fucking mobility scooters for the rest of your life. He won't fucking care what the reason is; whether it's another dealer taxing you or your tosspot buyers not paying, he won't care; he'll do your fucking knees mate. And if the filth get hold of it, you'd better hope they sentence you to fucking Alcatraz because you'll still owe him for it and he'll still collect. Get my drift, Lee?'

Summers did indeed get the drift of Joe's message. At an early stage in his employment he'd been invited, if that was the right word, to see what happened when Joseph Flynn had cause to express his disappointment with one of his staff. Joseph extended this invitation to all those who worked for him, in order to ensure their absolute and unswerving loyalty. He didn't consider attendance at an 'obedience demonstration' to be optional. The recipient of that day's corrective learning had been a debt collector, very similar in standing and function to Summers himself, who had simply added an additional ten percent to the amount he was demanding on behalf of the Flynns. Unfortunately, he had not seen fit to run this staff incentive scheme past Joseph Flynn before putting it into effect and benefitting from it. Joseph took a dim view of such innovation.

Summers considered himself a hard case and was happy to dish out a kicking at the slightest excuse. Even so he felt extremely uncomfortable at the sight and sound of the debt collector experiencing the dubious privilege of having his testicles connected by jump leads to a car battery.

'While I'm on the subject, keep your bloody wits about you, what you have of them,' Joe added. 'There's a mob been down this way from Birmingham. You know my dad's mate Robbo?' Summers did. They robbed his firm a couple of nights back. This lot stuck blue lights on their motor and got some of those yellow jackets so they look like coppers. These muppets in the other firm fell for it and stopped for the cop car when the blues came on. These tossers asked if they'd got any gear and said they would have to confiscate it, and just gave them a caution then told them to fuck off. They couldn't believe they'd got off so lightly till they told Robbo who went mental with them. They'd lost ten grand's worth of smack. I think Robbo's still trying to decide whether to cripple them or have done with it and just fucking dump them in the Severn. I know what my dad would've done, they'd have been fucking skinned alive,' Joe helpfully pointed out, before going on. 'Seeing as you're here, you can do my dad a favour. You don't want to go wandering around with that smack stuffed down your fucking trousers, do you? I've got a motor round the back that needs dropping off in Newport. Micky Phillips, you know him, runs a garage just by the Maesglas estate if you know that. Here's the directions.' Joe handed Summers a folded sheet of paper. 'There's Micky's phone number on it. Tell him my dad sent you over and he'll sort you out a lift back. I would drop that stash off somewhere safe first though if I were you. The car's round the back of the unit like I said. It's a Golf, you'll love it. Just don't fucking bend it or lose it.'

Summers didn't see fit to ask why the car needed dropping off in Newport as the Flynns ran their business on the basis of 'need to know', and they would have considered that Summers didn't. He would not have been particularly relaxed to learn that two of Phillips' associates had tried to rob a cash-in-transit van earlier that afternoon. In the end they had been put off by the number of potential witnesses and had bottled it, dumping the car on Joe and returning to South Wales by train instead. As their revised arrangements had required them to travel light, this resulted in their blagging gear remaining in the car. The kit comprised balaclavas, a pick axe handle and, even more fatefully for the evening's events, a loaded sawn-off shotgun. It didn't take Summers long to find these items under a blanket on the back seat.

Although technically competent to be in charge of a motor vehicle on a road, pursuant to the Road Traffic Act 1988, Summers had never seen the need to trouble the DVLA for a driving licence, nor did he view insurance as a must-have. He was also not the most considerate of drivers. However, he did love the feeling of power, physical and emotional, to be derived from driving a lively car, so he did not spare the accelerator. Approaching a road junction, he was vaguely aware of an oncoming vehicle which, legally speaking, should have had the right of way but Summers was confident of pulling out in front of it and accelerating away. His assuredness turned swiftly to a minor degree of concern as the other driver appeared to resent this impertinence and accelerated to keep pace behind the Golf. Concern morphed instantly to alarm when blue lights started flashing behind the front grille of the following car.

Before the street lights ended, Summers was able to see that his pursuer was a dark plain car without any apparent markings. The Brummie bastards, thought Summers, must have been lying in wait for him. He speculated briefly as to whether he had been set up by Flynn, before deciding it was academic. If he lost the drugs he was as good as dead regardless of his standing in the eyes of the Flynn family. He kept on driving out of town and the other car kept on following.

It soon became clear to Summers that he was in an unequal contest. Even driving slightly beyond his capabilities and relying on luck to keep him on the road, he could not rid himself of his dogged pursuer. He had to deal with this, he thought, before he fucked up badly and trashed the Golf. The only way out of this situation was, Summers realised, to rely on the tried and tested method of threatening or using violence. The answer lay on the back seat, under the blanket.

Stopping the car abruptly, Summers reached behind him. The first item he was able to grab was a balaclava, which he immediately donned. There was no point in confirming to these toe rags that they had the right man if they were indeed after him in particular. Summers also considered it unlikely that, if they weren't actually after him, they would decide he was of no interest and let him carry on his merry way along with his kilo of smack. They'd probably help themselves to the anyway. So either way, he felt he was on a hiding to nothing.

Putting his hand back under the blanket, he intended to take out the pick axe handle but as he reached for it he saw the driver's door of the other car open and a figure emerge. Joe had been spot on; the bastard was even dressed as a cop, but without his hat.

Summers' fingers closed round the cold metal barrel of the sawn-off. That would have to do instead. He grabbed the firearm, resting it briefly on the front seat to change his grip from barrel to butt, then got out of the car for the inevitable confrontation.

The yellow-jacketed figure was approaching him and showed no intention of keeping his distance. Summers knew he would have to out-bluff him. Raising the shotgun and aiming it at his opponent, he shouted 'Fuck off copper.' His forefinger had naturally found the first of the twin triggers and impulsively squeezed. Not being used to handling firearms, Summers had no real notion of how much pressure was required. In this case, it was not much. He was stunned when the shotgun fired and at that distance, the spread of pellets meant that he couldn't miss. The other guy went down, slumped against the front wing of his own car. There was a gaping cavity in his chest and he certainly didn't look long for this world.

Summers thought the other man looked vaguely familiar, he might even have been a genuine cop, but Summers knew his goose was now cooked. There were no other witnesses and the guy would probably die anyway so it seemed perfectly right to put him out of his misery. Summers fired the second barrel.

The damage to the other guy, be he a cop or another crim, was clearly too much for him to live. The penny dropped with Summers that, should he be caught, he would be so deep in the brown stuff it wouldn't be worth trying to swim to the surface. Stopping around to see what happened next did not seem to be the brightest option, so he got back in the Golf and floored it.

***

'You've used my fucking shooter and my fucking wheels to kill a cop? You fucking moronic, half-witted scumbag.' It was clear to Summers that Phillips was not best pleased with the turn of events. Thanks to the absence of living witnesses, and the scarcity of policing resources to carry out even routine traffic checks, the rest of Summers' odyssey to Newport had been blissfully uneventful. Phillips was not yet finished. 'What fucking use is this car to me now? The filth will be crawling all over looking for it and any blue Golf is going to be towed off for forensic examination at the first sniff of any criminal connections.'

'I told you there's no witnesses,' implored Summers. 'There was only me and him, and he's fucking stiffed. He won't talk. He can't,' he added.

'I'm not gonna take the chance. I'll have to lose the car and the shooter. I'll have to think on how I'm going to do that. STEVE!!'

'Yes, mate?' The voice came from the back of the workshop. A second man, whom Summers presumed to be Steve, came forward and joined them.

'This prize fuckwit has gone and offed a rozzer. Think you can get rid of the Golf? It'll need torching. The shotgun needs to disappear too because Brain of Fucking Britain here gave the poor bastard both barrels.'

'The motor, not a problem. It'll need to be somewhere remote. Up the Brecon Beacons is probably the best we can do right now. You don't need to know where, Micky, better that you don't, in fact. Give me the keys, I'll get it sorted. I'll give you a bell later when it's done and let you know where to pick me up if that's OK.'

Phillips chucked Steve the car keys. 'Yeah, I'll fetch you when I've sorted this plonker out, Steve.' He turned to Summers. 'I'll have to have a word with Flynny over this. My lads should never have dumped the car on Joe and fucked off like that, let alone leaving the shooter in the car. But then again nor should you have taken time out to reduce the size of the constabulary by one. So by any account, it's you that owes me, not Flynny. Now fuck off before I suggest to Steve we leave you in the car when he sets it alight. I am sorely fucking tempted.'

Summers' only real stroke of luck that day was that he had just enough cash on him to buy a rail ticket back home, although it was late evening by the time the train reached Stambridge. His bedsit was a half mile walk through the nearly-deserted streets, miserable enough on any wet and windy evening, let alone one which had seen worries of cataclysmic proportions descend on the hapless Summers.

Fate had not yet quite finished with Summers this day, however. As he wandered along the wind-blown, rain-soaked street, a police car slowly drew up alongside him. The passenger side window eased its way down and the street-lit face of a tired-looking police officer emerged. 'Evening mate, we just need a quick word with you if that's ok.'

Too drained to argue, Summers did as he was told. A routine check, he was told. 'There's been a serious incident outside Stambridge earlier this evening,' the cop said. 'Name, date of birth, address please.' Summers gave them his details. 'What you doing out and about?' the cop was curious to know.

'I've been to Newport,' he told him, thinking quickly. They'd probably have CCTV showing him getting off the train in any case. For that matter there was CCTV on the trains as well nowadays so they'd know where he got on. Big fucking Brother rules okay.

'Why did you go to Newport?' Cops were nosey bastards, as Summers well knew.

'I was looking at a car.'

'You obviously didn't buy it, did you? You should've done, saved yourself getting a soaking.' Not just nosey but chatty too, Summers thought. The local plods must be running another charm offensive. Wonders never ceased. 'Right mate, thanks for your cooperation. I'd get home and get dry if I were you.' The police officer wound the window up as the car drove off, trailing a fine mist of spray in its wake.

For a moment, Summers was relieved that the cops hadn't got out and searched him. Then, as realisation dawned on him that he'd left a kilo of heroin, with a street value approaching thirty thousand pounds, in what was almost certainly by now the smouldering remains of the Golf, his utterly miserable evening was made complete.

CHAPTER ELEVEN

To: *Assistant Chief Constable Harper,*
From: *Detective Superintendent Richard Whittingham,
SIO, Operation Witchford (Murder of PC Kerridge)*

Sir,

*As requested, the following is an overview to date of the
investigation into the murder of PC428 Nicholas Kerridge,
Western Division Roads Policing Unit, on 26th October last
year (Operation Witchford refers). First and foremost, the
Counter Terrorist Unit has assessed this incident as not linked
to terrorism.*

Circumstances

*PC Kerridge was on mobile patrol in an unmarked Volvo
V70, MW76, at approximately 1930hrs that day. His tour of
duty was 1400-2200hrs. He was single crewed at the time of
the incident. However between 1400hrs and 1910hrs that day
he had been on mobile patrol in company with PC875 Mark
Garrett in a marked vehicle, MW92. PC Garrett was
preparing a court file in the WDRPU office at Fordwell at the
time of the incident. This was authorised by PS Alison
Dunholme, the team's supervisor, and who was also in the
office at Fordwell at the time of the incident. Both officers have
been debriefed by Professional Standards Department and
their actions and activities prior to and after the incident were
wholly in line with established policy and procedure.*

*PC Kerridge was currently authorised to Advanced level,
for that category of vehicle, and was also Tactical Pursuit and
Containment (TPAC) trained. He was therefore fully
authorised to be carrying out the operational activity in which*

he was engaged, namely attempting to stop a moving motor vehicle following a suspicious incident earlier in his tour.

The suspicious incident, reported by George Thatcham, a member of the public, at 1534hrs that day, was recorded on the control log as:

15:34:07 TELEPHONE CALL VIA FORCE CALL BUREAU
CALLER STATES HE HAS SEEN A BLUE VW GOLF GTI FOLLOWING A CASH DELIVERY VAN ROUND STAMBRIDGE TOWN CENTRE. IT HAS BEEN UP AND DOWN THE HIGH STREET A COUPLE OF TIMES AND LOOKS A BIT ODD. THERE ARE TWO MEN IN IT WHO DON'T LOOK LIKE SECURITY GUARDS. THEY ARE A BIT SCRUFFY. HE THINKS IT IS SUSPICIOUS. PARTIAL VRM IS YZ57--- NO FURTHER DETAILS.

Mr. Thatcham has been fully debriefed by investigators and cannot provide any significant additional details. He is 73 years old and his eyesight is not perfect so he is unable to confirm the vehicle registration with absolute certainty. However he is adamant that the type of car is accurate as it is the same make and model as his grand-daughter's car. He saw the car in clear daylight so is certain about the colour.

Following receipt of the call, MW92 was despatched to Stambridge arriving at 1548hrs, but did not locate either the security van or any vehicle resembling the VW Golf. MW92 remained in the area of Stambridge carrying out routine operational activities (see attached log at Appendix One) taking their meal break between 1700 and 1745hrs at Fordwell. They resumed mobile patrol, again covering the area between Fordwell, Stambridge and the force boundary. The period of time between resuming from their meal break until returning to Fordwell at 1910hrs was uneventful.

MW76 was checked by PC Kerridge when he took the vehicle out and he signed the vehicle's logbook to this effect. There were no apparent or reported deficiencies being carried by the vehicle, with the exception of the front passenger seat heating system which was not working and was not considered a priority by Fleet Maintenance. The vehicle radio set was working correctly at all times and had been operated by PC Kerridge immediately prior to the incident.

The control room log of the Op Witchford incident is attached as Appendix Two. This commenced at 1935hrs on the outskirts of Stambridge when PC Kerridge informed control that he was following a VW Golf towards Severndale Forest. He was not able to confirm the registration number of the vehicle.

MW91 offered to assist MW76 in stopping the Golf and a divisional unit SB20 also made for the area, although stating they were not pursuit trained.

At 1938hrs PC Kerridge told control that the vehicle had stopped on a minor road in Severndale Forest. This road leads west eventually joining the A4344 near the village of Stoney Fold. The final contact with PC Kerridge was at 1939hrs but he did not give any description or state any intentions. The control room operator, Patricia Heald, states that he sounded perfectly calm.

Nothing having been heard from PC Kerridge for some four minutes Ms. Heald, being aware that PC Kerridge was single crewed and stopping a vehicle in a remote location, decided to check his welfare by radio call. There was no response. After a short series of further such calls, Ms. Heald raised her concerns with Insp. Raj Dhesi, the Force Control Room supervisor. No further contact was made with PC Kerridge.

MW91, crewed by PC Jane McKenzie and PC Stuart Williams located MW76 at 1951hrs. There was no sign of the Golf or its occupant. PC Kerridge was lying against the front nearside wing of MW76 having sustained what appeared to be gunshot wounds. PC Kerridge did not respond in any way and life was pronounced extinct at the scene by the paramedics who attended at 2015hrs. The post mortem established that he had been shot twice at close range by a twelve-bore shot gun. The opinion of the pathologist is that PC Kerridge was killed outright by either the first or the second shot. He did not appear to have moved since falling against the vehicle. The power and spread of the pellets suggest that the shotgun was a sawn-off.

PS Dunholme attended and preserved the scene. As on call SIO for the force I attended, arriving at 2055hrs, by which time the duty Detective Inspector, DI Heather Turner, and SOCO were also present. The on call ACC was Mr. Dickinson and I briefed him a number of times over the first few hours. The Press Office was also called out and a series of press conferences were held. Mr. Dickinson dealt with the media.

Post Mortem Examination

A PM was carried out by Dr. Tristan Habgood, a Home Office pathologist. The report concludes that PC Kerridge died of internal injuries inflicted by multiple shotgun pellets from two twelve-bore cartridges fired separately at close range. The injuries were not considered survivable. PC Kerridge was otherwise in good physical condition for his age, with no physical abnormalities or medical conditions worthy of note.

Forensic Evidence

MW76 has been subject to a full forensic and mechanical examination which was conducted by the Force Serious Collision Investigation Team in conjunction with officers from Op Witchford. There has been nothing found of evidential value to add to evidence found at the scene. FSCIT confirms that the vehicle was fully serviceable at the time of the incident.

There was no forensic trace recovered from MW76 that can be attributed to any suspect. It therefore appears that the offender did not enter MW76 or have any direct physical contact with it.

Evidence recovered at scene (see photographs) included numerous shotgun pellets from the front offside wing of MW76 which are identical to those found in the body of PC Kerridge.

There were fresh tyre tracks in soft mud on the road verge. Partial forensic lifts were made but these were not definitive due to the heavy rain. It has not been possible to identify the tyres responsible.

The road surface was very wet, and no footwear marks were seen or recovered. There were no cigarette butts found at the scene and no other discarded items attributed to the offender. A thorough finger-tip search has been made of the vicinity of the scene, and a complete search has been made of the roads, verges and adjoining areas along the road to Stoney Fold. Because of the narrowness of the minor road at the location, it would not have been possible for a vehicle to pass MW76 and there was no sign of any attempt to do so. However, further thorough searches have been conducted back to the main road, to no gain.

Local Enquiries

All farms, outbuildings and other dwellings in the vicinity have been visited and all householders have now been traced, interviewed and eliminated. No similar vehicle has been found in the locality.

House to house enquiries have been conducted in Stoney Fold. Three residents confirm hearing a vehicle passing at speed at or around 1945hrs. However it is not uncommon for vehicles to travel at speed at night in the vicinity so no one thought this unusual.

CCTV has been seized and viewed from Stambridge town centre, both the local authority system, which comprises two cameras, and local commercial premises. The Golf was acting as described by Mr. Thatcham, but it is not crystal clear because of the rain on the lens. The cameras in Stam-bridge were recording but not being actively monitored when the Golf

112

was visible. Although the details on the log were passed to the CCTV room, by the time the operator switched over to Stambridge the Golf and security van had moved on.

The crew of the security van, Matthew Abingdola and Harry Yates, has been fully debriefed. They were aware of the Golf but as it was following quite openly it appeared to them that it was just a couple of 'boy racers' messing about, as this often happens apparently. They did not make any stops while the Golf was following them, but went back later to finish off, when there was no sign of it. They called it in to their control room where it was logged.

Vehicle Enquiries

No blue VW Golfs have been reported stolen in the Stambridge area recently (the last such report was six months ago). Five such vehicles have been reported stolen in this force area in the past two years. Blue is not an uncommon colour for VW Golfs, even GTi models, though the most popular colours are black and silver. None have a registration number similar to YZ57. A batch search has been carried out on PNC for YZ57 blue Golfs. 24 blue Golfs were sold on a 57 plate in the YZ area, which is Yorkshire. Of these two have been written off, three others now bear personalised plates. However all registered keepers have been visited. Eight in total have been sold on; one of these has been sold three times in total. All but one of these vehicles have been accounted for. The outstanding vehicle was sold twice, the second time for cash and not subsequently re-registered with DVLA. This is YZ57WSB. This vehicle has been circulated on PNC and ANPR as wanted.

A trawl of ANPR shows that a vehicle with the registration YZ57WSB was picked up on the A48 towards Chepstow at 2011hrs on the evening of the incident. This is some twenty miles from the scene so would have required the Golf to travel at an average speed of 40 miles per hour to be consistent with it having left the scene a couple of minutes after PC Kerridge said he had stopped it. Whilst this is necessarily speculation,

113

it shows it is entirely feasible that the vehicle was directly linked to the incident. There was no trace from ANPR in the Gwent area and we are awaiting confirmation of the location of their cameras, such as they might be. South Wales Police confirm none of their ANPR logged the vehicle so it is possible that it went to the Newport area. It has not pinged ANPR since. Systems on both Severn Bridges show the vehicle definitely hasn't crossed either of them in the month before the incident or since.

I believe the Golf YZ57WSB is the strongest lead we have. Subsequent enquiries have been made with all filling stations in this force area and in Gwent in order to obtain any CCTV or other images when it was being fuelled. However most of these had wiped their systems as normal. They mostly only retain such images for a few days at most as they are usually just bothered about drivers making off without paying. We do have three images from Newport, the latest being four days before the incident, which show the driver to be a car dealer by the name of Michael Phillips (see below). The sales receipts show that he paid cash on each occasion.

Intelligence Checks

The Police National Database has been checked and YZ57WSB was not linked in Yorkshire. However it was stop-checked in Gwent force area two weeks before the incident. It was shown in trade at the time and being driven by Phillips. There is intelligence to suggest Phillips supplies 'clean' cars to some of the South Wales organised criminals, but his paperwork suggests the Golf was moved on a few days before the incident. It was a cash sale and the buyer gave his name as James Robinson without a verified address. The cash is all marked up in the books, so there are no tax or VAT issues.

Person Checks

On the evening of the incident all available staff were tasked with stopping and checking vehicles and anyone else considered worth speaking to. Details of some 2600 checks are held should any suspects subsequently come to light.

Suspects

Michael PHILLIPS attended Newport Police Station at our request. He has been interviewed and eliminated as the killer as he was definitely in Newport all that day, including on the evening in question. He was at work at the time as he had an urgent job on. He was with at least one colleague, a Stephen BEASANT, who confirmed PHILLIPS' alibi. Neither of them is known in this force. All we can show is that PHILLIPS was in possession of the Golf until three days or so before the incident. PHILLIPS has no significant previous convictions. The possibility remains that PHILLIPS supplied the vehicle to criminal associates or contacts as per the intelligence, and is covering for them. In that case it is not unlikely pressure is being applied to secure his silence. For that reason, PHILLIPS remains of interest to Op Witchford. Telecoms enquiries relating to PHILLIPS' business and personal landlines and known mobiles have not, to date, revealed any links of note. It is possible he has an unattributed Pay As You Go mobile, but so far none has been found.

James ROBINSON has not so far been traced. PHILLIPS gave a credible description of him as male, white, aged mid-forties, short fair hair, and no distinguishing features. He had an accent described by PHILLIPS as 'not local, probably London or something like that'. PHILLIPS admits that if someone wants to buy a car for cash he would be daft to turn it down. Plenty of other 'grey economy' businessmen routinely use cash, according to PHILLIPS, which is no surprise. We have searched PNC and PND and found 115 possible matches across the country. Host forces are assisting us in speaking to all of them but as yet we have not identified a definite suspect from this line of enquiry. In the case of PHILLIPS being leant on by others, it is considered quite likely that ROBINSON is a fabrication. If proven this implicates PHILLIPS in Perverting the Course of Justice, rather than simply Assisting an Offender.

Stephen BEASANT has been interviewed and his account also confirms that of PHILLIPS. There is nothing so far to link BEASANT directly to the murder of PC Kerridge. However, because of his account he is inextricably linked to PHILLIPS should the latter be found to be lying.

PC Kerridge had not reported any direct credible threats of harm to him or his family. Although it is to be anticipated that his work in roads policing might occasionally prove unpopular with some offenders, there is no one believed to hold a specific personal grudge against him. Over the course of his career, including recently, PC Kerridge's workload was slightly above average but he did not have a reputation for being over-zealous. At the time of the incident, he was not subject of any outstanding complaints and his disciplinary record overall was in line with expectations for an operationally effective roads policing officer. There were no known issues in his private life that might conceivably have resulted in anyone seeking to harm him.

No identified strong suspects have thus far emerged and the only tangible lead, short of a source or a member of the public coming forward, is the VW Golf YZ57WSB. It is essential that this vehicle is located and the identity of its driver established for the evening of the incident.

Ongoing Enquiries

1. I am due to appear on Crimewatch next month to try and re-establish some momentum in the enquiry.

2. I have also directed that there be a renewed tasking of sources, and have authorised enhanced payments for relevant information.

3. There is an advertised reward of £100000, also linked to Crimestoppers, for information leading to conviction.

4. We have repeatedly contacted the media, though in the absence of progress their interest is increasingly difficult to sustain; indeed certain newspapers have become somewhat negative in their coverage so we have the issue of reputation management to consider.

5. Warning markers on PNC are still valid and, as mentioned above, ANPR has been updated to keep the registration live. However, it is as if the Golf has disappeared and we have to face the possibility that it has been permanently disposed of in an untraceable manner.

6. Although we have recovered shot gun pellets, in the absence of cartridges and the firearm itself, these are of no evidential value. All forces have been notified that the firearm is still outstanding and any recovered will be forensically examined.

7. An intelligence requirement has been disseminated to Gwent and South Wales forces for PHILLIPS and associations with organised crime nominals.

Sir, I have to report that the above is the most accurate update and overview that I am able to give you at this time. I would appreciate your views on the continuing scale of the investigation into the tragic death of PC Kerridge.

Yours sincerely,

Richard Whittingham,
Detective Superintendent.

That, I thought as I carefully replaced the SIO's report in his in-tray, explained a lot. No eye-witnesses, no forensics and no suspect to link them to even if one turned up. I was annoyed that I hadn't had the chance to remove the tape masking the registration number and pass the details on to control. At least they would have had a fighting chance of stopping the vehicle if it could have been circulated sooner. I'd never heard of Phillips so didn't know how he was linked to Summers, if at all. Summers, who had actually done the dastardly deed, didn't even feature in the report, unless he was amongst the 2600 people stopped and checked. At the moment, at least in the expert opinion of the SIO, everything hinged either on Phillips coughing that Summers had had the car, or else information being received in expectation of the reward. It was nice to know that grassing up my killer was worth a hundred grand, but even that might not outweigh the threat of concrete wellies and a trip to the bottom of the River Severn should the wrong person get to hear about it.

The progress of what I thought of as 'my' investigation had been bothering me since I'd been back to retrieve Don't Jump Derek. Chris, to be fair, understood my angst, though her initial counsel was to try and move on. In the end she'd not demurred when I said I was going to go back and see what was happening. Nigel in Reception had let me out into the alleyway and I had a pleasant enough trip back to my old stamping ground. I was tempted to drop in at Fordwell to see who was around but common sense prevailed. It would have been a bit upsetting for me to see them and not be able to communicate with them. However materialising would have been a disastrous idea and quite likely have resulted in getting myself banned from traveling back, which would mean no job of course. Direct communication with the living was strictly forbidden, that much had been made clear time and again. For that matter, visiting any of my old haunts would not have been entirely helpful at this stage in my transition, of that I was in no doubt.

The Major Investigation Department was, in my force, responsible for investigating all homicides other than those that occurred as a result of road traffic collisions. This had always grated with me. The chances of getting killed on the roads was three or four times that of being murdered, but road deaths still didn't seem to be taken quite as seriously as murders. That was bizarre, I'd always thought, because the victim was just as dead and the cause was probably just as academic to all the grieving relatives. Be that as it may, my untimely demise was the prime concern of MID and specifically Detective Superintendent Whittingham, to whom I would be eternally grateful, should he somehow manage to pin the charge on Summers.

MID's modern offices sat anonymously in the middle of a business park on the outskirts of Bracewell, a market town situated an inconvenient distance from both Fordwell and Stambridge. It was, by virtue of the detective work carried out there, something of a fortress and entry was strictly by authorisation or invitation. Unless, of course, you happen to be a ghost, so I just breezed in like I owned the place. No one could have stopped me and no one tried, because I chose to remain ethereal and invisible. As a mere plod, and a traffic one at that, no one had ever considered that there was any benefit to them in inviting me to have a look round the place, so I hadn't got the faintest idea where to go. There were three floors and my years of experience with the complete absence of variety in policing premises suggested to me that the specialist departments such as Scientific Support, those with most potential callers, would be on the ground floor. That kept the riffraff confined as close as possible to the outside world, where they belonged. The top floor, with its panoramic views of whatever lay beyond the business park, would be the preserve of senior management who would not want to be disturbed by lesser mortals, even within their own department. By a process of deduction that left the middle floor, which is where I started. There were three rooms set aside for major investigations and my ego was gratified to see that my apparently moribund investigation was awarded the signal honour of languishing in Incident Room One.

Inside the large open-plan room were the usual rows of desks, each with a dedicated terminal. At one end was a row of three smart-boards. All of these were inactive, mainly because I had chosen to visit on a Sunday evening. Overtime was clearly being rationed as the room was unoccupied. The far end of the room was partitioned into two internal offices, one each for the SIO and Deputy SIO. Rank still had some privileges. There were windows between the offices and the main room, all of which featured blinds to provide privacy when desired. I didn't know D/Supt. Whittingham personally or by reputation, but I imagined that the lack of progress in the investigation would have tested his humour at times, so the staff would be spared his scowls if the blinds were closed.

Of the two long walls, one comprised a series of tinted windows, no doubt reflective on the outside to thwart curious window cleaners. The other featured a number of white-boards, on which was displayed a wealth of information, contact numbers, photos from the scene and of numerous persons of interest. Two such images were a custody photograph of Summers, looking a few years younger and slightly less haggard than when I had last seen him, and one marked '*Michael PHILLIPS 24-03-1969*' looking a lot younger than the age suggested by his date of birth. In marker pen under the photograph of Summers was the comment *'Seen Stambridge 2320hrs, off Newport train. Not linked to PHILLIPS (yet)'*. That was something, I thought. At least he was but one link away from being a decent suspect. In a moment of devilment I picked up a marker pen and drew an arrow to Summers' mug-shot, writing in neat (and untraceable, I hoped) capital letters: SUMMERS IS YOUR MAN. I couldn't afford to have anyone doing a handwriting check; if it was matched to mine that would cause major ructions, so I kept it as neutral as possible. I had no doubt that there would be something of an inquisition into who had written it, and on what basis of fact. On the other hand, a diligent Detective Sergeant might think someone was mucking about and erase it, but hopefully the seed would have been planted. Realistically, and short of giving the game away, under the circumstances it was all I could do to assist them.

CHAPTER TWELVE

'Michael Phillips, James Robinson and Stephen Beasant are the only names they've got to go on. Summers only features because he was checked out wandering around Stambridge later on.'

I was back in the Intelligence Office, along with Danny and Gordon. I'd filled them in on my trip to MID and both had bought into my personal mission to get Summers brought to justice. Danny, after his arrival here, had felt a sense of annoyance about his own gangland murder, until he checked up and found that his executioner had been locked up and sentenced to thirty years minimum. I had no doubt that Danny was relishing a forthcoming reunion when the bastard's time came. Gordon was probably just along for the ride as the passage of time, I imagined, had lessened his own hunger for vengeance. Plus he probably hoped there was the chance of going back and killing some bad guys. Whatever their reasons, I was grateful for their support and encouragement.

A penny dropped with Danny as soon as I mentioned Phillips' name. 'Micky Phillips from Newport? Car dealer bloke?'

'That's what the report said. Do you know him?'

'When I was undercover we used to rent motors off him,' Danny continued. 'He had a guy called Steve who worked for him, I don't know his last name. James Robinson doesn't ring a bell though. Where does he fit in?' Small world, I thought, but if Danny's previous work showed that Phillips had been linked to serious crime it would certainly strengthen the case against him. If, that was, the investigation team could get to know about it.

'Robinson's the bloke who supposedly bought the car off Phillips. They haven't tracked him down yet; for all anyone knows, Phillips might've made him up.' I was fairly certain that was the case; it was not entirely unknown for people to lie to us, even in serious crimes for which they were not personally responsible.

'Look at what we know and what the investigation team knows,' suggested Danny. 'We need to be able point them in the right direction. It's them who have to be able to prove it. Shame really as it would be a laugh seeing Nick giving evidence in court. That would get them talking.'

'We know Summers had the car; I saw the plate and it was definitely the part registration they passed out. But it's all very well me knowing that, for them it's just a line of enquiry. For all they know it could be another car entirely,' I mused. 'They've got to show that Summers had the means, the motive and the opportunity to kill me. I know he had the means and the opportunity but I could only hazard a guess at his motive. From what I can remember of him he was just a small-time toe-rag. He was handy with his fists but I don't ever recall him having a firearms marker. He was a drug dealer but never got convicted of it as he wasn't all that high on our list of priorities. I know he was a runner for the Flynns who were what passed for a home-grown OCG. I never had him down for a blagger though.'

'Can't we just go and sort the blighter out ourselves?' suggested Gordon. 'I'm sure we could persuade Paul to get him put in some really unpleasant Redevelopment Unit for a few centuries. There are some tough ones for the child rapists and war criminals. That would be better than him getting mollycoddled in some cosy prison for the next thirty years, as you chaps keep moaning on about. In my day at least he'd have swung for it early one morning.'

'I'm not sure even Paul would go for that one, not if he's only killed one person, even someone as revered as our esteemed colleague here,' Danny considered. 'It's too much grief from Fate Planning for what it would achieve, it's really only important to us. We can have a look for his file, see if he's overdue, which is a long shot. If he is, he's fair game.'

Gordon stood up and went to the furthest rack. 'It's a useless system for tracking anyone down by name,' he muttered. 'We can't guarantee he's here as he might not be due yet. Was Summers born and bred in Stambridge? That would make things a tad easier.'

'Yeah, I'm pretty certain he was, from what I remember,' I told him. 'While we're looking for him, is it worth looking in the Newport files as well, in case the other guys are overdue?'

'Wilco, Phillips and Robinson?' confirmed Gordon.

'Yes. Phillips is probably shown in Newport but Robinson could be anywhere, if indeed he exists,' I suggested.

I turned back to Danny. 'If they find the car, as long as it's not been totally trashed, they might just be able to forensically link it to Summers, but even that on its own wouldn't put Summers at the scene. It would be a cough or nothing, unless of course the shotgun turns up as well, with Summers' fingerprints on it. Even then he might be able talk his way out of it though he'd need to be pretty damned convincing. Going 'No comment' would sink him.'

'Even if they had the car, placed Summers in the car by forensics and put the shotgun in his hands, it would still be circumstantial. We need Summers with the car and the firearm at the scene, at the right time. The registration number wasn't complete and there's no transfer of material between you and him.' Danny was getting into his stride. 'But bearing in mind it wasn't his motor, and he's not known to have been into firearms, the circumstantial evidence would be that bit stronger. What we really need, and what the investigation team really needs, is to get Summers linked to the vehicle either just before he shot you, or just after. Preferably both, because then he'd be really stuffed. Answers on a postcard?'

'It looks from the SIO report like he headed straight over towards Newport, or at least Chepstow, so in all likelihood he was returning the car to Phillips,' I added. 'The team thinks that as well so it's just a matter of proving that. In the absence of Summers coming clean, then they need to find the car still in Phillips' possession, or get Phillips to cough to it and grass Summers up. Phillips certainly won't want to go down for murdering a cop so I'm sure if push came to shove he'd come on side.'

'The other possibility is that someone else saw Summers take the car back to Phillips and could give witness evidence to that effect,' Gordon chipped in. 'Was there anyone else there?'

'Steve Beasant gave Phillips an alibi, so that's a possibility,' I conceded. 'The other question is how Summers got the car in the first place. Did he get it from Phillips or someone else? Phillips said he sold the car to this James Robinson. Personally, my bullshit detector went off at that, it's just a little bit too coincidental as he'd had the car so recently and then after the shooting it's clocked heading back towards Newport. Shame it didn't hit ANPR on the way to Stambridge, you'd have thought it would have taken a similar route as it didn't go over the Severn Bridges.'

'Mobile ANPR?' I suggested.' Very good for picking up vehicles driving past that are already wanted but it's a bit hit and miss otherwise. It all boils down to a number of possibilities: there was no ANPR when Summers set off from Newport, he used a different route or he picked the car up from someone else. Two people know the answer to that, Summers and Phillips. May be Beasant if he was there too.'

'Unfortunately the people who don't actually know are the investigation team, and us,' Danny mused.

'Bizarre, isn't it, when you think of it,' I commented. 'We know who did it but can't link the suspect to what the investigation already knows. They, meanwhile, have found out a few odds and ends that we had no knowledge of, but they don't know what's relevant and what's a red herring. And we've got no way of letting them know what we know.'

'Like we've already said, though, it's one thing putting Summers in the frame, another entirely providing any tangible evidence. And then we'd have to find a way of communicating with the team that didn't blow our cover.' Danny stood up. 'I'm going to fetch a brew, you two fine legal minds want one as well?'

Having accepted our orders for drinks, coffee for me and finest Earl Grey tea for the formerly intrepid aviator Gordon, Danny loped off in the direction of the canteen. I went to give Gordon a hand ratching through the files of the inadvertently undead. Gordon soon exhausted the relatively small number relating to the residents of Stambridge and had moved across the Welsh border, bureaucratically speaking, and was checking out Newport. I occupied my time looking for places near Stambridge, just in case the Grim Reaper's intelligence system was more accurate than that of my former employer.

'Why are you so hell-bent on nailing this Summers bounder, if you don't mind me asking?' Gordon was slowly working his way along the racks of files.

'Because I was seriously hacked off that some scrote deprived me of my pension. But I can accept, I suppose, that I was never intended to collect on that despite the exorbitant amount I paid into the scheme, money I now wish I'd totally wasted on having a good time. Worse than that, though, it's because I dropped my guard for an instant and the same toe rag got the better of me. It goes against everything I'd worked for all those years. How about you, weren't you angry when you got brought down by the Red Baron or whoever it was?'

'Not angry, no. I was shocked at first, and totally gutted as I thought I'd had a lot to look forward to. There was this popsie of a WAAF that I thought I was on a promise with, for a start. As for the Hun who shot me down, there was no point in getting too upset about it. He only lasted a week longer than me. Life expectancy for aircrew wasn't brilliant, regardless of which side you were on. 'Learn to fly, then you die' would've been an appropriate motto for all of us. As soon as I adjusted to being over here I started going to the Flying Club which is where a lot of the aircrew types meet up. I'll take you over one evening. It's equally popular with the ordinary decent Hun fliers, which it turns out is most of them. They were only following orders after all, and they believed they were defending their homes which we were trying to flatten.

'Anyway during the war there were so many of us turning up that we couldn't meet everybody individually but still wanted to catch up with our mates. We'd post our details on a board, stuff like squadron, where and when we were killed, that kind of thing. One evening this night-fighter bod got in touch and said he'd shot me down. He shook my hands and actually apologised for the inconvenience he'd caused me! We've had many a beer over the years. We're good mates now, after all that, so there was no point in me going on about him. He'd had an engine failure on take-off a few days after shooting down my Lanc. He ploughed into an SS barracks. I pointed out the irony that he'd probably done more damage to the Third Reich than I'd managed on all my ops put together.'

He digressed easily, did Gordon, but he'd answered my question.

'I just want to get Summers potted, as much for my colleagues as myself,' I volunteered, rather selflessly I thought. 'When there's an unsolved murder of a copper, the pressure's on my colleagues to get it sorted. They get put upon by the bosses, because it's always bad form to have an unsolved murder on the books. Next thing is the press latch on to the lack of a result so gives the force a kicking. Usually they go on about how we should call in the Met, like no one else can get a result. Unless of course it's the Met that can't solve a crime, then the papers bang on about them being arrogant and a law unto themselves who would do well to learn from other forces. Worst of all, as far as I'm concerned, is knowing that there's a cop killer out there, laughing at us and, for all we know, waiting to get another of us. So, yes, it's personal and yes, I want Summers brought to justice and for as many people as possible to know about it.'

'Well in that case...' Gordon paused theatrically. 'You might be interested to know that, even though we haven't found Summers, at least your Mr. Beasant missed his date with fate. He's two years overdue.'

'Tell me more,' I said, intrigued.

'He's now thirty five years old and survived a car crash which was supposed to finish him off. It appears that there was a bit of a SNAFU and they got his passenger instead. So he's in play if you want him.'

'We could bring him in then and see what he knows,' I pondered. 'I don't suppose Phillips is overdue as well?'

'No sign of him so far. To get more than one of them would be stretching our luck.'

'Stretching our luck in what way?' Danny had just wandered back in with a tray of hot drinks, so we congregated around the table.

'No sign of Summers but we have found out Phillips' alibi witness, Beasant, should've been here two years ago.' I informed him. 'What do you reckon, Danny, should we bring him in or hope that the investigation team get there without us?'

'Well, he could tell us whether Phillips is or isn't lying

126

about the car. He might even know where Summers fits in so that would be handy. But unless we can find some way of getting what we find out across to the investigation team, there's not a lot of point.'

'How often did you used to start an investigation in the vague belief that it would all come together in the end?' I asked him. 'It didn't used to stop us, did it? We can Beasant bring in, that's perfectly legit and won't scupper the official investigation. We've got a much better chance of wringing out of Beasant what really went on with Phillips and Summers than they have. There's bound to be some way of imparting that to the team one way or another, even if I have to go back and do the old 'writing on the wall' trick.'

'Sounds like a plan then,' said Danny. 'Or, rather, two plans. One is to fetch in this Beasant bloke and the second is to find someone who can pass the info on without it coming out that it's from us.'

'Yup, that's about the shape of it,' I told him. 'Now, how can we get hold of Mr. Beasant?'

CHAPTER THIRTEEN

We decided it would be better if I didn't get directly involved in retrieving Beasant, so that task was left to Danny and Gordon. I was quite confident that they would tell me all about it in any case. Once he was here I would get the chance to speak to him and it was not as if we were short of time. We didn't do release without charge after 24 hours. In any case, I had something else planned. Call me vindictive if you like, but I wanted to put Summers under a bit of pressure, in the hope that he might feel compelled to confess. The best way I could think of to achieve that was to frighten him witless.

After the other two had departed, I went back to my room and went through my wardrobe. Having realised that the closet would contain whatever I wanted it to, I found my old uniform, including my rather bedraggled and blood-stained high visibility vest. I hadn't seen it since my arrival, but now I wanted it, there it was. I rolled the vest up and stuffed it under a more innocuous-looking casual jacket. There was no point in making a scene till I was ready.

By now, Nigel was used to my passing through to the other world, so I didn't need to explain myself. He barely glanced up from his crossword as he pressed the buzzer to let me out.

I was still invisible and intended to keep things that way, at least for now. My first call was back at my old office at Fordwell. I had tried to time things for when it was least likely to be occupied, so I waited until I knew the late shift would all be in the team briefing. It wasn't to spare their feelings, as they couldn't see me, but I still thought it might be a bit painful for me. I eased my way into the RPU office and scoured the pin boards on the walls till I found what I was looking for.

I'd remembered seeing Summers' details on the wall when I'd worked there, but couldn't quite recall his address and, as luck would have it, he still featured on the list of our priority nominals, specifically because he was known to drive without the niceties of driving licence or insurance. 28A Springbourne Gardens, Stambridge. Very nice too, it sounded, though I knew it was anything but. A red brick council-owned dwelling on a run-down sink estate, the Summers residence was a squalid first floor flat.

I had what I needed from the RPU office so made myself scarce. It's the same feeling you get when, having left somewhere you knew well, you go back to it. There are usually too many memories and you realise that the place has moved on without you. I could understand why some spirits might try too hard to hold on to what they had lost, condemning themselves to the purgatory of rattling round in places once so familiar to them but where they were now just lost souls. I hoped for such entities it didn't take too long for them to realise that the sooner they accepted their new lot after life, the better. For that reason, I definitely didn't want to see any of my old mates, so I departed in search of Summers.

For my, admittedly somewhat malevolent, plan to work, I needed Summers to be on his own. If he was lying in bed in the middle of the night, that would be ideal, but his being alone was vital. I intended to really put the frighteners on him and I didn't want any witnesses, any more than he would have wanted anyone there when he shot me. As it was only mid-afternoon, there was a good chance that Summers would be out and about, doing something not very beneficial for the community, but I would wait if I had to.

It was a seven mile walk from Fordwell to Stambridge, which occupied a couple of hours or so. Being back on Earth, everything wasn't automatically to my liking and it was, once again, raining. This bothered me not one bit as I chose to remain insubstantial. That way I wouldn't get run over, which was one benefit. I amused myself thinking of my colleagues' shock and bafflement if they turned out to a report of a pedestrian knock-down and found that the victim was me. The paperwork on that one would occupy the bosses for years, I thought.

Arriving in Stambridge I made my way to Springbourne Gardens which was an anonymous cul-de-sac on the Westfield estate. This was situated towards the outer edge of the housing development, which by virtue of it lying on the rising side of a hill was known as the Top End. The residents of this insalubrious area considered themselves a cut above the denizens of the even grottier part of the estate further down the slope. This was known, with startling originality, as the Bottom End. Knowing what I did about the living standards of these vertically-discriminating latter-day snobs who wasted their lives at the Top End, I shuddered to think how the other half lived.

Finding Summers' bijou hovel precisely where I had left it after my last professional visit a couple of years earlier, I walked straight through the closed door. No need here for a door ram; this was much easier.

The flat emanated the all-pervading smell I associated with so many similar addresses. When I was young in service I had attributed the acrid stench, which defined all such dwellings, to incontinent cats, and wondered why our clientele put up with such unsociable pets. Eventually it had dawned on me that this was the smell of people who rarely or never washed themselves or their clothing. Summers was certainly in this category, the scruffy herbert. Being dead had done nothing to diminish my sense of smell which was fine when it came to enjoying the aroma of fresh mown grass, or the perfume of flowers. Summers' unwashed underpants did not fall into this pleasurable category however and his whole flat stank.

It didn't appear that Summers himself was particularly house-proud, nor did he appear to live with a partner for whom domestic bliss was high on the agenda. The place was a complete tip. From the kitchen, every working surface piled with unwashed pots and plates, take-away food containers liberally strewn about with total abandon, to the single bedroom which was a pile of unkempt sheets, a duvet and clothing, there wasn't a single part of his abode that looked cared for. He could have been burgled repeatedly and no one would have noticed; in fact the burglars themselves, rather than ransacking the place, would have done better to tidy it up, not that I expected they'd have found anything worth stealing in the bedroom. For all I knew, Summers probably welcomed the occasional police raid just for the free spring cleaning it represented.

There being no immediate sign of my unwitting host, I settled down to wait. I decided that, of the few rooms available to me, the lounge was my preferred option. Having seen the state of the bedroom and kitchen, I certainly didn't feel any compulsion to check out the bathroom.

The lounge, at least, had some discernible space for me to relax while I awaited my killer's return. It was painted in tasteful magnolia, featuring added grubby handprints, especially around the light switches. As a beneficiary of social housing, I expected that Summers could call on the council to pop round every couple of years to spruce up the decor if, that is, they could find the walls through all the clutter. The rest of the room was equipped in what I liked to think of as Benefit Scrounger Chic; an unnecessarily long settee dominated the room on the horizontal plane whilst vertical extravagance was represented by a hideously large flat screen television, the channels provided by a satellite box. Surprisingly the remote control was readily accessible; Summers clearly had his priorities. I pressed the standby button and the screen came to life. In my previous life, this would have constituted an offence of abstracting electricity, but that legal nicety didn't bother me now. Flicking through the channels I chose BBC One as it was about time for the news so I thought I'd catch up on what I'd been missing which, it transpired, was not a lot. Ongoing conflict in the Middle East was providing, from my current perspective, an apparently inexhaustible supply of new arrivals on our side of the divide. I couldn't see how anyone there could survive long enough to come to the attention of my team and certainly I hadn't been aware of any of my colleagues being despatched to Damascus or Tehran to seek out overstayers. Closer to home, matters in Europe still seemed to be perplexing this country's political masters, probably distracting them from their second jobs and their lavish expense accounts, I thought, unless things had changed dramatically since I'd left. There was the obligatory feature on the unseasonably cold and wet conditions; seeing as it was Winter I couldn't see what was unseasonable about either of these but the BBC clearly felt that global warming was to blame for the cold weather. No longer my problem, I was relieved to think.

The national bulletin ended, and the Beeb moved seamlessly on to the local programme. Nothing much had changed here either, it would appear. Problems with hospital services in the area, though nothing that the local trades unionists and opposition politicians thought couldn't be resolved by pumping in even more money from the long-suffering tax payer. Just before the weather forecast, a brief report mentioned delays caused by what the local police had described as 'a serious road traffic collision' just over the border on the Newport road. The delays were expected to last for several hours. This sounded to me like a fatal incident, reading between the lines. When the reporter mentioned that the crash had occurred in otherwise quiet road conditions, with a witness saying that the vehicle had inexplicably lost control, I had to wonder whether Danny and Gordon had anything to do with it.

The Beeb and I moved on to an early evening light entertainment show, almost joyfully witless in the jocular treatment of the topics it covered, thence to its flagship soap opera, which I had always found to be spectacularly dismal, even turgid. I hadn't missed television and could well understand why no one else seemed to be badgering to have it introduced to the Afterlife. Halfway through, the latter programme descended into a gripping re-enactment of a domestic dispute, consisting of an almost incomprehensible cockney tirade by the two protagonists, neither of whom thought of calling the police to sort it out. The neighbours were all at the pub, as it happened, so they didn't summon assistance either. Without anyone acting the part of the cops, there was no policing procedure for me to criticise. I was about start channel-hopping when the flat door opened and in lurched Summers.

He was clearly the worse for wear, having, I immediately assumed, been enjoying the hospitality of some local drinking hole. Still, I thought, better that than burgling folk, or whatever it was that he got up to of an afternoon. Summers looked momentarily baffled to find the television on and a screenful of Londoners airing their dirty linen in public, then shrugged in recognition of the possibility that he'd left it on earlier. He picked up the remote control and found a football match that had just started. I was amused to note that the Grim Reaper's particular favourite team, Arsenal, was involved. Rather than the hated Manchester United, they were taking on some hard to pronounce side which looked from its name as if it hailed from Eastern Europe. Five minutes in, and still no score but it was early days yet, according to the cliché-spouting commentator. Summers settled down to watch it, so I succumbed to the temporarily inevitable and sat at the far end of the settee to enjoy the match. Timing, for me, was important. I wanted him to remember what he was about to see, but for him not to be entirely certain whether it was real or imagined. In time, the memory would gnaw at him.

Summers rolled himself a cigarette, adding some herbal material, then lit it and lay back, sharing smoke and the sickly sweet odour of cannabis with the room. At least passive smoking no longer worried me. After a few minutes, the football match lost its grip on Summers, his eyes closed and he drifted off into an alcohol-fuelled snooze. I stood up, took the high-visibility vest from beneath my jacket and put it on. The vest was shredded by the passage of numerous shotgun pellets, and heavily stained with my blood. The overall impression was of massive trauma to my chest, which was exactly what I wanted to convey. Having put the vest on, I made myself visible, then stood and waited.

The match ground its way torpidly through the first half, enlivened only when Arsenal scored, admittedly against the run of play. I didn't think Paul would complain. At least it allowed the home team's supporters to break into their obligatory rendition of *'One nil to the Arsenal'*, a chant they managed to sustain till half time.

Ten minutes into second half, Arsenal showed that they had clearly been invigorated during the interval, either by the inspirational leadership of their manager, or perhaps by someone slipping something into their tea. Whatever the cause, for what might have been the first time in recent history, they scored again, followed unbelievably soon after by a third. *'Three nil to the Arsenal'* was now being sung with gusto by the increasingly incredulous crowd.

Their fervour managed to percolate its way into Summers' somnolent consciousness, and he stirred. I stood next to the television in my bloodied uniform and waited for him to open his eyes. As he returned to the muddle-headed state of semi-wakefulness that marks a groggy awakening, he was looking right at me. His face whitened with shock and his jaw dropped, a stream of drool running from the side of his mouth. I looked him straight in the eye and slowly raised my right arm till I was pointing at him, at which he shrank back against the backrest of the settee looking aghast. When I slowly but clearly mouthed the word 'Murderer...' I was delighted to see that he wet himself. Satisfied that, if nothing else, I would give him a few sleepless nights, I faded from his view and left the building.

Tactfully I removed my bloodied vest before casually sauntering back to the alleyway in Queen Street and buzzing for access. One of Nigel's colleagues was on duty and seemed completely unfazed by my arrival. Different team, different department, it was not for him to question the comings and goings of colleagues at all hours of the day and night. That spared me any awkward questions. To further reinforce the notion that I was on legitimate business I casually asked if Danny and Gordon had been in with their prisoner. The Reception Unit supervisor informed me that they'd returned a few hours earlier.

'Did they have a retrieval by the name of Stephen Beasant with them?' I enquired.

'Yes, very straightforward really. He should've come over a couple of years back so no issues on the face of it, but they've asked me for a lie down. Said they'd be back in the morning, possibly with you if you were back in time.'

'Thanks mate. Yes, I would like a word with him. Is he on his rest period right now?' There was no time like the present, I felt, but my enthusiasm was quashed by the supervisor who confirmed that Beasant was not to be disturbed just now.

'It's been a bit of a traumatic day for him, as they so often are. Best you speak with him in the morning. He's not going anywhere,' he commented. I accepted that and went for a quick shower and change of clothes, then wandered off to the bar.

CHAPTER FOURTEEN

When I arrived in the bar, I was delighted to find Danny and Gordon who were happily chatting up, respectively, Rachel and Lizzie. To make my social life complete, Chris was sitting with them but clearly letting them get on with their mutual flirting. As I strolled over, she gave me one of her wonderfully warm smiles and moved over on the bench seat to make room for me.

'My knight in shining armour, you've saved me from a dreadful fate as a gooseberry.' She sounded as pleased to see me as she'd looked, which stirred me no end. 'What have you been up to?'

'I've been visiting an old friend,' I told her, to which she looked me in the eye and murmured 'Why doesn't that surprise me? You can tweak the rules, but only up to a point, though I'm sure you know that. Just tell me you haven't actually gone off the rails and that I don't have to cover things with the Boss...'

'I just pointed something out to him,' I said, which was true, strictly speaking.

'I can't let you guys out of my sight, can I?' she whispered, rolling her eyes. At the same time I felt her gently squeeze my arm, which showed that at least I wasn't in too much trouble, at least so far.

There was a break in the deep and meaningful conversation involving our companions, so I asked Danny 'How did it go? I gather Mr. Beasant is now in our tender care.'

'Yes he is, and you'll probably also be aware we've got him a lie down overnight,' he told me. 'When you're ready in the morning, we'll have a chat with him and see what he can tell us.'

'Let's do that,' I agreed. 'Go on then, tell me how you potted him today. It wasn't a car crash by any stretch of the imagination was it?'

'Yes it was. It seemed the most straightforward way,' Danny replied.

Unless you were one of the traffic officers tasked with sweeping up the mess, I thought rather ruefully.

Danny went on. 'We went to Phillips' place as I remembered how to get there, and the two of them were there. We hung around a bit in case they started talking about what had happened, but that must just be going over old ground for them as it never cropped up in the conversation. Anyway, they'd been fixing an old shed, an Astra, and Beasant said he'd take it out on a test run before they gave it back to the customer. Gordon and I went along for the ride. I've not staged a car crash before, you know traffic was always more your scene than mine, so we had a bit of a chat about how to go about it. Anyhow, young Gordon here is more at one with the world of machinery than I am so I just let him crack on with it.'

'Plus I've crashed before of course, so I knew what to expect,' Gordon added. I noticed that Lizzie was following his every word with rapt attention. Maybe she thought crashing your Lancaster was a bit of a bird-puller though I'm certain that wasn't what Gordon had had in mind at the time. 'It was straightforward in the end. We sat in the back seat and waited till he was on a clear stretch of road as we didn't want any of what they now call collateral damage. I put my arm over his eyes and materialised so suddenly he couldn't see where he was going. Because we were doing about seventy miles an hour at the time, it only took a twitch of the wheel with my other hand and we were straight into a tree. Wizard prang, and all that.'

'It worked a treat, naturally enough,' Danny ventured. 'I even felt some sympathy for the traffic lot when they turned up as he was a right mess. Beasant himself was seriously upset, as you might expect. He kept wandering around in despair, moaning 'Is that me, is that me?' while we were trying to keep his head together till the transport turned up. Luckily William got to us before he lost the plot, and he'd calmed down a bit by then.'

'I take it he didn't say anything about my job, I mean after he'd calmed down,' I asked.

'Not a dickey bird,' answered Gordon. 'Mind you, we didn't mention anything about it and he doesn't know you're with us yet. The supervisor says you can have a crack at him in the morning, before he goes across to the Greeters. After that he goes into his post-arrival sleep so wouldn't be around for a few days so best make the most of it.'

I decided that I'd wrung as much out of my colleagues as I could, so went and got a round of drinks in. On my return, Danny and Rachel were chatting quietly whilst Gordon continued to fascinate Lizzie with the tactics of area bombing or some such enthralling topic which involved waving his hands around manically.

That meant I had Chris to myself, so engaged her in conversation about this and that, culminating with an update on the developments in rock music after she left the scene. At least I was able to reassure her that much had endured that she would recognise, with the addition of many new forms of music that seemed to be named after outbuildings but were just so much noise, in my opinion at least.

Eventually, our drinks finished, I asked Chris. 'It's a bit early to turn in. Fancy another?'

'Not right now, if that's OK. What I do fancy is a stroll. Have you looked outside, it's a beautiful evening.'

The landscape was clearly moonlit, the trees like silver-white ghosts of their daytime forms. It sounded like an invitation that I wasn't inclined to turn down, so we stood and bade our companions a pleasant evening and goodnight.

'Nothing I ever saw before can compare with this.' Chris took my hand as we walked away from the bar. We were, once more, on the path that I now knew would lead us to the lake shore.

Chris was more assertive this evening, something, I was slowly learning, she saved for work rather than out of hours. It suggested she was caught up in the enthusiasm of her idea for the walk. I loved it that she was keen, finding it quite infectious. She looked gorgeous in a blue and white floral dress and white cardigan, with a pair of low-heeled slip-on shoes. She had returned briefly to her room and collected a bag, suggesting that we might enjoy another glass or two of wine in the open air. Her deep blue eyes managed to sparkle even in the moonlight shining through the canopy of leaves above us. Her obvious joy at the prospect of a romantic stroll was equally inspiring to me.

Having seen the lake a couple of days previously, I knew it was my favourite kind of beauty spot; and here there were no shops or other tawdry nonsense, whilst it was but a short walk from where we lived now. Being out of sight of the office and accommodation, I hadn't been too spoiled and, I felt, there was little chance of becoming bored through constant exposure to the vista.

The lake looked magnificent, reflecting the silvery light from the moon and stars. The far shore was visible only as an indigo line across the distant horizon, the densely-wooded slopes only becoming more detailed closer to us. The substantial path that ran along the shore, which had led us to the restaurant, appeared to circumnavigate it, wending its way through the pines that grew in abundance. We wandered, hand in hand, along the trail listening to the music of the night, soft birdsong from some nocturnal flocks that had joined us in our particular part of heaven.

We left the path and found a comfortable spot on a small hillock. Chris took a travel rug from the bag, which we spread out and sat down on, gazing across the water.

'Open this, Nick, if you like,' she said, passing me a chilled bottle of wine. I unscrewed the top, rummaged in the bag and found two wine glasses which I filled generously. Chris sat close to me, putting her arm around me, her hand resting on my hip. I put mine round her waist, pulling her in close, feeling the loose fabric of her dress, playing with it with my fingers as I stroked her waist. She turned her face towards me and kissed me softly on the cheek, then rested her head on my shoulder.

'This is lovely, I could stay here all evening given half a chance.'

'There's no rush, is there? Let's make the most of it.'

'Mmm, you're tempting me now.' Her hand made its way under my shirt as she turned to me again and gave me a long, lingering full-on kiss. I opened my lips and mouth to accommodate her as I felt her tongue seeking mine. We kissed with our eyes open and I saw Chris's blue eyes with the dark pools of her irises gazing into mine. I pulled her closer to me, reached up and stroked the back of her hair.

Her hands now slipped under my shirt and caressed my skin, stroking up and down slowly as we extended our sensual though gentle kiss.

We stretched out side by side on the travel rug, kissing more passionately now. The ground beneath the rug was spongy, thick with pine needles, and soft to lie on. We were in a natural dip, fifteen feet or so above the level of the path and thirty yards into the woods. I was confident that no one would stumble across us, and felt encouraged to continue with my gentle seduction.

We knew that now the time had come. Turning each other on with mouth and hands had been but the appetiser for the full expression of our loving.

She moved next to me on the travel rug, lying on her back and pulling me on top of her. I wrapped my arms around Chris holding her close as we made love.

'I think that was long overdue,' she sighed afterwards, between kisses.

'Well I was too much of a gentleman to ask.' I wanted to lie there with Chris for as long as I could, relaxing and softening slowly, my physical passion spent but emotionally still as deeply committed as I had ever known. I was delighted to find out that some things never changed, regardless of which life we were in.

We lay in each other's arms in the intimate emotional bonding that follows love-making with someone you suddenly realise means so much to you. The night birds continued to sing, the wind sighed in the trees and the sound of water running into the lake lulled us as we lay there, spent.

CHAPTER FIFTEEN

'Stephen Beasant, my name is PC Nick Kerridge. Do you know who I am?' Danny and I were sitting at a table in one of the Reception Unit interview rooms. Opposite us sat Beasant, who appeared quite calm and composed. He certainly wasn't quaking in his boots; if anything he looked dismissive and slightly arrogant.

'Should I? You famous or something?' His manner bore out his appearance.

'I was murdered by Lee Patrick Summers. Do you know him?'

There was a flicker of recognition, and some conster-nation in Beasant's eyes, followed straight away by a denial that he'd ever heard the name. I liked that. It suggested that he knew something and what he knew worried him.

'Stop messing about, Beasant. Just start helping us out,' Danny said. He'd started to write in anticipation of a full and frank account, which was clearly not going to be extracted easily from the recalcitrant individual sitting across the table.

'I don't know what you're talking about. I've never met this Summers, I swear down. What's all this about by the way? This time yesterday I was carrying on as normal, went to work for Steve then you and that other goon turned up and made me crash.' The latter part was obviously aimed at Danny.

'Do you ever watch the news?' I ignored Beasant's denials and tried to get back on track.

'Yeah, course I did, at least when I got a break from running around on Micky Phillips' behalf. So before you ask it again, yes I do know who you are. What is this, Life on Mars or something?'

'Something like that,' I commented quietly then carried on. 'You'll know Phillips was taken in for questioning about the Golf that was used.'

'Was he? He never discussed his business with me.'

'You know he was, Steve. You gave the police a witness

statement saying he was in the workshop all evening, didn't you? So don't take me for a fool.'

'Where's my brief?' Beasant sneered. 'I know my rights, and you can't keep holding me here. As soon as it's twenty four hours you've got to charge me or let me go.'

'That's where you're wrong, smart arse.' Danny was not impressed with Beasant. 'You forget, old son, that PACE doesn't count here. You're not far wrong when you go on about Life on Mars. DCI Gene Hunt might not be here but if you don't start playing ball I can find somebody equally horrible, so don't push your luck, sunshine. You won't find a brief here, we've got all eternity to hold on to you and if you really want to be awkward I will make your worst nightmares come true.'

Beasant wasn't that easily swayed. 'If I've given a statement that's the end of it,' he smirked. 'It must be true because I signed the bit at the top that says so.'

'Perverting the Course of Justice is the least of your worries, mate,' Danny threw in. 'Eternal damnation should be at the forefront of your mind right now.'

Beasant gave this option due consideration, before offering his opinion on it: 'Fuck off.'

This was getting us nowhere fast. I thought I'd give it one more try. Still feeling mellow from my late night sojourn with Chris, I was determined not to let this tosspot wind me up.

'I know that Summers shot me, and I know that the Golf he was driving came from Phillips. You know that the police asked Phillips about it, because you gave them a statement saying you were with him at the workshop all that afternoon. I'm not saying that you were involved in my murder, but I am saying that you can tell us a lot more about the Golf. Let me make it easy for you. Who did Phillips lend or hire the car to that day? Who brought it back? And what happened to it afterwards?'

'If you read my statement, you'll know he flogged it a few days previous.' Beasant still to stuck to his story. 'Therefore, Inspector Clouseau, it never left the workshop on the day because it wasn't there in the first place. And hence it never come back either. As for what happened to it afterwards, let me make it easy for you.' Beasant leaned forward thrusting his face towards mine and spat. 'Fuck knows.'

'Who did he sell it to?' I asked him, unfazed.

'I dunno; some gadger called John Robertson or some such.' Beasant looked like he didn't give two hoots and I had already formed the opinion that that was an accurate summary of where he stood. I was rapidly taking a dislike to this bloke.

'Who did Phillips help out from the Cardiff gangs?' I thought I'd change tack slightly. I'd only got one real chance to wring out of Beasant what he knew after all.

'What do you mean?' Mister 'I Know Nothing' came once again to the fore.

'What I mean, and I will phrase it a la Life on Mars, is that your friend Micky Phillips had some rather tasty buddies in the South Wales underworld, who used to hire his motors, my old son. That tells me that Phillips isn't just some hard-working entrepreneur but is intrinsically linked to organised crime. You're his loyal assistant and know who's who and what's what. So start naming names.'

'Well he was one of them.' Beasant pointed at Danny. 'What're you doing here?'

'This is my day job,' Danny told him. 'I've moved on since we last met.'

'I'm getting bored with this.' Beasant stifled a transparently mock yawn. My totally unprofessional desire to give him a smack in the teeth was edging closer to the surface now.

I tried again, as much to focus on keeping my cool as in expectation of any progress. 'You really need to consider your position. You've got absolutely nothing to lose by helping us clear all this up. No one will know you've helped us out and they're hardly in a position to have a go back at you. Why not make things easier for yourself?'

'I'm dead now, aren't I?' Beasant sneered. 'How much worse can it get?'

'Oh, it can get a lot worse than this, believe me.' Danny looked him straight in the eye, holding his gaze. 'You've not been allowed into the nice bit of the Afterlife yet. It's up to us where you go from here. There are plenty of options. Where do you think all the nonces, child killers and mass murderers go? And defence lawyers, for that matter? Did you think it's all forgive and forget?'

'I'm not a fucking pervert, and I've never killed any-one!' Beasant's voice rose an octave in protestation of his innocence. 'Anyway, who the hell are you to say what happens to me? You the Grim Reaper's sidekicks or some-thing?'

'Funny you should say that,' commented Danny. 'What if we were, would that make a difference?'

'I've never believed any of that bollocks,' Beasant continued. 'I'm hardly wetting myself with you two clowns.'

'Let's take a break here,' Danny decided. 'You can think about where you want to go from here, Steve. Help us out, like I said, and you'll find that you'll adjust very quickly and this is a wonderful existence. A good word from us with the Decision Maker and the job's a good 'un. A bad word, on the other hand, and it's a Redevelopment Unit for you. It's especially difficult to come to terms with what they think are your major shortcomings if you haven't really done anything too bad, but the staff won't know that. Nor will they particularly care as, like us, they've heard it all before. Millions of evil souls they've dealt with over the eons, sad to say. What's the odd miscarriage of justice, eh?'

'Fuck off.' A man of few words, our Steve.

'Stay here. We'll be back,' promised Danny. He looked at me. 'Time for some legal advice.' We left the interview room and went for a coffee break in Nigel's small kitchen behind the Reception desk. He didn't mind, as long as we made him one as well.

'What do you reckon, truth or lies?'

'He's an arrogant, lying toe-rag, in my humble opinion.' Danny stirred his coffee.

'He's not bothered is he? We could do with a Plan B,' I told him.

'I might just have one. You go back in there and make a play of going through his previous. Make it look like you're trying to get some mitigation. Big up the hell that awaits him in the RUs. Then whatever happens,' Danny was smirking so was quite obviously up to something. 'Don't look surprised and for fuck's sake don't laugh.' Now there was a challenge.

Beasant stubbornly refused to take any of my hints that

things were going to go further downhill for him, and made a point of examining his grubby and untidy finger nails as I went through his previous misdemeanours with him. Fate Planning had, very swiftly and efficiently I thought, produced his file. Our misdeeds truly were noted down as we wended our way through life. Instead of appearing on a scroll, to be read out by some Old Testament-style bloke with beard and robes at the Pearly Gates, they were stuffed into a manilla folder and kept in a cupboard pending the arrival in the Afterlife of the person to whom they related. I now leafed through the file which I made a point of considering in great depth.

I had reached Beasant's early twenties, at which time his sins largely consisted of fraudulent benefits claims and obtaining sexual services from girlfriends by the deception that he really loved all of them, when there was a commotion out in the Reception area.

'STEPHEN BEASANT, YOUR TIME HAS COME!' boomed a stentorian voice in doom-laden tones. 'BRING THAT MISERABLE SINNER BEASANT OUT NOW TO FACE HIS JUDGEMENT.'

'Who's that? What does he want?' Beasant was stirred.

'Better go and see what he wants,' I suggested. 'Any last words before you meet your Maker?'

The booming continued unabated. 'BEASANT, YOUR TIME HAS COME. PREPARE TO SPEND ETERNITY IN HELL.'

The door opened and Danny stuck his head in. To his credit, he appeared fraught, a similar look that I had seen many times at work on the face of a sergeant or inspector, usually marking the unanticipated arrival of the top brass to cheer us all up. 'Get him out here now Nick! Shit, this has gone pear-shaped.'

To be fair, Beasant's face had gone a whiter shade of pale as he started to get the faintest inkling that the cards might not wholly be stacked in his favour. He stood up, and I noticed that he was trembling now.

'Come on Steve,' I said in as kindly a tone as I could manage, leading Beasant from the room. 'You've had your chance now, I'm afraid.' I was trying to keep a straight face, as Danny had urged, but part of me wondered if we had bitten off more than we could chew. I'd been pushing my luck a bit recently and at the back of my mind was the thought that I to might have gone too far. Perhaps Paul had got wind of our investigation, the unofficial trips back and, God forbid, my cameo appearance in Summers' flat.

I led the now-sheepish Beasant out into the Reception desk area where we were met by the awful sight of the black-cloaked, hooded figure I had, at the back of my mind, been anticipating since my arrival. Beasant looked as if, had he been back in the old dimension, he would have needed to change his underwear. He stood stock still in the doorway, his mouth open, clearly lost for words.

The Grim Reaper, in the same manner as when I had visited Summers, slowly lifted his right arm and pointed a finger at Beasant. Not even reducing the volume now that his victim was quivering before him, the dreadful figure commanded that Beasant kneel before him. 'I STAND HERE IN JUDGMENT BEFORE YOU,' he continued, like the Foghorn of Doom. 'YOUR WORTHLESS LIFE ON EARTH IS ENDED, YOU WHO HAVE ACHIEVED NOTHING, LEARNED NOTHING, NOR DONE GOOD FOR ANYONE BUT YOURSELF!'

Steady on, I thought, his file wasn't that bad in comparison with many scrotes of my acquaintance, but it would have been counter-productive to point that out just now.

Dropping the volume till it was slightly below the threshold of pain, the Grim Reaper continued. 'Even given the opportunity to redeem yourself, the darkness in your heart proved too strong to let any virtue shine through. You have failed to take that last chance to avoid roasting in hell fires for all eternity. Speak now before I condemn you, Stephen Beasant!'

As far as interview techniques went, this would definitely count as oppressive under our previous rules, but here no one, with the exception of Beasant, was batting an eyelid. Nigel had his head down, seemingly intent on his crossword, while the Judgment of Doomsday continued unabated at its original decibel level.

'SPEAK NOW, I COMMAND YOU, OR FACE A TORTURED ETERNITY IN THE FIRES OF DAMNATION!' Even I decided that I would be a paragon of virtue in future, so I could only imagine what must have been going through Beasant's mind.

He was obviously taken in completely, and hadn't got the faintest idea what he was supposed to say. Some incomprehensible stammering emerged from his trembling lips as his previously-stoic facade crumbled. Eventually he managed to compose himself. 'What can I say to make things right? I don't want this. I've done nothing to deserve it.'

'Why should you have one more chance? You could've redeemed yourself by helping to right the wrong when you were asked about it, but you care more for what remains of your miserable soul,' ranted on the Reaper, who seemed to get a real buzz out of seriously frightening people. I'd misjudged Paul, I decided. He was clearly a raving psychopath.

'Alright, alright, I'll tell them what I know. I don't want to go to hell, I used to go to church, and I wish I'd never stopped going now.' Perilously close to crying, Beasant had apparently seen some sort of a light, albeit from an unusually dark source.

'I will grant you a further ten minutes to bare your soul to these fine servants of the Lord.' Either the Grim Reaper was quick to take advantage of Beasant's apparently Damascene conversion, or there was something he'd omitted to mention about the existence of the Almighty when we'd last spoken. The hooded figure spun on his heel and strode grimly from the custody suite. In the absence of the booming voice from beyond the grave, you could have heard a pin drop.

'Better get on with it before he comes back. He's a stickler for time and he said ten minutes.' Nigel looked up briefly from his crossword, fixing Beasant with a cold stare. Poor Beasant must have realised that he might have had plenty of friends in the past world, but they were in precious short supply in this one.

Danny, a somewhat chastened Beasant and I sat down once more in the interview room.

'Want to tell us about the car, Steve?' Danny was all sweetness and light now.

'If I tell you, promise me he won't come back,' begged Beasant.

'We don't make the promises. It's between you and him. We know all about you, you're aware of that from my colleague's file. So we can tell if you're lying. You've got about nine minutes left by my watch.'

'OK, OK. Micky didn't sell the car. I know what happened to it, I torched it, it was Summers brought it back and Micky had a right go at him...' Beasant was babbling now, nearly incoherent in his haste to bare his soul.

'Slow down Steve,' I urged him. 'You've got to tell us but it needs to make sense. One thing at a time.'

'Have I got time, what if he comes back...?'

'I'm sure we can get what we need in the next...' I made a show of checking my watch'...Eight minutes. One question at a time, and one answer. First, where is the car?'

'It's up in the Brecon Beacons. I torched it, like I said.'

'Where exactly?'

'You go up the A40 to Crickhowell, then there's a minor road takes you up past Talybont Reservoir. There's a farm just at the far end of the reservoir, no one lived there when I went up there. Just past that, quarter of a mile or so on the right, there's a track into the woods. I took it up there and there's a turning, bit a clearing. It's in there.' Hallelujah, I thought, in keeping with the religious turn matters seemed to have taken. We appeared to have found the car. Anything else would be a bonus.

'What happened when Summers brought the car back?' I pressed on, keeping Beasant on the rack. 'Seven minutes left, I make it.'

'Micky went bloody mental with him, called him every name under the sun for the grief he'd caused. He told me to sort it out, which I did.'

'What happened to the shotgun, was that in the car?' I made prolonged eye contact with Beasant; I hadn't thought to ask about the firearm before, for some reason, and didn't want him to think of denying it. 'Six and a half minutes,' I added helpfully.

'It was; that numpty Summers had just left it on the front seat. He'd have been totally stuffed if he'd been stopped on the way over.' But he hadn't been, I thought, as I asked Beasant 'What happened to that?'

'All I could think of doing was cutting it up with an angle grinder, and then I put all the bits in a bucket of cement till it

147

set. My mate's got a boat down the coast. He owed me a favour and doesn't ask questions, so took us out into the Bristol Channel, about three or so miles off shore, and it went over the side. They won't find that.'

'Was it Summers that took the car in the first place, or did he just bring it back?' I wanted to know.

'Nah, it wasn't him, it was two of Micky's lads. They wanted it for a blag on a cash-in-transit van.'

'Lads?'

'Sons of his mate. The Llewellyn brothers, Stu and Adie. A pair of totally fucking useless wasters. A bit like Summers really.'

'How come Summers had the car then, when he came back with it?'

'Micky got a call. The Llewellyn boys bottled out of the blag and came back on the train, leaving all their gear in the car. They dumped it on Joe Flynn, Joseph's boy from Stambridge, and Summers worked for him. Joe got Summers to bring it back. Tell you how much of a fuckwit Summers is, he rang us after to say he'd left a kilo of smack in the car and to ask if he could have it back. Too late, I told Micky, it had gone up in smoke with the motor, which is true. I wasn't bothered about clearing the car out; I didn't want anything on me that might link me back to that copper's death.' He turned to me. 'Sorry mate, I meant your tragic death, I keep forgetting. There's a lot to take in.'

'It's all right Steve, we've got there I think. Do you swear on your own soul that's all true, because that's what's at stake if you're lying? The Hoodie from Hell is due back in a minute.' I hoped that there was still a fair amount of menace in my implied threat to him, though I was starting to believe he was being straight with us now.

'Honest to God, that's what happened, I swear it on all that's holy.' Beasant had belatedly bought into religion in a big way, it appeared. I seem to remember the Bible went on about it never being too late to repent, but with the impending reappearance of the Grim Reaper, Beasant probably thought this was cutting things a bit fine.

I was satisfied with what we had now, and Beasant, try as he might, couldn't think of anything further that might conceivably placate his hooded nemesis. At the end of the interview, he simply pleaded with me. 'Have I done enough? Will you put in a good word for me with him?' I told him I would see what I could do.

'Stay here,' I told Beasant and gestured to Danny to come with me. My instruction was probably superfluous. Whilst there was any chance that the Grim Reaper was still lurking around waiting to pounce I didn't think that the Four Horsemen of the Apocalypse would stand a chance of dragging Beasant out into the Reception desk area.

We wandered over to Nigel who was battling with clue 24 down. He looked up. 'Was it a straight cough?'

'It worked like a dream,' Danny told him. 'He'd have admitted to anything we put to him I think.'

'Better make it convincing. Go up to the canteen for ten minutes whilst you have a brew. Make it look like you're consulting the boss, then we'll give him the good news.'

'He's not actually coming back down, then?' I asked Nigel.

'Is he heck. Once is enough for one day, as far as I'm concerned.'

We left the suite and made our way upstairs. Sitting at a table in the canteen with the obligatory cups of coffee were Gordon and Chris. Gordon gave me a broad grin whilst Chris gave me a more subtle and gently smouldering smile. I returned it with pleasure. I presumed they both knew what had occurred in Reception this morning.

'How did you get Paul to go along with that ruse?' I asked the pair, eliciting laughs from both.

'Paul? He's been out all morning arranging an earthquake,' Chris told me earnestly. Gordon looked deadpan, as he pointed at me and said in his grimmest tone 'I command you to confess to me what you two got up to last night...'

Chris had the modesty to blush while I nearly fell off my chair laughing.

Returning to Reception, we fetched the trembling Beasant from the interview room. 'Good news,' I told him. 'The Grim Reaper says you have atoned for your sins and he is relinquishing his claim to your soul. You are free to enter the Afterlife.'

Beasant thanked us profusely for our help and apologised

for his earlier attitude problem. Suitably chastened by his recent experience, he was actually quite a likeable character. We wished him all the best as he went through to Reception.

'Shall we go and have a look for the car?' I suggested to Danny.

'Seeing as we virtually had to unleash the Hounds of Hell to get the information out of him, it would almost be rude not to,' he replied.

I was accepting what Beasant had told us in good faith. If a personal appearance by an annoyed Reaper didn't do the trick, nothing would, I figured, and what he'd told us seemed credible.

Traipsing out to that bit of the sticks that languished in the Brecon Beacons represented something of a challenge as it was far beyond the capability of public transport to get us there. In the end, though, it didn't present too much of a problem to us; we simply waited by traffic lights for a vehicle to stop and invisibly hitched a lift. This got us as far as the Talybont Reservoir, after which we had to walk.

The farm was where Beasant told us, and still appeared to be deserted; a silent victim of the rural recession. There were few people around. I'd made some notes during the interview, and just hoped that Beasant's memory had been accurate. There was a lot of countryside to cover if it wasn't. There was a track pretty much where he'd said, so we turned off the road and made away through the trees. It was peaceful, certainly, and the sounds of nature were all around us, birds, the wind in the trees and the distant sound of running water as a woodland stream made its way down to the reservoir. I'd been spoilt, however, by the lake and the woods around my new home, and they'd taken on a special significance after last night. I was looking forward to seeing Chris again, to see what she'd made of our romantic encounter.

The track became increasing overgrown; Beasant would have struggled to get the Golf through, I'd have thought, but then he had every incentive to make sure it was well-hidden. His memory didn't let him, or us, down though. A bit further on the track terminated in a small clearing, in the centre of which sat the blackened hulk of what looked like a burnt-out VW Golf.

CHAPTER SIXTEEN

'He told you everything then, in the end?' Gordon, having finished his stint of amateur dramatics, was keen to learn more. We'd just returned from checking out Beasant's story, which had taken the best part of the afternoon because of its inconvenient location.

'Yes, the boy done good,' I commented.

'I do wish you wouldn't talk like a football commentator,' commented Chris, who had also joined us.

The six of us were, by now, sitting once more in the bar. My social life was certainly starting to take off. I'd knocked on Chris's door on my return, purportedly to give her an update but in reality to see what kind of a response I might get after the previous night's passion. I needn't have worried. She took my arm and pulled me into her room, kicked the door shut and gave me a long and passionate kiss. 'I've been thinking of you all day,' she murmured when at last we came up for air. 'I want you to myself tonight, so we won't stay too late.' I couldn't have agreed more.

The rest of the team were already well into the drinks when we joined them .

'Go on then, what was the crack with the Grim Reaper costume? I was sure that was Paul.' I still had to smile at the memory, but hadn't followed Gordon's later direction to spill the beans on my nightcap with Chris.

'Danny came upstairs and told me about what an awkward sod your Mr. Beasant was, and we kicked around a few ideas about how we could get the penny to drop with him. He said it was a shame we couldn't rope Paul in, so we went up to the office to see if he was around. He is actually up for a laugh when he's in the right mood. When we got there, Chris told us he was out all morning, trying to find some counter-measure to GM crops, which he thinks are going to reduce the effectiveness of famine as a tactical option. Anyway she lent us the Grim Reaper outfit which he usually only brings out for parties these days anyway. If he came back unexpectedly, she'd tell him it was away for cleaning. He doesn't get too interested in that kind of detail. Fortunately it's a bit too small for Danny but fits me reasonably well. I'm thinking of asking if I can have a job as stand in for him.' His broad grin suggested to me that, so far, Gordon hadn't considered this seriously; I thought he'd made an excellent fist of his impersonation in Reception earlier and told him so. 'Thanks, damned decent of you to say so old boy.' Gordon continued. 'I presume it had the desired effect?'

'Yes it worked a treat. It's all checked out unless it's a hell of a coincidence, which I feel is unlikely. We've got the car, we know who Summers got it from, and we know what happened to the shotgun though that, sadly, has gone for a Burton,' I summed up.

'Now we need to return to the thorny question of how to break all that out to the investigation team.' Danny clearly hadn't made any progress on that front.

'What about a good old-fashioned séance?' Rachel suggested. Danny rolled his eyes, though I couldn't see which particular aspect of the idea he found hard to believe. As a fully signed up member of Spirits R Us, he was proof of existence beyond the grave, and he was a dab hand at communicating with the living, even if they didn't continue living very long after he'd got in touch.

He went on. 'How would we go about organising one of those? We can't really go and stick up a notice in the Village Hall. 'Come and meet your neighbourhood spooks. Tuesday at 7.30 pm. Tea and buns afterwards.' I can't see that happening, to be honest.'

'We don't organise it, you dozy pillock,' Rachel laughed. 'We find one and gate-crash it. Then we tell the medium we've got a message for someone who's there and that they've got to go to the police with it. We give them enough information to make it credible but not so much that it's a bit fishy.' She turned to me. 'Nick, you're always going back and forth, couldn't you see if there's one advertised somewhere?'

'No need even for that,' Lizzie chipped in eagerly. 'There were a couple of ladies at my old place who kept saying they'd

152

got the gift. They'd have a séance every so often, to try and keep in touch with their loved ones who'd already passed over. I think they were bothered that their husbands were getting up to no good on this side whilst they were stuck over there in the old folks home. I never believed in all that of course, which goes to show how wrong you can be.'

'Did they ever actually get through to anyone, or do you think they were just kidding themselves or each other?' I asked. A few months ago I'd have shared Danny's skepticism but now I knew better.

'One or two of them seemed to believe it, and the rest just wanted to hope.' Lizzie looked wistful as she thought back. 'I was never quite sure how they did it, but the two old girls who set it all up did seem to say the right things a lot of the time.'

Them and a few thousand other assorted frauds and charlatans, I thought, but kept that to myself. Instead I asked her 'Who were the main movers and shakers in this spiritualist group, Lizzie? It might be worth having a quiet word with them next time they start rattling the tables and chucking up ectoplasm, or whatever they get up to.' I'd never been to a séance myself, and it suddenly seemed to be a good wheeze to attend one from the other side of the curtain, so to speak.

'Like I said there were two of them who went on and on about it. Doris and Barbara, they're called, I can't remember their surnames but you'll find them easily enough. They tend to stick together. They're like an old married couple, always bickering with each other and one will contradict the other. But if anyone tries to come between them they stick to each other like glue.'

'What excuse would they use for a séance, Lizzie?' Gordon was getting interested now as well, it seemed.

'Sometimes they didn't need an excuse. If there nothing on the television they'd just do it out of boredom. There's not a lot to do if you're in your seventies or eighties and been parked in an old folks home by your family. We couldn't even go down to the pub. Other times though, if somebody had recently passed on, one of their family or someone like that, they'd try and make contact.' Lizzie paused to take a sip of her drink. 'They made out it was to check they were alright but really I think they were trying to see if there was life after death. You wonder a lot about that as you get closer to it,' she added.

'Did they try and contact you, Lizzie?' Rachel wondered.

'I don't know. I haven't had any messages. How would they let me know?' Lizzie had a point, I supposed.

'You might get a tannoy message,' Gordon pointed out, cupping his hands over his mouth to imitate a loudspeaker. 'Message for Lizzie Roberts. Would Lizzie Roberts please go the nearest darkened room for a call from the other side? Hello, Lizzie Roberts, is there anybody there...?'

'Oh Gordon, do be quiet!' Lizzie chided him. 'I was only joking. It wouldn't make any difference anyway as they couldn't really contact the spirits, they were just pretending.'

'They'll be in for a surprise when you lot come through loud and clear,' said Danny, whose doubts had obviously prevented him from joining in fully with the conversation. 'What are you going to say to them? You can hardly expect them to ring the incident room and relay a message in real time.'

'We could pass them the basics,' I told him. 'Tell them where the car is and that Summers did it. That's all they would need to kick start the enquiries.'

'They get all kind of fruitcakes and weirdoes ringing them with that sort of stuff. It never solved a case before as far as I'm aware.'

'Yeah, well they've got stuff all else to go on and all we've got to do is get them to check out the spot where the Golf was dumped. They wouldn't say it had come from a medium, they'd just treat it as anonymous intelligence but I'd hazard a guess they'd check it out,' I told Danny. In fact I'd come across that previously when some psychic rang in with a tip about where we'd find the body of a missing person. It was all rubbish, as it happened, but we still got sent to some desolate spot in the forest to take a look at the totally undisturbed earth. A courting couple found the decomposed body a few days later, about three hundred miles away. I expect that cooled their passion.

I turned back to Lizzie. 'If you could give one of them a prompt, do you think that might do the trick? Materialising in front of one of them in the middle of the night, telling her you've got a message you need to pass on, that sort of thing.'

Rachel looked quite keen on this idea. 'Fancy a trip back, Lizzie, if you wouldn't find it too upsetting?' she asked.

'I wouldn't find it at all upsetting,' Lizzie replied. 'I was sick to death of the place, it was just life generally I didn't want to let go of. I'm not sure about going back on my own though. You guys seem to think nothing of it but I'm not sure how I'd get on. The other thing is, wouldn't someone try to stop me? I was an overstayer, you told me. They might think I was trying to escape and send me to a Redevelopment Unit

'I'll come with you,' Rachel reassured her. 'I'll just tell the Reception supervisor you're being trained up. There's no issue with that, is there, Chris?'

'Not that I can see. I'll tell Paul you're thinking of joining us and want an experiential attachment. He'll be cool about it, I'm quite sure. He's always looking for free help. He'll probably give us a hit list to take with us. 'Every Little Helps' seems to be the in-phrase at the moment. I'm not sure where he gets all these phrases from, but he seems to come up with a new one every week.'

'One of his management meetings, I expect,' I told her. 'Our lot were always competing with each other to come up with some new buzz word. Every other week it would be 'Run this up the flagpole and see who salutes', or 'More bang for your buck', or other such drivel.'

'Right then, chaps and chapesses, what's the plan?' Gordon asked.

'I would suggest that Lizzie and Rachel go back in the dead of night, as Rachel just said,' I told him. 'Lizzie wakes up Doris or Barbara, gives her the message and suggests she holds a séance the next evening. Then we turn up at the séance and give them the low down on the car and Summers. It might be best if I go with Lizzie for that one so the old dear can say she heard it direct from me. I'll stay invisible but I'll have to make myself heard by the so-called medium.

'A loud whisper should be alright,' Lizzie added. 'They're all as deaf as a post so no one else will make out what you're saying. Doris is probably the best as she's less hard of hearing than the others and she's always convinced that she's getting messages from beyond.'

***

'This is Doris' room,' Lizzie told Rachel as they lurked invisibly in the corridor. It was three o'clock in the morning and their journey to Lizzie's former rest home in Penarth had been uneventful, largely because Gordon had grabbed a car and driven them over there himself. Danny and I would have had to go by bus. He'd parked round the corner out of sight whilst Lizzie and Rachel popped inside for a quick haunt.

Rachel had given Lizzie the usual crash course in walking through walls, appearing and disappearing at will. Lizzie hadn't quite been convinced that it worked because, of course, we can see each other all the time. Fortunately there was a large and ornate mirror in the vestibule. It transpires that mirrors will only reflect us when we choose to be visible, so Lizzie was able to practice switching herself on and off till she'd got the hang of it. In fact, Rachel was a better instructor than Danny and showed Lizzie how to fade in gradually so that, even when visible, she appeared ethereal rather than solid. This, Rachel explained to her, would be useful as she now looked many decades younger than she did when Doris had last seen her, and her younger self might be unrecognisable to the still- mortal residents of the home.

Doris was sleeping soundly when they entered her room via the side wall. Her blue-rinsed hair was splayed across the pillow as she lay on her back, snoring lightly, a gossamer-thin stream of saliva easing its way from the corner of her mouth and down her cheek. To Lizzie, who by now had fully settled into her new existence, Doris looked like an ancient relic.

To disturb her sleep, Rachel, still invisible, stroked Doris on the forehead. The old lady stirred, mumbled indistinctly and drifted back off to sleep, so Rachel repeated the action.

Doris' eyes flickered open and peered myopically into the gloom. A voice, strangely familiar but quite out of context, filtered through her mental fuzziness. 'Doris....Doris....can you hear me? I need to tell you something.'

'Who's there? Do you know what time it is?' Doris answered, seemingly annoyed at the disturbance.

Rachel, who was of course still invisible and inaudible to

156

Doris, was quick on the uptake. She urged Lizzie. 'Just tell her before she wakes up fully, and then go back to insubstantial. She's going to be bright as a button in a sec.'

Lizzie had managed to stay fairly vague in form but her words were clear. 'Doris, it's me, Lizzie. You remember me, I was here till recently. I've got an important message. I need to come through to you this evening. Get the others tonight in the lounge. You know you've got the gift. I'll be there later. Goodbye for now, Doris.' Her tactic of not letting Doris get a word in edge ways appeared to work, leaving Doris momentarily confused. Doris could see a blurred and misty form but recognised her former friend's voice. She was however, too dumbfounded to reply coherently as Lizzie faded away, leaving Doris, by now sitting bolt upright in her bed, to ponder what she thought she had just heard.

***

'So far, so good,' I told Rachel and Lizzie over breakfast when they told me about their nocturnal chat to Doris. 'What time will she call them all together?'

Lizzie considered this for a moment. 'It depends on when the managers go home. They don't approve of the residents trying to commune with the dead. It's probably against council policy I expect,' she smiled. 'When I was there, most of the night staff didn't worry what we got up to. There were usually only one or two on at a time anyway. A couple of them were fervent believers anyway and would join in. The late manager normally finishes about nine-ish and Doris will be full of it after last night so I think nine thirty would be a good time. We can always wait around if we have to, can't we?'

I wandered off after that; Lizzie, Rachel and Gordon had retired to their various beds as they were, effectively, on nights. In the office I met up with Danny who was just off with William and a couple of the others to cause a small train crash, so I decided to join them. It was mildly entertaining in a ghoulish kind of way; by now I had settled in and was beginning to appreciate the value of what we were doing. Amongst us we picked up three overstayers from the total of five who made the trip back with us, the other two being due now in any case so it was all neat and tidy. Paul would doubtless be well pleased when he heard about the job.

At about nine o'clock, we went out through Reception. Rachel, Lizzie and I would do the séance while Gordon once again drove the getaway car, so to speak. As far as transport was concerned, it was clearly a case of who you know. Gordon's protective side was quite apparent, at least as far as Lizzie was concerned. As a lead driver, he seemed to have unrestricted access to vehicles whenever he wanted, and I wasn't going to query that. In any case, as he pointed out, public transport was a bit thin on the ground at night.

We reached the nursing home in Penarth at about half past nine, and went inside. Five elderly ladies sat in the lounge. The television was broadcasting some reality show that involved wannabe personalities making dinner in turns whilst generally pratting around and slagging each other off. That's entertainment for some people, I thought. A couple of the residents were playing cards, one was knitting and the final two were flicking through lightweight magazines with plenty of competitions. No one was watching the food-and-bitching show, except us.

A few minutes later, a middle-aged and slightly condescending woman stuck her head round the door. 'That's one of the day managers,' Lizzie told me.

'Good night ladies, don't be late to bed. You've got Jocelyn looking after you tonight,' the manager said to her guests, the official ones at least. There were a couple of mumbled responses from the residents, which conveyed a sense of agreement for its own sake, rather than indicating enthusiastic compliance. For the life of me, I couldn't see why the residents had to go to bed early. For all the difference it made, they could have stayed up all night knocking back the Horlicks and snorting cocoa. I suppose it made less work for Jocelyn if they were stacking the zeds. The day manager left them, and us, to our own various devices.

Jocelyn, it turned out when she stuck her head round the lounge door, looked to be a large woman of apparent West African heritage. Dressed in a bright green, red and yellow robe she exuded an air of energetic efficiency. 'Good evening my friends, now who would like a hot drink before bedtime?'

she asked them, eliciting much more enthusiasm from her audience. They all would, as it happened, so Jocelyn bounced off back to the kitchen.

Doris and her backing group were obviously comfortable with Jocelyn, as her impending return did not stop them pulling a drop-leaved table, along with five dining chairs, into the centre of the room. 'Switch the TV off, Joan,' Doris commanded, taking a glass tumbler from the sideboard and placing it inverted on the wooden table. The five ladies sat round the table, its leaves up so that it was circular. Doris had dimmed the wall lights. The room seemed larger in the dark, the effect enhanced by the red velvet curtains and flock wallpaper which blended together in the gloom. Lizzie, Rachel and I took advantage of the revised seating arrangements by dumping ourselves on the longest settee.

The makeshift coven appeared to be no strangers to the process of trying to contact the dear departed. I hadn't got the faintest idea what went on apart from the clichés of joining hands and asking if anyone was there. Either this was accurate or Doris and the dabblers had seen the same programmes and films as me, because that was exactly what they did.

'Is there anybody there?' Doris asked. 'We don't mean you any harm.' That was a relief; the last thing I had envisaged was being mugged by Hell's Grannies. Having seen the upturned glass, I initially wondered if Doris was going to get out some lettered cards and conduct a Ouija session, but it seemed not. 'If you're there, give us a sign,' Doris intoned. 'Move the glass to my right and back again to show me you can hear us.'

'Should we move it?' Lizzie asked me.

'Not yet,' I decided. 'I'd rather we just whispered in her ear. I don't want to give them all clear proof that we exist; I just need Doris to believe what I'm going to tell her. Let her get into the swing of it first though.'

'What if she really is psychic?' Rachel grinned. 'Should we try and find out? The others would never know, unless they share her gift.'

'Give it a go if you like, but I'd be gob smacked if she was,' I said. 'Make sure you haven't accidentally gone visible or audible though.'

Rachel stood and walked over to stand by the table. When

159

Doris repeated her question, Rachel replied, quite casually, 'Yes, there are three of us here to speak to you but we're forming an orderly queue, don't worry.' This drew no response whatsoever from Doris, or indeed her companions. 'Is there anybody there yet?' the makeshift medium carried on, like a stuck record.

'Yes, yes, I am you daft old bat!' Rachel shouted at her. Still no reaction was forthcoming. 'In for a penny,' I thought. I reached forward between Doris and Joan, leant over the table, made myself substantial but not visible, and nudged the glass ever so slightly. I then carefully withdrew without making any contact with either lady.

'It moved, the glass moved!' Doris squeaked.

'Well I didn't see it,' Joan rebuffed her. I couldn't resist tapping Doris twice on the shoulder causing her to look round whilst giving out a most unladylike squawk. 'Someone touched my shoulder! Was that you Joan?!'

'I didn't, honest, Doris. Are you sure you're not imagining it?'

'No, someone definitely tapped me on the shoulder. I felt it clear as day.'

The three of us were now back on the settee, rolling around in fits of silent and incorporeal laughter. Then, getting a grip, I remembered we had serious work to do.

'Go and whisper in Doris' good ear, if she's got one. Tell her it's you. Don't let her see you though,' I urged Lizzie.

Lizzie placed her mouth close to Doris ear, a task made slightly more difficult as the old woman was getting a bit twitchy now. 'Doris, Doris, can you hear me? It's Lizzie. I came to see you last night, remember?'

This time, Doris leapt up, knocking her chair backwards with a loud clatter. 'She's here! Oh my God it's Lizzie, she's come back to us!' Doris was panicking now, breathing rapidly. Her companions were dumbfounded. Things were not going to plan.

Matters escalated a few seconds later, with Doris gasping for breath, leaning on the table for support. The lounge door flew open and the large form of Jocelyn bustled in. 'What on earth are you doing, you silly girls?' she enquired.

'Oh, bloody hell, it's Jocelyn. That's all we need.' I said to

160

Rachel, not bothering to lower my voice as I was still inaudible to mere mortals. But not, however, to Jocelyn. 'What you mean, 'Bloody hell it's Jocelyn'?' she demanded, pointing straight at the three of us on the settee. 'And what, in the name of all that's holy, are you three doing in here?'

'Oh shit.' I muttered to Rachel. 'Don't tell me this one really is psychic.'

'Now don't you sit there talking about me like I'm not here. I know where you're from. I seen plenty of you before back home before I came here. Get back to where you belong, you bad spirits!'

All this was too much for Doris, who promptly expired on the carpet.

'Now look what you've done, you've killed Doris,' yelled Jocelyn, for whom ghosts obviously were nothing to be feared. 'Be gone with you before I call a priest and have you all exorcised. And make sure you take Doris with you. I don't want anyone else hanging around haunting this house.'

Next to Doris' body which was now lying collapsed on the lounge floor, there stood a much younger woman, who seemed to be in her twenties. This came as no surprise to me by now, naturally enough. I realised that we couldn't hang around with Jocelyn the Ghostbuster on our case. I took Doris by the arm. She didn't flinch this time. 'Don't worry, Doris, you're perfectly OK,' I lied to her. 'Come with me.' Doris was still looking like a stunned mullet, so I led her gently out of the room. Being in contact with me seemed to make it easy for her to walk through the walls.

When we got outside I asked Lizzie to look after her old friend, whilst I went off a short distance with Rachel. 'What are we going to do with Doris?' I asked. 'It must've been her time. Does someone come and fetch her?'

'There'll be a Greeter along shortly if they're expecting her. We'd better make ourselves scarce or there'll be some awkward questions. They get really nosey if they think we're involved.'

'I went to a train crash earlier on today with Danny,' I said. 'Two of those we brought back were due and there didn't seem to be a problem just taking them with us.'

'That was because you were on a pre-planned job, not just

161

winging it,' Rachel retorted. 'No one knows we're here so they'll just turn up for Doris as normal. She won't go anywhere near our Reception. If they see us they'll know there's something dodgy going on and we'll get grassed up to Paul. He'll go ballistic as he hates any kind of casual contact unless it's unavoidable.'

That was me told, so I went back to Lizzie and Doris. I decided just to bluff my way out. 'We've got to go now, Doris, but someone will be here in a minute. Don't go away. Come on Lizzie, I'll explain later.'

I grabbed Lizzie by the hand and took her round the corner. I just caught sight of two figures making their way across the lawn towards Doris. The Greeters had arrived.

'That went well,' I told Danny, ironically, when we finally got to the bar later that night. 'As Gordon would say, a bit of a SNAFU. We just need to hope that Doris is so bemused that she either doesn't mention us or doesn't make sense if she does.'

'Well, my friend, you can't say I didn't warn you, but there you go.' Whilst I didn't remember a specific warning from Danny, he hadn't hidden his overall lack of enthusiasm for the idea. 'What are you going to do now?'

'Shame we can't just ring Crimestoppers.' I murmured as another light came on in the dim recess of my mind. 'Can we make phone calls when we go back there?'

'I don't think so.' Danny took a drink from his glass. 'That would constitute direct contact so would be against regulations. I suppose you could try indirectly.'

I tried another tack. 'Do you think we could influence someone to make a phone call for us?'

'Maybe.'

Give us a hand here, Danny, I thought, but no ideas came from my colleague.

'Tell me what you have in mind,' he ventured after a brief pause.

'Suppose we could find someone suggestible enough to pick up on the information. All they would have to do is call Crimestoppers and pass it on. The call handler wouldn't need to know where it came from as it's anonymous, so the source doesn't even need to be credible as long as they can string a couple of sentences together.'

'What's Crimestoppers?'

Gordon, of course, had missed out on the evolution of the British criminal justice system subsequent to 1943, so I explained to him.

'It's a charity that takes information from people who don't want to speak to the police directly. If you know something, you ring their number and speak to a call taker. You don't need to leave your details; they just give you a code number or something and you go to a bank and they sort out a reward for you if it's right. What it means is that the people who really know what's going on can pass stuff on without it being traced back to them, so they don't wind up wearing a concrete overcoat.' I hoped that would explain it succinctly for Gordon who, after all, would never actually need to ring Crimestoppers but still seemed keen to get his knowledge up to date.

'Aha, I see. So we need someone who we could tell, but wouldn't be credible enough to be believed if he started spouting on about messages from the Hereafter, but without that context, the information itself would be taken seriously?'

'Aren't there loads of cranks who hear voices? Wouldn't one of those do?' suggested Chris. 'We all used to have a resident loony on our beats who would contact us because their kettle had started telling them that their cat was in league with Satan, or stuff like that.'

That rang a bell with me. 'When I was on the beat before I went onto traffic there was a bloke like that. He used to write long rambling letters to the Chief Constable about the Government beaming thought rays into his living room and giving him strange dreams. He was convinced that this was all down to the Prime Minister practicing mind control on him, to get him to go and start wars on his behalf, or some such drivel. He didn't know why the Prime Minister had picked on him, of course, but he was convinced that the Chief was in the same lodge as the PM and could get him to pick on someone else. I had to go and speak to the bloke on a number of occasions, when he wanted to tell visiting Royal dignitaries about what was going on. The Chief was a bit bothered about it for some reason. I added mischievously. 'Maybe it was all true...'

163

'Yes, he would do,' surmised Gordon. 'Where did he live?'

'Fordwell, a road called, let me think now...' I reached into the depths of my memory to dredge out this particular nugget. 'Windsor Crescent, number nine as I recall.' Blimey, I thought, I'd been wasting memory cells with that useful nugget of information for years. 'Mr. Winston Golightly, he said his name was. Poor sod.'

'Think he'll still be there?' Danny didn't look too hopeful, as if loonies on his own patch had routinely disappeared without trace rather than hanging around for years bothering us. Maybe they had.

'It must've been about twelve years ago,' I remembered. 'And he was around fifty then and as daft as a brush. Can we check if he's passed this way?' I asked Chris.

'No problem, I'll check with Fate Planning and see if they've got an address for him,' she offered. 'I'll let you know so you can go and have a quiet word with him. Just act like ordinary living humans for a change.'

CHAPTER SEVENTEEN

Mr. Winston Golightly hadn't moved home since I had last visited him. Nor had he been able to shake off the conviction that he was still being singled out for experiments in mind control. Prime Ministers had been and gone but each newcomer seemed as intent as their predecessors to communicate specifically with him. His sleep was disrupted by strange and disturbing dreams and his waking hours by a constant stream of murmurings in his ear and bizarre concepts filtering into his brain. The thought that he might be stark raving bonkers had not occurred to Winston; to him the perceptions were all too real.

He was used to the brush-offs he had received from or on behalf of the various Chief Constables to have held office since he had been compelled to take them into his confidence; by now he was resigned to the fact they were all part of a massive conspiracy. His neighbours tended to give him short shrift too when he tried to engage their enthusiasm for fighting this telepathic scourge.

The six of us discussed long into the night how we might convince Winston to pass the information on to Crimestoppers. Chris, having verified that he was to be found exactly where I had thought, also added that he was not an overstayer and was, in fact, due to keep banging on about mind-bending politicians for several more years yet. For once I felt sorry for the current and next few Chief Constables.

We considered who should visit Winston, how they should appear and in what form the message should be passed on. Right at the outset, we decided that my involvement would once again be a non-starter; Winston might well remember me from previous encounters and in all likelihood would have noted from the news that I was no more, at least as far as his dimension was concerned. We didn't think that there was much merit in frightening him out of his wits; he was suggestible, certainly, and would be open to the idea of contacting the authorities. We just needed to make certain that he didn't waste the information by trying to pass it to someone who would, seeing its source, stick it straight in the 'yip yip wibble' file.

In the end, we decided amongst us that Rachel and Gordon would make a suitably credible team. Gordon, though young in appearance, had shown considerable gravitas when posing as the Grim Reaper whilst Rachel had demonstrated when dealing with Derek on the suspension bridge a certain propensity to wind middle-aged men round her little finger.

Lizzie was rather sorry for Winston, feeling that we were taking advantage of a poor, befuddled old man. Danny, cynical as ever, expressed the view that Winston was in a minority of one in thinking that his head was being interfered with, and would probably be quite happy to have this confirmed as it would prove to him that he wasn't going mad after all. The whole episode, Danny enthused, would probably do him a world of good. Lizzie wasn't overly convinced but gave us the benefit of the doubt. I suspected that Gordon would make the most of an opportunity to explain it all in great detail to her later on.

There being no time like the present, we decided to go to the bar; Gordon and Rachel would go and see Winston in the morning. I remembered to give them detailed directions.

***

Another morning dawned, grey with low cloud and, yet again, rain beating against his kitchen window as Winston Golightly contemplated his kippers. As soon as he'd finished his breakfast, Winston decided, he would wash up, clean the house and then go to the library where he would use his free internet access to research the many fiendish plots being inflicted on the luckless populace by the Government. The fact that he actually did exactly the same thing every day didn't occur to Winston. Had it done so, he wouldn't have been bothered as his mission was to expose the inconvenient truths that, alas, only he could see. Conspiracy was rife,

Winston knew, and he alone was able to expose it.

Winston couldn't use his own computer, of course; he was absolutely convinced that it was monitored live time by MI5. As an added bonus, if he went to the library to conduct his thorough research, the Government's Thought Ray would not be able to focus on him, interfering with his mind in a bid to eradicate the evidence from within his brain.

Three kippers downed and one to go; it was Wednesday. Starting on each and every Sunday, he alternated between three and four kippers. On Saturdays, in the spirit of self-denial familiar to all the martyrs who had gone before him, Winston only ate one kipper, but had an extra bowl of porridge to compensate. This was a hardship as he didn't like porridge, but its special ingredients, he was convinced, lined his brain with a gooey substance that made it harder for the Prime Ministerial Thought Ray to penetrate.

As Winston poured himself another cup of tea to accompany the last kipper, he sensed a presence. He looked up and saw two people had silently joined him by the table, a pleasant-looking young woman with shoulder-length fair hair, and an equally-young gentleman, taller and with the upright bearing that suggested a military background. This latter impression was emphasised by his magnificent handlebar moustache. Both his visitors wore formal suits, the style of each befitting their respective genders.

'Do you mind if we sit down, Winston?' Rachel asked. For once, Winston was lost for words, so flapped his hands as if to indicate consent. They sat.

'Wh – who are you?' Winston stuttered. He was unaccustomed to visitors at all, except for the police when they called to make veiled threats about his bothering the Chief Constable.

'We are from the Prime Minister's Special Information Unit,' said Gordon, his clipped tones sounding to Winston like a throwback to the days when BBC presenters wore dinner jackets to read the news.

'What are your names?' Winston was getting slightly more relaxed. He'd never heard of members of the Security Services arresting anyone while they were actually sitting down themselves. Usually, he was convinced, they would smash down the door, throw in a couple of stun grenades and he'd have been trussed up like a turkey before he'd realised what was happening. He was equally sure that the snatch squads didn't join their victims for breakfast.

'Our names do not matter,' Gordon replied. 'It is what we have to say that is important. You are, are you not, Mister Winston Golightly?' Winston confirmed that this was true. They clearly knew that without him telling them.

'Good,' continued Gordon. 'You have come to our attention because, despite our best efforts, you recognise the truth and cannot easily be persuaded to ignore what is right.' He stroked his moustache with his finger. 'This puts you in a very small minority.'

Winston had known this to be true all along and was secretly relieved to have it confirmed, even if by a member of the secret inner circle of Government. 'What do you want?' Winston asked.

'You have been selected specially, by the Prime Minister himself, to pass on a message. This is highly sensitive and contains specific details encrypted in the wording. Would you like to finish that rather splendid kipper, by the way? Shame to let it go to waste.'

Winston, all of a sudden, was no longer very hungry. 'No, thanks, I've had plenty,' he replied. 'Would you like it?'

'Very decent of you, but no thanks all the same. We've not got long and this is tremendously important.'

Rachel considered the kipper with a degree of unease, patently not sharing Gordon's apparent enthusiasm for smoked fish as a delicacy. Fortunately, however, she was not called upon to join Winston in his repast.

'Why should I help you?' asked Winston. 'All you do is plague me with Thought Rays. You've been giving me some right bad dreams recently.'

'You are to do exactly what we ask and, crucially, not to breathe a word of our existence, let alone the fact that we've visited you,' explained Rachel. 'The Prime Minister will be most vexed if he gets to hear that you've let him down and will turn the dream machine up to maximum. On the other hand, if you simply relay to a certain telephone number what we have to tell you, we will ask the PM to go easy.'

'Can I ask why he would want me to pass on this message?' Winston was clearly a bit edgy.

'No you can't,' answered Rachel sweetly.

'Have you got a telephone, old boy?' Gordon enquired. Winston confirmed that there was one on the hall table. Gordon stood up and indicated that Winston should lead him to it. When they got to the phone, Gordon took a piece of paper from his pocket and gave it to Winston. 'Dial that telephone number,' he instructed, pointing to a sequence of digits at the top of sheet. 'Then read that message word for word, repeat it, and make sure they read it back so they've got it right. Then forget the telephone number and the message. Can do?'

Winston nodded, picked up the telephone handset, and started dialling.

The telephone call complete, Gordon took the piece of paper back and led Winston back into the kitchen. 'Fancy making a brew, old chap?' Gordon asked. Winston went to fill the kettle. When he turned back from the sink, there was no sign of the visitors, who had departed as silently and suddenly as they had arrived.

CHAPTER EIGHTEEN

To: Assistant Chief Constable Harper,
From: Detective Superintendent Richard Whittingham,
SIO, Operation Witchford

Sir,

I am pleased to report that significant progress has been made in the investigation into the murder of PC Nick Kerridge last year.

Last week the Op Witchford team was contacted directly by the Crimestoppers team in London. They had received single source intelligence as below. It is, inevitably, anonymous as always the case with Crimestoppers intelligence.

'I have got important information about who killed PC Kerridge in Severndale Forest last year. Please don't disregard this. I know you've been looking for the car that was involved and I know where it is.

PC Kerridge was murdered by a criminal in Stambridge called Lee Summers. Your officers spoke to him that evening. Summers picked up the Golf car from a lad called Joe Flynn. It was left with Flynn by two men called Stu and Adie Llewellyn from the Newport area. They left a shotgun in the car. Summers was asked to drive the car back to Newport to give it to Micky Phillips. On the way, Summers was stopped in the Forest by PC Kerridge so Summers shot PC Kerridge. I'm not exactly sure why, but Summers had a kilo of drugs in the car which might have been something to do with it.

After he took the car back to Phillips, Summers went home to Stambridge where your officers spoke to him. He had left the drugs in the car. The car was driven up to the Brecon Beacons by a bloke called Stephen Beasant. You have to go to Crickhowell, and then up alongside the north side of Talybont

Reservoir till you get to a deserted farm at the top end of the lake. Go past the farm about quarter of a mile and take the track on the right. You'll find the car up there. Beasant burnt it out, still with the drugs in it. He cut up the shotgun, mixed it up in a bucket of cement and dropped it somewhere in the middle of the Bristol Channel. Beasant is dead now, he died a few days ago in a car crash outside Newport. Check on all this stuff I've told you and you'll find it's true.'

I can report that the above intelligence contained some details known to us but not publicised, such as police officers speaking to SUMMERS, so we took it seriously. As a result the burnt out car was recovered in the location stated. The Vehicle Identification Number verifies that it is the VW Golf we have been seeking. Forensic evidence has been very limited as the car was comprehensively incinerated. However, traces of heroin were found. The following individuals were all arrested, initially on suspicion of murder:

Joe FLYNN denied murder but admitted supplying one kilo of heroin to Lee SUMMERS, and has been charged with the latter offence. FLYNN admits asking SUMMERS to return the car to PHILLIPS.

Stuart LLEWELLYN and Adrian LLEWELLYN both denied murder but admitted Possessing a Firearm with Intent to Cause Fear of Violence.

PHILLIPS has made no comment throughout. He has been charged with assisting an offender (namely SUMMERS) and Perverting the Course of Justice.

SUMMERS has made no comment throughout. He has been charged with the Murder of PC Nicholas Kerridge and with Possessing a Controlled Drug of Class 'A'. Should Summers be convicted of the murder of PC Kerridge, the source will be eligible for the £100,000 reward.

The above charges represent the conclusion of the investigation into the murder of PC Kerridge. This report is submitted for your information.

Yours sincerely,

Richard Whittingham,
Detective Superintendent.

It took well over a year for the case to reach trial. Once I had read the SIO's final report I knew that matters would go quiet for a while. Summers had inevitably been remanded in custody after charge, so I left him in as much peace as he could expect to get inside. I didn't enjoy visiting prisons in any case; they are soulless places, stinking of unwashed bodies and frustrated testosterone and, in my opinion, best avoided.

I did go to a couple of prisons with Danny in the intervening months, to collect overstayers of a particularly nasty kind. One was a notorious child rapist and murderer; he'd been banging on in the press about wanting to be allowed to die and had been on constant suicide watch for years, so that one took a bit of planning. In fairness to him, he was not really a deliberate overstayer but if the authorities really want to keep you alive they can make it very difficult for you to do otherwise. In the end Danny just used the stun gun and gave him a heart attack, though not before we had woken him in the middle of the night and told him in no uncertain terms what lay in store for him in the Redevelopment Unit. After we had collected him, his soul was equally unpleasant, exuding menace and creepiness even after death. I began to realise that some people were genuinely and irremediably evil, and wondered what it must have been like to encounter war criminals and the like when their own time came.

The other inmate was considered less of a suicide risk so gave us a bit more scope for creativity. Another killer, this one had beaten his ten month old son to death because he couldn't hear the football commentary on the television over the baby's crying. The fact that his son was crying because he was undernourished and starving cut no ice with the cruel bastard. With a supreme sense of irony, Danny interfered with the television in his cell, timing it so he expired during a European Champions League football match. The fact that the killer was a Manchester United supporter and we fixed it so that he carked it as injury time approach with the 'must win' match poised at 1-1 made it even better. The icing on the cake was that we stayed around to watch their opponents score a dramatic winner. Oh, how we laughed.

My mission to secure justice, or as some might see it,

vengeance, in the case of my own murder was in abeyance with Summers in chokey, so I threw myself into my new career with enthusiasm. In a despairingly short period of time I had lost my distaste for causing the demise of overstayers, though perhaps not to the extent that I could yet emulate Gordon in my passion for death and mayhem. Paul had still been getting grief from his own bosses, and we had the makings of a good squad, especially since Lizzie had also qualified as a team member. She and Rachel began to work together, dealing with some highly emotive tasks which generally involved families. I still fought shy of collecting children, not that there were many juvenile overstayers as by and large they didn't have that much control over their own destiny. Lizzie and Rachel, however, had a particular empathy and were able to face up to what was a very difficult job. That meant that Danny, Gordon and I were able to handle the more straightforward operations, sometimes bringing several clients back in a day between us. This certainly kept Paul off our backs.

Since our evening by the lake, Chris and I had spent as much of our free time together as possible. There were many advantages to being dead, I was discovering. No housework, no household shopping, just plenty of time to go where we chose. The sex was pretty spectacular too. When you can have anything you want, I had found, pursuits of material things are pointless. The true purpose in our lives was getting to know each other for who we really were. Like on Earth, Chris told me, relationships in the Afterlife could peter out or endure; it was down to the individuals. Some couples we met had been together for centuries, measured by Earth time; they were the true soul mates. Even though we worked together, Chris's job and mine were sufficiently different for our paths only to cross every so often during the working day. Although she came out with us to the other world occasionally, she didn't get out very often. Paul kept her far too busy for that.

CHAPTER NINETEEN

'All rise.' As the time-honoured cry of the Court Clerk rang across the packed benches, Summers watched the briefs, assistants, press and public stand in homage to the judge. His Honour Mr. Justice Rupert Benson, robed and bewigged, strode to his throne-like perch from where he would gaze imperiously at the assembled multitude before him. He ran his time-served eyes over the line of barristers, the defendants in the dock, and the twelve good persons of the jury. His Honour regarded all of them with equal contempt. He did not even bother to look at the press seats or the ghoulish spectators in the public gallery; they had no role to play in the proceedings so would be ignored, unless they did something to annoy him.

'You may proceed with the charges, Mr. Ramsbottom,' His Honour informed the Clerk, who bowed his head to the judge.

'Lee Summers, you are charged with the offence of murder. How do you plead?'

Summers, standing in the dock, had lost all his normal cockiness and was too nervous to give a coherent answer. His barrister, Mr. John Stanningley, got to his feet. 'Your Honour, my client wishes to plead Not Guilty to the charge of Murder. He is also entering a plea of Not Guilty to a charge of Possession of a Class 'A' Controlled Drug.'

'Thank you, Mr. Stanningley,' the judge announced, peering at the barrister over the rim of his glasses. "I will take it as read that the other defendant is similarly devoid of the gift of speech, so will take a plea from counsel on his behalf."

The brief for Phillips separately confirmed that his client had nothing to do with the murder of the police officer, even as peripherally as assisting Summers and doing his best to scupper the investigation. Phillips had refused to say a word to the police and it appeared likely that his vow of silence continued.

His Honour nodded sagely, as if this was only to be expected. Turning his face to the prosecution team's bench, he addressed them. 'Mrs. Warrener, I understand you have recently taken silk. I am sure you will conduct this case with all the gravitas and decorum that honour merits.'

Mrs. Susan Warrener, QC, having recently been elevated amongst her peers, nodded respectfully to the judge, secretly relishing the chance to act for the prosecution in such a high profile case. Securing the conviction of the defendants for murdering a police officer would immediately ensure that her profile was raised. She cared little about the defendants themselves, or even about the victim; had she been so briefed and paid, she would equally happily have defended them, especially as an acquittal for a cop-killer would look even more impressive on her CV.

'Your Honour, I am obliged for your guidance.' She turned to address the jury. 'Ladies and gentlemen, you will hear evidence from police officers and expert witnesses that reveals a chain of events that led to the callous murder of an upstanding police officer.'

I appreciated the unintended irony as I was indeed standing up at the back of the court, observing the proceedings. After all, I hadn't attended my own funeral in spirit, though I assume I was there in body, and going to the trial of your own murderer was definitely a once in a life time event.

So I watched with interest as Mrs. Warrener QC waxed eloquent about the calamity of blunders initiated by the hapless Summers. By the time her character assassination was complete, the jurors would have been forgiven for concluding that those who had been implicated in killing me had studied the art and ethics of murder at the feet of Pol Pot.

She asserted 'A man by the name of Joseph Flynn supplied a kilo of heroin to Summers, in order that the latter could bolster his criminal enterprise by selling it at inflated prices to tormented drug addicts across the region. Summers, the prosecution case will show, was in possession of the drugs and driving a car provided, as admitted, by Mr. Flynn, when he was stopped and checked by Police Constable Nicholas Kerridge.

'PC Kerridge, of course, cannot tell us what happened, or

175

why. All is not lost because the forensic evidence will show you exactly what happened. Only Summers, if he has the personal courage, can tell us why but if he chooses not to admit his terrible guilt, then we can only surmise.

'It matters not, however, if the prosecution cannot prove the actual motive beyond reasonable doubt; it will suffice to show merely that there was a reason for Summers to wish to cause serious harm to PC Kerridge who was, after all, carrying out his lawful duty to keep the community safe and feeling safe...'

Mrs. Warrener certainly gave me a good character reference, extolling my virtues as she virtually went through our Chief Constable's statement of values, a comprehensive and inspirational piece of managerial waffle for cops which in essence told us not to shout at victims, beat up the general public or fiddle the tea fund. It appeared I had adhered with almost promotion-seeking zeal to the letter of this worthy guidance. Shame there wasn't one for the criminal fraternity, I thought, starting with 'Thou shalt not kill coppers'. My colleagues would appreciate that kind of mission statement.

By the time the prosecutor had finished outlining the case against Summers, I was ready to fetch a noose and string him from the rafters, but then I had every excuse to be biased.

Mrs. Warrener then moved on to outline the parts played by the assortment of ne'er-do-wells originally implicated in Summers' misdeeds. 'Mr. Flynn, who set this whole unfortunate chain of events in motion, does not sit in the dock, ladies and gentlemen, as he has had the courage to admit his part, in that he supplied no less than one kilogram of heroin to Summers. Mr. Flynn, you might wish to note, has served a suitable term of imprisonment which reflects not just his wrongdoing but also his contrition which was exemplified by his admission at the earliest possible stage.'

Contrition, I thought, along with a script for the judge which asked for leniency to reflect Joe Flynn's finger pointing unwaveringly at the idiot Summers. A three year sentence which meant that after eighteen months Flynn was back out on the streets, albeit on licence. The bastard was back in business before this trial had even started.

'There were others involved in the aforementioned chain

who also, by virtue of their acceptance of their wrongdoing, do not appear before this court with the accused,' she droned on. 'They played no direct part in the murder of PC Kerridge, and could not have foreseen the consequences of their unfortunate actions.' Stu and Aidy Llewellyn, in other words, who had unwittingly made a sawn-off available to Summers, thereby costing me my existence on Earth. Cynical as I am, I had not been unduly surprised by the even more lenient sentence handed down to Tweedle Dum and Tweedle Dee, and they were out of prison even before Flynn. Those security vans don't rob themselves, of course, so no doubt they had soon reverted to their own ways. I could only hope they came to a sticky end, and I made a mental note to check with Fate Planning when they were due for their comeuppance. I might just go and say hello, I decided.

'The Crown will be calling on the aforementioned Joe Flynn, Stuart and Adrian Llewellyn as witnesses,' announced Mrs. Warrener. 'They will tell you how the car and sawn-off shotgun fell into the hands of Summers, and how it was ultimately provided by Phillips, who appears in the dock alongside Summers. Unlike Flynn and the Llewellyn brothers, Phillips lied and lied again to detectives in the course of the investigation and caused the said vehicle to disappear after the murder, thereby causing significant delay and expense. Had it not been for a single piece of information leading to the car being recovered and forensically examined, PC Kerridge's killer and his associates might never have been brought to justice.'

I wondered how the Crimestoppers intelligence would play out in court, but the prosecuting counsel moved swiftly on, presumably because the information had actually proved to be spot on. At least the prosecution could now tell the jury that they had linked the car and shotgun to Summers, and thereby to the car chase and stop that had been my last acts.

Mrs. Warrener then waxed lyrical about the wealth of forensic and other evidence that could be presented if required. Most of it, admittedly, simply corroborated what was already known, so it appeared that there would little if any doubt that Summers had been in the car and that the car had, to all intents and purposes, belonged to Phillips. The jury, by now, seemed to be reaching saturation point with the information being extolled by the prosecution. It was a shame, I reflected, that we couldn't introduce Beasant's confession and his confrontation by the Grim Reaper. That would make them sit up and take notice.

His Honour Judge Rupert had also had a brain full by now, so he decided it was time for an early lunch. Court was adjourned accordingly, Summers and Phillips being taken back down to the cells for the recess. Being incorporeal, I didn't need a sandwich so I thought I'd nip downstairs after them for a quick bit of haunting. No peace for the wicked, and all that.

I'd already visited Summers on a few occasions, usually when he was either drunk or half asleep. Whilst this was against our rules of engagement, as any manifestation had to be necessary to accomplish our task, it was at least deniable. I'd toyed with the idea of appearing in court, in a manner of speaking, but that would have caused no end of a stink and would inevitably have come to the attention of Paul, if not his bosses, and it would have resulted in a one way trip to the Redevelopment Unit for me. A private appearance it would have to be then. It might appear that I had, by now, become something of a phantom stalker as far as Lee Summers was concerned, but the fact of the matter was that I wanted to freak the bastard out. Despite our best efforts, and the ebullience of Mrs. Warrener, I was less than convinced that there was a conclusive case against my killer and the more neurotic I could make him, the better. Direct confrontation with the Grim Reaper, albeit Gordon dressed up in the boss's outfit, had worked wonders with our friend Beasant and I still remained hopefully that we could get a trembling confession from Summers. Haunting Summers in the lunchtime adjournment was an entirely different matter from the private appearances I had previously indulged in. There were people around for him to shout to, and there was always the possibility that someone might just look through the cell hatch. I also needed to check for CCTV; I wasn't quite sure whether my ghostly image would be captured but a starring role in *Most Haunted* would not go down spectacularly well back at the office.

Sauntering down the steps from the dock to the cells, I

drifted effortlessly through the heavy iron grilled gate. I've always liked old courts, and this was one such. Stambridge Crown Court retained all the majesty of its Eighteenth Century origins, dark wooden paneling in abundance around the walls of the court room itself, surmounted by a cornice displaying the coats of arms of local distinguished families. Most of those, I surmised, would long since have either been reduced to penury or emigrated to retain a more amenable lifestyle in the Colonies. There is no place in modern Britain for the historical landed gentry, as the levelers and *Guardian* readers of the modern meritocracy constantly remind us.

Inside Stambridge and similarly traditional palaces of justice, it was still easy to imagine Mr. Justice Benson donning his black cap and telling a trembling Summers that he would be taken to a place of lawful execution and thence hanged by the neck until dead. The Eurocrats would have a collective thrombie if that ever happened of course, which didn't mean it was a bad idea.

The feel-bad factor was reiterated downstairs, the stone walls featuring peeling whitewash and a general air of despondency, matched only by the miserable demeanour of the court security staff. I felt a degree of sympathy for a hard-working and put-upon group of individuals who didn't get to see much sunshine in their dismal world, but reflected that, for the most part, they worked for a large private enterprise organisation and were free to leave at any time, unlike our mutual clientele.

I'd given the staff a few minutes to stick Summers and Phillips back behind bars and disappear to the rudimentary kitchen to prepare them their low-budget microwave lunch. The coast now being relatively clear, I stuck my head through a couple of cell doors before finding first Phillips and then Summers. At least the private enterprise wannabe cops, who now did what used to be our job here, had not put them in the same cell, which was something. Summers was lounging on the plastic-covered mattress which served to make the ancient wooden bench slightly and, in my view, unjustifiably more comfortable. He was picking his nose which at least gave him something constructive and challenging to occupy his mind. I hadn't seen him engaged in this particular activity in the dock;

179

even he would have realised it would not endear him to the jury, so he presumably had a bit of catching up to do.

I had thought to bring my blood-stained high-vis jacket along, just in case this opportunity arose, and I was wearing the garment so I knew Summers would recognise me. There was no camera in the cell, so I silently materialised before his very eyes. As usual, I pointed at him and in a low voice growled 'Murderer', then for good measure added 'Confess your crime, or you will lose your soul'. I thoroughly enjoyed seeing Summers' gaunt and pallid features, eyes wide and jaw dropping, his right index finger immersed in one nostril as he gawped witlessly at the apparition before him. Deciding I had better quit while I was ahead, and still undetected, I faded quickly from his sight, though not before flicking him a crafty V-sign. I'm not a very nice person deep down, I realised by now, and in any event, Summers could hardly complain about my lack of courtesy. As I drifted back into the corridor I could hear Summers yelling for the security staff and banging loudly on his cell door, imploring them to release him from the cell which he was now maintaining was haunted. Needless to say this resulted in short shrift from the officer at the desk who told Summers to wind his neck in if he wanted to go back in court.

Abandoning Summers to his blubbering, I went back upstairs and popped into the Jury Room just on the off-chance that they had already decided to convict Summers and were simply marking time until the judge asked their opinion. I was disappointed, of course. They were lounging around the table, scoffing sandwiches and swigging tea and talking variously about the previous night's football, the exploits of Britain's Most Talented dancing dog; anything in fact except the matter in hand. I could only conclude that Silky Sue was boring them rigid and hoped that something would spark their interest before they completely lost the will to live.

The afternoon session continued in much the same vein as the morning, though I noticed that the prosecution team was now being supported by a middle-aged gent whom I vaguely recognised as the SIO, Detective Superintendent Whittingham. I now recalled having seen him in occasional copies of the force magazine, usually celebrating some outstanding achievement in bringing villains to book.

Inclining now towards stoutness, he still cut something of a dashing figure in his navy blue pinstripe suit, grey hair immaculately trimmed and sporting an expensive pair of designer spectacles. No doubt he would feel compelled to intervene if the prosecution brief wandered too far off track.

Mrs. Warrener, having earlier outlined what the prosecution would say, now started saying it. Trials for serious crimes are long on detail and, despite the impression given on television or the cinema screen, invariably short on drama and excitement. Details of a multitude of reports and submissions were laid out, all of which had been accepted in advance by the defence who did not dispute what had happened to me, only that it was Summers who was wholly responsible. This, at least, meant that we were spared a lengthy parade of experts to read out what was already available in documentary form.

Eventually, the first day of the trial drew stultifyingly to its close, so I made my way back to the Afterlife, and went to the bar.

As ever, the gang was there already. Chris gave me her customary smouldering look as I walked in; she knew that I was following the trial and hadn't objected too strenuously. Her take on it might have been a bit different had she known that I had been making myself known to Summers, but I figured that what she didn't know would probably not harm her. Danny and Rachel were engrossed in a seemingly sensible conversation whilst Gordon appeared to be instructing Lizzie in the finer points of some drinking game. Having in past times been a fan of war films like *The Dam Busters*, I half expected him to persuade her to put a sooty paste on her bare feet and make black footprints on the ceiling. On the other hand, maybe he kept that kind of thing for the flying club.

'I've never seen a trial', Gordon informed me as he brought a round of drinks back to our table. His drinking game had proved a tad challenging for Lizzie given that she and the others had already enjoyed a few glasses prior to my arrival.

'Don't worry, you're not missing much,' Danny retorted. 'A load of self-important, over-educated loudmouths try to bore some random members of the public into a catatonic trance in the hope that they will agree with the respective cases put to them. You might as well toss a coin at the outset and

181

save a shed load of time and money'. Our resident cynic had lost none of his world-weary contempt for the criminal justice system, it was abundantly clear.

'Sounds like plenty of politicians I could name,' I commented. 'Still, if you're interested in seeing a bit more of our world you're more than welcome to come with me. It's all words, though; there's no flak and no night-fighters so you might find it a bit tedious.'

'Yes, well, if I could reciprocate, old boy, you'd probably want to be on an op that was similarly lacking in excitement so I'm sure I can contain my boredom'. I couldn't have agreed more.

The following day, therefore, there were two of us lurking without form or substance at the rear of Court Two at Stambridge Crown Court. Silky Sue called her first witness, who was none other than Stu Llewellyn. This being a rare court appearance in which he was not actually the defendant, Llewellyn was wearing his normal apparel which consisted of a stylish Ben Sherman shirt and jeans, rather than the more traditional ill-fitting suit. He had, however, not lost the naturally shifty demeanour that I presumed was his norm whenever he was in front of the judiciary in whatever capacity. The prosecution brief led him carefully through his statement, not least because he gave the impression of wanting to deny everything. It must have been ingrained in him. Mrs. Warrener eventually felt compelled to reassure him that he had nothing further to worry about, from the legal system at least.

'You've done your time, Mr. Llewellyn, so you might as well share with the ladies and gentlemen of the jury the details of what happened on that night nearly two years ago. I know a lot of water has flowed under the bridge, and if necessary I will refresh your memory...'

Stanningley was on his hind legs immediately. 'I do hope that the prosecution isn't planning to put words in the mouth of their witness,' he interjected. His Honour Judge Rupert looked down his nose at the defence barrister as if he just suffered an abrupt and voluminous outbreak of wind.

'I am quite capable of ensuring that no one breaks the rules in my court, Mr. Stanningley. Will that be all?'

'Yes, Your Honour,' conceded Stanningley, taking his seat

once more.

'It'll be all for now, but I wouldn't mind betting he can't shut up for long,' I said to Gordon.

Mrs. Warrener led Stu Llewellyn through his rather stilted statement, made to the police after he was charged with Possession of a Firearm with Intent to Cause Fear of Violence. Llewellyn confirmed that he and his brother had used the car to travel from Newport to Stambridge, and that they'd left a pick-axe handle, loaded sawn-off shotgun and two balaclavas under a blanket on the back seat. He was rather less willing to say why he felt it was necessary to travel on to my patch armed to the teeth but, as I pointed out to Gordon, that didn't really matter. Llewellyn did point out that, once he and Aidy had decided that abject cowardice was the better part of valour, they had been at a loss to know what to do with the blagging kit, sawn-off shotguns and pick-axe handles not being overly welcome on the local rail service. They had decided between themselves that the 'do nothing' option was easier than trying to think of a feasible alternative, so they had simply left the kit in the car, which they foisted off on Joe Flynn before legging it to the station.

Given the chance to stick his oar in, Mr. Stanningley set to with relish. He made the most of the opportunity to emphasise to the jury that Llewellyn had been convicted and imprisoned for the offence which he was now offering as evidence. 'Laying it on bit thick, isn't he?' I pointed out to Gordon, who replied 'With a shovel, old boy,' grinning broadly.

Eventually Mr. Stanningley got round to his main points. 'Mr. Llewellyn, you say that you left in the car...' Pausing theatrically to place his reading glasses on his nose at he made a show of consulting his sheaf of papers though only the most feeble-minded of onlookers would have forgotten what Llewellyn had been talking about.

'A sawn-orf shotgun'. Fair play to him, he managed to make it sound as if Purdey & Co had taken to producing a slimmed-down version of their finest piece.

'A sawn-orf shotgun,' he repeated, presumably in case any members of the jury had been suddenly stricken with amnesia. 'And, pray tell the jury, Mr. Llewellyn...' Another theatrical pause. 'Where precisely is this sawn-orf shotgun now?'

'I don't know, mate,' responded Llewellyn, affably.

'I'm not your mate, Mr. Llewellyn,' came back Stanningley as an aside. 'You don't know,' he emphasised slowly and with gravity. 'Did you ever see the sawn-orf shotgun again, after you abandoned your car and felonious equipment in Stambridge?'

'No m... I mean Sir. I left it by there and never saw it again.'

'You never saw it again.' Again, the emphasis, with eye contact with the line of jurors to ensure that they were all still with Stanningley as he pursued his line of forensic interrogation. 'So, Mr. Llewellyn, you cannot say if it was in the car when the car was returned to Newport, or indeed wherever the prosecution is going to maintain it went to after you left it.' Specs off now, and I noticed that Stanningley was in the habit of chewing the end of one arm of his glasses.

'No, that's right, I can't,' Llewellyn conceded, slightly too helpfully for my liking.

Stanningley was no fool, and knew to quit while he was ahead. He made to sit down, but just before doing so he asked, almost as an afterthought, 'Oh, Mr. Llewellyn, what was the registration number of the car, by the way?'

Llewellyn was flummoxed by this apparently simple question, which it appeared no one on the prosecution team had thought to check. 'I don't know, I didn't look.'

'I see. Thank you Mr. Llewellyn. That will be all from me', the defence brief told him gratefully. I looked over towards the prosecution tables and saw the unedifying sight of the SIO with his head buried in his hands.

'That went well,' Gordon pointed out brightly.

Joe Flynn's attempts to further the cause of justice was even more peremptory once the defence flak barrage got him in their sights. He was absolutely certain, when asked by the prosecution, that it was Summers that had collected the heroin and the vehicle from him. He knew it for a fact, Flynn confidently announced, as he had been there when Summers drove away.

'And when you say you were there, Mr. Flynn,' Stanningley probed when he rose to cross-examine the witness. 'Exactly where do you mean?'

'I was at my place, like I said,' Flynn replied.

'At your place.' Again Stanningley spelled this out in much the same way that a weary teacher would try to interact with a mentally-challenged problem child. 'Were you inside your 'place', as you put it? Or outside waving to my client as he drove away in Mr. Llewellyn's car?'

'Erm, I was inside, in fact,' Flynn confirmed.

'Oh, indeed.' Stanningley clearly felt that he was getting warmer. 'So did you, perhaps, watch my client from your window?'

'Not exactly, no.'

'Not exactly. I see. But you saw my client get into Mr. Llewellyn's car and then drive away?'

'Umm, not really.'

'Not really? Is that more or less precise than 'not exactly', Mr. Flynn? Or do you really mean 'no' in each case?'

'Yes,' replied Flynn, looking like he really didn't want to be there. I knew how he felt.

'Is that 'yes' as in you meant 'no'?' went on Stanningley. 'You might wish to answer 'it is' or 'it is not' so we don't confuse the jury,' he added smugly.

'You're confusing me', mumbled Flynn.

'I'm so sorry, Mr. Flynn', fired back Stanningley. 'Let me make it simple. I put it to you that you did not, in fact, see my client get into the car that Mr. Llewellyn had left you your place. Am I right?'

'Yes, you are', conceded Flynn reluctantly.

'Thank you Mr. Flynn, for clarifying that. So whilst we are making matters so much clearer for the ladies and gentlemen of the jury, perhaps you could confirm whether you did in fact see the sawn-orf shotgun in Mr. Llewellyn's car before my client got into it?'

'Umm, not...I mean, no I did not', admitted Flynn.

'So, to clarify matters absolutely,' Stanningley pontificated, thumbs hooked into the lapels of his gown. 'You know that Mr. Llewellyn left his car at your, err, place. You don't know whether there was a sawn-orf shotgun in it. You also cannot say whether my client actually took the car away when he left your place.'

'Yes, I suppose so, but the car was gone so I assumed it was Summers as I'd told him to take it.'

'Ahh, you assumed.' Stanningley was evidently pleased about that utterance by Flynn. 'But you don't actually know, do you?'

'No that's right,' conceded Flynn. 'But the car wasn't there when I went out about half an hour later, so I thought he must've taken it.'

'Ah, but there might be another explanation, might there not?' asked Stanningley. The way he was dragging this out, I was beginning to think briefs were carefully trained to drag things out as much as possible.

'I suppose if you earn a thousand pounds an hour, or whatever the rate is, you would try to take as long as possible', I told Gordon.

'Well I suppose it might've been stolen,' Flynn said flippantly, not for one moment expecting Stanningley to take him seriously. This was, of course, a mistake.

'Precisely, Mr. Flynn,' announced Stanningley, as if this alternative was glaringly obvious to all but the most simple-minded. 'Thank you for clarifying that. I have no further questions', he added, taking his seat whilst Flynn was left slack-jawed and unable to dig himself out of the hole, on the edge of which the prosecution case now teetered.

It appeared that the prosecution's case was in danger of collapse before lunchtime on the second day. 'Worse than England's batting against Australia,' was Gordon's verdict. I felt sorry for the investigation team, having watched Detective Superintendent Whittingham gradually turning a more vivid shade of purple as the morning wore on. Worst of all, Summers and Phillips had taken to smirking quite openly at the discomfort of the prosecution.

'What can you do about it?' Gordon asked me as the lunchtime adjournment approached.

'I tried spooking Summers yesterday, but it didn't have any effect,' I told him. 'He's seen me before as you know, but I think all I'm doing is making him think he's going round the bend.'

'What about the other blighter, Phillips? Have you had a go at him?' Gordon asked.

'Not yet. He doesn't seem the type to take any notice of a vision.' I sounded despondent but I was seriously thinking that things were going to go pear-shaped.

'Where's Paul this afternoon?' Gordon suddenly enquired.

'Dunno. Chris said something about him going to a conference on increasing the headcount in natural disasters, which sounds like the usual barrel of laughs. I think that's him sorted for the week.'

'How long till lunch?'

'Should be about one, so maybe ninety minutes?' I hoped that the trial lasted that long.

'I've got an idea. I'll need to speak to Lizzie and see if she can sort something out for me.' Without a further word, Gordon vanished through the back wall.

The morning ground remorselessly on, a series of technicalities having seemingly given Mr. Stanningley more chances to put some bullet holes in the prosecution case. Each of these was vigorously contested by Mrs. Warrener, perhaps more in the hope than the expectation that something would turn up. It was not looking good.

Judge Rupert eventually decided that lunch was in order about thirty minutes earlier than normal, but at least matters were still in abeyance so all was not yet lost.

I hung around the temporarily deserted courtroom, awaiting the return of Gordon, however he might manifest himself. I had a sneaking feeling I knew what was coming.

True to form, a short while later the Grim Reaper materialised through the back wall, complete with cloak, hood and scythe. Having witness his performance with Beasant, I was no longer too fazed by this. He didn't even bother shouting this time.

'I asked Lizzie who had a quiet word with Chris,' he explained before I had even said anything. 'I thought I might try leaning on Phillips to see if he'll come over to our point of view'.

'Oh, right.' It was worth a go, I thought.

'I didn't ask you because if it all goes tits-up then I'll carry the can,' he added cheerfully.

We went downstairs again, completely invisible of course. I checked a couple of cells before finding the one holding Phillips, who was getting stuck into a vile-looking mess of stew and potatoes. I went back to where Gordon was lurking.

'He's in there. There's no camera so you'll be OK but you'd better make it snappy as he'll scream blue murder when he sees you, and the staff will be in like a shot'.

'Don't panic, old boy. We'll get through it. Just follow my lead'.

We walked through the metal door. Phillips was pre-occupied with his lunch as we materialised. He looked up to find Gordon's hooded figure pointing at him whilst I stood in my blood-stained jacket looking as tragic as I could manage. Phillips was nearly sick with fright.

'You will tell the truth', intoned Gordon in a doom-laded tone. 'This man was murdered most foully and you have played a part. Confess to your sins or come with us...'

Phillips dropped his lunch on the floor as he cringed in the corner of the cell. He screamed for security, as predicted.

We heard footsteps approaching along the cell corridor, the clatter of keys and then the door opened. As it did so we dematerialised.

'What the hell's wrong with you pair?' asked the security guard. 'It was your mate yesterday and now you. What's the matter?'

Phillips was still curled up in a terrified ball on his bench, pointing at us even though he could no longer see us. 'Ghosts...' was all he could manage to utter feebly.

'Ghosts? What ghosts? There's nothing there. You're fucking mental, you are'. The guard slammed the door as he left. Diversity training was clearly at a premium in the private security industry, I told Gordon whilst we were invisible and inaudible.

As the footsteps receded, we materialised once more. Phillips freaked out again even before Gordon spoke. As he yelled and screamed, my colleague told him once again that confession would be good for his soul, in this case literally. We were out of sight of the cell hatch so stayed in Phillips' view as the guard returned. This time, the hatch dropped rather than the door opening.

'What is the matter, Phillips?' demanded a clearly rather annoyed voice.

'It's them, they're here...' Phillips was pointing at us, face white with fear. 'They just keep walking through the wall'.

The keys clattered once more and the door opened, at which we disappeared, unhelpfully as far as Phillips' credibility was concerned.

'There is nothing there. You're bloody imaging it. Have you been on the wacky baccy or something? You got a secret stash in here or what? I can arrange for a body search if you like. Body search, that's a good one,' the guard sniggered.

'They were here. I could see them. A blood-stained copper and the hooded Death thing with the scythe, like in a horror film. I swear down. He was talking to me, the Death bloke'.

'Oh yeah? What was he saying then? Come to get you, has he?' Another snigger.

'He wants me to confess, say what happened, or else I'll die horribly and he'll take me with him'.

'Confess? Bloody good idea. Do that and we can all piss off home. Want your brief, do you? Now fuck off, you're spoiling my lunch.' That metallic crash peculiar to cell doors accompanied the guard's departure.

'You're coming with us, then, Micky', Gordon told Phillips with an air of finality as silence descended once in the corridor of doom. 'If you won't confess your sins, your mortal remains will stay in this cell while we cart off your soul for final judgment'. He waved his scythe in a suitably menacing fashion, which would have come close to taking my head off had I not been dead already.

'Nooooooo...' wailed Phillips. 'I'll do it, get my brief. What do you want me to say?'

'Just the facts,' replied Gordon, like a rather poor Sixties detective programme.

'I will, I promise. Will you still be watching me?' Phillips was actually in tears now.

'Oh yes,' confirmed Gordon. 'We'll be watching and listening to you every step of the way. Fail us and you'll find yourself headless from the neck down.' We left.

The start of the afternoon session was unaccountably delayed for thirty minutes and when Judge Rupert took his seat, Mr. Kiran Sharma, barrister for Phillips, rose first. Mrs. Warrener was clearly in on developments as she didn't make the usual song and dance about the defence raising an issue.

'Your Honour, my client, Mr. Phillips, wishes to change

his plea to Guilty to the charge of Perverting the Course of Justice. I have discussed this with prosecuting counsel and she has agreed to offer no evidence on the further charge of Assisting an Offender, on the grounds that it has not yet been determined that Mr. Summers is an offender, and Perverting the Course of Justice is the more serious charge. Further, my client, for reasons he will not divulge, now wishes to appear as a witness for the prosecution.' He paused, glancing across to Silky Sue. 'My learned friend for the prosecution is amenable to this course of action.'

'Perhaps not surprisingly,' murmured the judge, peering over the rims of his spectacles. 'Very well then. Ladies and gentlemen of the jury, you might wonder why Mr. Phillips has had what might be a Damascene change of heart, but you must of course consider what Mr. Phillips has to say with equal weight to the other witnesses. Please continue, Mrs. Warrener. Your witness, I believe.'

Summers was absolutely aghast at this turn of events and tried to take a swing at Phillips, requiring the dock security staff to grab his arm and earning a stern warning from the judge.

Phillips made his way to the witness stand and took the oath. The reference to Almighty God seemed especially heartfelt, probably because Phillips was now convinced that he would quite likely be granted a personal audience in the near future.

'May I make a statement please, judge?' he started.

'Technically it's Your Honour but don't let me stand on ceremony,' Mr. Justice Benson informed him. 'Yes you may, but remember that you are under oath and may be cross-examined by the defence.'

'I've had a change of mind and decided to tell you what happened. That car was the right one, Summers brought it back and told me that he'd killed the copper. The shotgun and the other stuff was still in the car...' Phillips, true to his word, gave a full and frank account of what Summers had told him, and how Beasant had disposed of the evidence before his own tragic demise.

Mr. Stanningley, for once, was unable to punch any significant holes in Phillips' account. He actually seemed

190

rather respondent whilst, in the dock, his client sat slumped and alone. Phillips was bailed pending sentence for the offence to which he had admitted his guilt, and walked from the court leaving Summers to his fate.

Whilst that happened, I saw Summers signal to his brief, who engaged in a brief but earnest conversation. There appeared to be a difference of opinion between the two, with Summers apparently adamant in his opinion. Reluctantly, Stanningley acquiesced, eventually shrugging his shoulders in resignation.

The prosecution team had run out of witnesses and exhausted its evidence, so Mrs. Warrener conceded that their case rested. His Honour had had enough for the day, so adjourned until the following morning.

We reconvened accordingly, Gordon having decided to retain the Grim Reaper gear 'just in case it comes in handy,' as he explained.

Mr. Stanningley, for what remained of the defence, cut a somewhat lonely figure as he stood up to present the case on Summers' behalf.

'I would like to call my first witness, Your Honour. Mr. Lee Summers, the defendant in this case.'

This was gambling everything on a single roll of the dice, I thought, as Summers was escorted to the witness stand where he swore an oath, somewhat less fervently than Phillips, I considered. He gave his evidence flanked by security staff, giving the appearance of being a rather scruffy rock star accompanied by minders.

'Mr. Summers, would you be so kind as to tell the court exactly what happened on that wet and wild night, nearly two years ago?' Stanningley asked by way of introduction.

To his credit, Summers displayed a hitherto hidden genius for creative story-telling.

'It's true, I did get the heroin from Joe Flynn, and he needed me to take this motor back to Phillips in Newport...'

'Which motor, Mr. Summers? You do need to be specific if you want the ladies and gentlemen of the jury to make the right decision,' interjected the judge.

'The Volkswagen Golf that he had at his house. Some Welsh lads had dumped it on him and 'cos I work for his dad

I said I'd do it. I didn't know there was a shooter and stuff else I wouldn't have taken it...'

'But you did take the vehicle, Mr. Summers, and with the most tragic and unfortunate circumstances, not least for Police Constable Kerridge who sadly is no longer with us,' Stanningley prompted Summers. I wished I could point out that I was actually still there, but it wouldn't have helped much.

'Yes that's right,' Summers confirmed.

'What happened next, Mr. Summers?' prompted Stanningley, evidently keen for his client to shed light on the mystery.

'I'd just left Flynn's place when I saw a hitchhiker. I thought 'That's unusual, you don't see a lot of people hitching lifts these days,' and it was pouring down with rain, so I stopped to give him a lift.'

'Very public-spirited of you,' chipped in Stanningley. , earning a withering look from the judge, suggesting he was overdoing the good citizen bit. 'Do continue, Mr. Summers. Where did you go next?'

'Well, I was on my way to Newport and thought I'd go round the top way rather than on the motorway. It's longer but wasn't my petrol, and I'd have had to cough up to go over the bridge.' Bang goes the good citizen, I thought.

'Who was it you gave a lift to?' Stanningley knew the prosecution would be curious to know, so thought to get that one in first.

'Dunno. It was dark and he had a big storm jacket on with the hood up. I couldn't really see his face and he didn't say much, just said "Thanks, mate" and sat there dead quietly.'

'So under the circumstances, you couldn't say who he is, is that right?' Stanningley continued to cover his bases.

'Yeah, that's right,' Summers was only too happy to agree. 'I'd never seen him before, neither. Nor since,' he added helpfully.

'So apart from expressing his gratitude, albeit rather less than effusively, was there any other conversation between you? Did he tell you anything about himself, where he was from, where he was going, that kind of thing?'

'Um, no, nothing. I just thought he was probably foreign or

something. He was just sat there, till the cop car tried to stop us.'

'Would you like to tell the court about what happened then, Mr. Summers?' Stanningley encouraged his client.

'Yeah well I was just driving out of Stambridge and there was this car drove up behind me and I thought 'Why don't he overtake?' but he didn't and next thing was the blue lights come on. I would've pulled over but the guy says "Fucking hell, it's the pigs, put your fucking foot down, mate." I tried to argue but he reached behind me and pulled the blanket off the back seat. I thought he was going to put it over his head to hide, which would've been a bit stupid, but there was this shooter on the back seat. He told me "Get us out of here or I'll blow you away and the copper." I reckoned you don't argue then, you just do what you're told.'

'You just do what you're told,' parroted Stanningley, as the theme from *Jackanory* ran through my mind. 'So, in effect, Mr. Summers, did you consider you had been hijacked at this point?'

'Hijacked? Yeah, that's right,' Summers said, as if the concept of being diverted at gunpoint had only just occurred to him, which in the scheme of things was not far from the truth.

Stanningley waited a few seconds on the off-chance that his client was going to add something meaningful but he did not. Maybe, I thought, his creative faculties needed a bit of a rest, having been working overtime recently. I didn't know if he actually believed what his client was saying, or just adhering to what defence briefs consider to be their code of ethics: that if the defendant tells them something is true, then it must be. Most cops would describe this stance as somewhere gullibility and perverting the course of justice. If asked to describe Summers' account thus far, I would have been hard-pressed to avoid describing it as 'a load of bollocks', but my opinion was not sought.

The barrister for the defence continued to help Summers along the path of complete fabrication. 'Please continue, Mr. Summers. What happened next?'

'I did like he wanted, floored it and tried to lose the copper but he had a faster car so I had no chance.' Nothing about my superior prowess as a trained pursuit driver, I noted. 'In the end, I told him we had to stop or we'd wind up dead anyway. We was up in the woods somewhere, I'd lost my way, so I just pulled in and sat there.' Yeah, right, I thought. 'Then the other guy took the gun and got out of the car. Next thing I heard was this 'BANG, BANG' and I thought he'd just fired it to scare the copper off. He jumped back in the car and told me to drive off, so I did. I was scared stiff by this and thought I'll not argue, I'll do what I'm told.

The stranger, perhaps inevitably and certainly conveniently, in the cynical view of almost everybody except those twelve good citizens and true in the jury box, had disappeared without trace into the night, leaving Summers to face the music alone.

The trauma, in the expert opinion of the psychiatrist magicked up overnight by the defence, explained why Summers could not offer any explanation in interview, hence his refusal to comment. This supported the contention by the defence that the jury should not infer anything untoward from Summers' earlier silence. Summers admitted possessing the heroin, all of it for his own personal use, but asserted that he would never harm a fly, far less an upstanding custodian of the law. The jury bought it, hook, line and transparently unlikely sinker.

Convicted of Possession of a Class 'A' Controlled Drug, but acquitted of Murder, Summers was let off with a fine, which he had no ability to pay, or intention of doing even if he could. He walked out of court a free if somewhat chastened man.

He would like to have been able to thank his erudite and learned brief for pulling off the miracle of an acquittal, but unfortunately Mr. Stanningley had come to a sudden and regrettable end shortly after the trial, having succumbed to an unanticipated heart attack as he walked away from a pub. Local CCTV showed a cloaked and hooded figure apparently pursuing the barrister waving a large scythe shortly before his fatal collapse. Diligent and extensive police enquiries had failed to trace this witness, sad to say.

CHAPTER TWENTY

'What's the story with this lot?' Danny asked, perched on the edge of Paul's desk.

'We're going for several over-stayers at once. It's more efficient that way.' Paul lounged in his executive chair, legs stretched out and crossed at the ankles. He still looked more like a Shakespearean actor than the harbinger of doom. I wondered how much competition there had been for the post.

We'd been summoned to his office by Chris, who told us 'The boss wants you to give him a hand. All hands to the pump, or some such motivational nonsense.' That meant Danny, Gordon, Rachel and I for a start.

'Why don't you come along as well, the more the merrier?' I'd suggested. Chris said she'd think about it.

'There are two families on one street. They've been at each other's throats for a while and between them they've got four overstayers. Gary, Thomas and Wayne Potter, and David Harris, apparently known as Dai. His neighbours will probably nickname him Dai the Death after we've been round. How very appropriate. We might as well bring them all in at the same time. Dai one, get three free, you might say.'

I shuddered to think how much worse the puns could possibly get. 'One for each of us then, Paul, I presume?'

'Almost, but I will come along on this one. Keep an eye on you, and all that.'

Danny managed, diplomatically, to contain the more apparent signs of his undoubted disappointment. 'Are you riding shotgun or is it an inspection? I was just wondering, like.'

'Oh it's not an inspection. Don't worry about that. I really want to get out of the office for a change, though it's so hard when I've got targets to meet, as I've told you before no doubt.' I looked at Chris who was loitering in the doorway.

'If you're all going shall I join you? You never know how these things might go, Paul...' Danny looked like he'd got a pretty good idea how this job might pan out.

Paul nodded. 'Yeah, what the heck, let's have an office day out. It's not like we've got to worry about the budget.'

It was early evening when we emerged into the alleyway. Cardiff is not the driest place in the country and I wasn't too surprised to find that, once again, it was raining. There were plenty of people around as the three of us walked towards Queen Street station. It must be Saturday, I thought, looking at the mixture of shoppers, laden down with bags, and those clearly dressed for an evening out. I must admit I hadn't thought to ask Danny what day it was; the calendar now seemed somewhat superfluous to my daily existence. I'd never been a big fan of shopping, unless it was for something that I had decided came under the heading of 'Must Have'. That usually meant some gadget or other, not unnaturally.

'The train to Rhymney, that's what we need,' Paul told us having glanced at the itinerary in his folder. We have to get off at somewhere called Abersyfiog then make our way uphill. It's in the Valleys, used to be a mining community.'

Danny remembered the area from when he was a probationer, he told us. 'We came out here for the miners' strike. Loads of overtime in return for standing around all day being shouted at by the miners' wives.' He added 'We've got to walk up a bloody steep hill, I expect.' I suspected that his level of enthusiasm for the task was inversely proportionate to the likely level of Paul's involvement.

'Makes sense I suppose if the railway's in a valley. I shouldn't think they would have put the railway at the top of the hill, so the only way is up.' Gordon, on the other hand seemed doubly delighted, firstly by the involvement of a moving vehicle and secondly by the prospect of gaining some altitude.

I didn't know the area myself but enough of my colleagues had spent time policing the strike in the Valleys and further afield. Old memories died hard, and we still weren't well thought of in certain pockets of the UK. When it suited the populace, uniforms were no more popular nowadays on the remnants of the South Wales coalfield than they had been in the Eighties. It was fairly academic in our case, I supposed; there had to be some advantages from being invisible.

CHAPTER TWENTY-ONE

Members of the Potter family weren't any more popular with their neighbours than my erstwhile colleagues, not that this bothered them in the slightest. They hadn't got on with their previous neighbours either, which was why the council had moved them from their last home. This was on an estate in Newport, which for all its faults was at least on the beaten track. The estate provided rich pickings for the extended Potter clan, kids to bully and tax for their phones and pocket money, customers for their drug dealings and the elderly to harass and relieve of their pensions. The Potters weren't very nice. Now they'd been resettled in a village in the Valleys. Abersyfiog was not popular with the Potters, and the feeling was mutual.

There wasn't much work in Abersyfiog; indeed there hadn't been since the pits had closed in the Eighties. This at least gave Eddie Potter, head of the family, the sense that being out of work was not his fault. He chose to forget that he had never done an honest day's toil in his life, even when the Jobcentre had suggested he might like to get off his idle backside and try a bit of labouring for a change.

Eddie had spawned three equally indolent sons and two rather unpalatable daughters in the twenty-two years he had spent with Anne, his wife. He didn't actually fancy the old rat bag any longer but their active and noisy sex life gave them something to do and was guaranteed to annoy the people either side of their terraced house. By almost any measure, they were well matched. Overweight and bone idle, each sported an impressive collection of totally meaningless tattoos, each could out-shout and out-swear the other when the mood so took them, which it often did.

The Potters were noisy, uncouth and thoroughly ill-mannered. Of an evening, assuming it wasn't actually raining, they were given to sitting and socialising on the pavement in front of their house. This usually involved drinking, smoking and swearing at each other. When failed by their vocabulary, which happened often, they resorted to violence, against passers-by or acquaintances. They weren't all that choosy.

Tommo Potter, eldest son of Eddie and Anne, was proud of his recent spell inside and now at the tender age of twenty-one considered himself to be a criminal mastermind. This opinion, shared by no one outside his direct family, was fuelled purely by his fantasy of building a drugs empire amongst the young people of Abersyfiog. His twin brothers, Gaz and Wayne, were younger and thicker even than the intellectually-challenged Tommo. They were gullible enough to be roped into assisting as he set up a supply chain for heroin and cannabis. This usually involved one or both of the twins picking the gear up from Tommo's dealer, who lived the other side of Newport and running it through to Abersyfiog in his decrepit Ford Mondeo. It goes without saying that the requisite driving documents were conspicuous by their absence.

Tommo was not particularly good as an entrepreneur, and had somewhat overestimated the ability of his customers to pay off their tabs. He lacked the ruthlessness necessary to enforce payment. This soon became common knowledge around the village, especially when Dai Harris, one of his early customers, found that punching Tommo in the face in lieu of payment for a wrap of smack brought no repercussions. Unfortunately, this lack of business acumen also meant that Tommo had been unable to pay his own supplier, Lee Summers, who was apparently very capable of being ruthless. Summers was also getting fed up of waiting for Tommo to stump up the readies for drugs previously supplied to him. Tommo was, in more ways than one, living on borrowed time.

As is often the custom in the Welsh Valleys, Harris had a nickname to differentiate him from everyone else called Dai, of which there quite a lot. He was known to one and all as Dai Morphine, in recognition of his heroin addiction. The Harris family lived a few doors up Evans Street from the Potters, which was handy for all concerned as it provided endless opportunities for them to wind each other up. Hailing from Abersyfiog, the Harrises distrusted any outsiders and in particular those who did not recognise the rightful place of the

Harrises at the top of the local pecking order. Special loathing was reserved for the Potters, whom they blamed for Dai's drugs habit, even though it had pre-dated the latter family's arrival by some years. Logical thought didn't feature prominently as a Harris hereditary trait.

The Potters and the Harrises had much in common, soaking up similar sums in benefits payments whilst contributing nothing in return. Owen and June Harris had done the decent thing when June had fallen pregnant at the age of seventeen. Their first daughter, Sheena, had swiftly been joined in the Family Allowance book by Aaron and Dai. All three were now in their early twenties. None of their names had ever featured on a payroll.

CHAPTER TWENTY-TWO

Tommo was not having the best of days. A little bird had told him, via a text message on his mobile, that his supplier Summers was no longer willing to extend him the credit that he had built up. Not only that, but unless he repaid the outstanding sum of five thousand pounds by the end of the week, he wouldn't be walking for a while. He would still owe his supplier five grand and being housebound would further dent his ability to earn the money, so he was starting to sweat a bit. Tommo was never big on creative thinking and his solutions inevitably revolved around further drug dealing or a spot of acquisitive crime. He thought resentfully of his biggest debtor, Dai Harris, who he estimated now owed him at least three grand. He was realistic enough to know that even if Dai had that amount of money, the last person he was likely to hand it over to would be Tommo. His brain was starting to ache with the effort of resolving his dilemma, and outside the legitimate economy, he didn't exactly have the option of arranging a consultation with the business adviser at a local bank, not that Abersyfiog had a bank.

Scrap metal. A small dim light came on in the recess of Tommo's brain. He'd seen, briefly on Sky News, a report about the burgeoning theft of virtually any forms of metal that could be unscrewed or pried loose and carried away. How much scrap, he wondered, would bring him five grand? Like buses, ideas kept Tommo waiting then two would come along at once. He had encountered Owen Harris a few days previously at the Legion, propping up the bar as usual. Owen didn't buy Tommo a pint, but had been holding forth to his cronies about how he had persuaded the council to stump up for a new central heating system for the Harris residence. Boiler, radiators, pipes, the whole works, had been installed the previous week. Owen reckoned it must have set the council back several thousand to ensure that his family was kept warm. The penny hadn't dropped with Tommo at the time but now there was a new imperative. A new boiler might just provide an acceptable deposit for Summers, thought Tommo, and he could probably cash in on the information about the address it came from which would provide rich pickings for anyone with the means to remove the pipes and radiators. His only challenge now was to find a way of getting his hands on the boiler, which he would consider as an, albeit unwitting, part payment by Dai of his debt.

Tommo might have been reading Summers' mind, as the only remaining blot on his own personal horizon was the money he owed Flynn. He had been given three months to come up with the readies; being a reformed character he set about this task with alacrity. Summers'' debtors list was slowly shrinking as did the amount outstanding to Flynn, and five grand would make a big hole in what remained. It was time to visit Tommo and collect what he was due.

There was a rugby international that Saturday. Wales were on their travels, this time to Twickenham where the entire Principality was confident that the hated English would get their comeuppance. For those unable to attend in person, the next best option was to watch the match in the convivial social atmosphere of one of Abersyfiog's numerous pubs or social clubs. The Harrises, Abersyfiog born and bred, saw their natural venue for such an occasion as the Working Men's Club, a fact that was well-known to Tommo. No one had ever seen fit to comment on the apparent irony of their family membership of a social club established to provide hard-earned liquid sustenance to the labouring classes. The Potters, less woven into the fabric of local society, would be staying at home.

Gaz Potter had offered to go over to meet Summers, in an attempt to persuade him to extend Tommo's deadline for the five grand. If he could swing it, he'd also try and get another package of drugs out of the supplier as a gesture of goodwill, Gaz told his brother, demonstrating a lamentable lack of understanding of how 'goodwill' actually worked in such circumstances. Tommo, all too glad not to have to face Summers in person, told Gaz to give him a call when he returned, on his unattributable Pay As You Go mobile, a method of communication favoured by drug dealers the world over.

As soon as the national anthems of the two teams rang out, each accompanied by cat-calls and booing from the respective groups of opposing supporters, Tommo knew that his chance for instant material gain had arrived. He muttered something to his recumbent parents about nipping out to see someone, gestured to Wayne to join him and left the house. The timing of the match, in the early evening, gave the brothers cover of darkness. From what had, in earlier days, been a coal shed attached to the rear of the house, Tommo took his toolkit, containing a torch, wrench, screwdrivers, a hacksaw and a selection of other such useful implements. They set off down the back lane that ran parallel to Evans Street, their destination being the, by now unoccupied, Harris abode.

Gaz Potter was wondering how good an idea it was to have called on Summers. The latter had just made it absolutely clear that, firstly there was to be no extension to the payment deadline and, furthermore, if Gaz or Tommo thought that Summers was going to let them have any more gear on credit, then they must be from a different planet. Payment was due, it was due now and if Tommo didn't pay up today then he would most likely find himself testicularly challenged. Gaz wasn't entirely sure what this meant, but it sounded impressively painful. Summers wasn't entirely sure either, to be honest, but it was a phrase he'd picked up from Flynn so probably had unpleasant insinuations.

'Where is that toe rag brother of yours?' Summers wanted to know.

'Dunno, he didn't say.' Summers' reputation as a hard man had been enhanced at his trial, the patently ridiculous defence case being further evidence of his invincibility in the murky circles in which he moved. Gaz thought he'd maybe try and mollify Summers a bit. 'He's fixing some central heating just up the road, he said, which is odd because I didn't know he was trained in that. I've to give him a ring and meet him with the gear I was supposed to get off you.'

'Like that's going to happen,' thought Summers, though keeping that to himself. An idea occurred to him, and he turned on his inconsiderable charm for the benefit of Gaz. 'I've got some new gear here, smack it is, from a new supplier. Try some before you go, just a bit. You can tell Tommo how good it is.'

'I've got to get back, give him a hand...' Gaz sounded dubious.

'You'll be fine, chill out for half an hour.' Summers went into the kitchen and prepared a syringe, using heroin that he had not yet got round to cutting. This would blow the mind of even an experienced user. Returning to the lounge he passed it to Gaz, who sat back on the settee, found a half decent vein and injected himself. Gaz's final thought before he passed into oblivion was that this was awesomely good gear.

CHAPTER TWENTY-THREE

'All quiet in there.' Tommo was peering through the kitchen window into the darkened interior of Chez Harris, or 19 Evans Street, as it was more properly known. There was no sound, no apparent movement, so Wayne took a pair of mole grips and attacked the lock on the back door. This did the trick and the door opened without a problem. The two thieves entered the kitchen, their way illuminated by Tommo's torch.

The new gas-fired boiler was sitting quietly in its cupboard next to the sink. A few days after its comprehensive refit, the kitchen was still reasonably uncluttered, something that would no doubt have changed due to June Harris's natural proclivity for bone idleness. As it happened, the state of the kitchen was shortly to become several orders of magnitude removed from mere untidiness. Tommo, complying with sensible health and safety precautions, switched off the main electric fuse to prevent any inadvertent sparks, then he and Wayne quietly set to work uncoupling the hoses and pipes from the boiler in preparation for its removal.

Summers thought that Gaz, following his self-injected dose of high-purity heroin, seemed dead to the world, a status that would likely remain the case for some time. In this he was nearly right; Gaz was indeed dead, but to more than the world. The unaccustomed concentration of the drug had killed him quickly. Gaz was no longer an overstayer, though we had no way of knowing that at that particular time.

Taking Gaz's car keys, Summers also helped himself to the late Potter brother's mobile phone. He shut the door of his flat and walked out to Gaz's car, parked helpfully at the front of the building.

On this occasion, Summers' drive to South Wales did not feature any murders or other events of note. It was a bit of a trek, taking him a good hour to reach his destination. As luck would have it, he got to Abersyfiog at about half time in the rugby international. Parking up on the street a few yards from Tommo Potter's house, to which he had been an occasional though unwelcome visitor, he sent Tommo a text message on Gaz Potter's mobile phone.

Were u at bro? Spelling was not Summers' strongest suit, even in the abbreviated lingua franca of texting.

Two or three minutes passed before the phone pinged with Tommo's reply: *We r at no 19. Where u bin u r l8.*

Be there in a mo. Just parkin car, Summers sent back.

CHAPTER TWENTY-FOUR

We few, we happy few, we band of avenging angels, made our way from the railway station up the steep streets that led to our destination. We'd made our usual invisible, ticketless, way from Cardiff to Abersyfiog. To have called the wayside halt a station would have been a considerable exaggeration, but at least the train stopped there, which saved us having to leap off it at speed. The dark evening, wind and incessant rain would, in that earlier time, have made for a miserable evening but it didn't affect us. We didn't get wet, or even really feel it. Danny had stopped moaning and was exchanging some pithy ex-copper comments with Rachel, doubtless about our present surroundings, the litter, unkempt houses and preponderance of satellite dishes. Paul and Gordon were navigating by street map whilst also comparing notes on ways to process mass casualties, something in which they shared a disturbingly intense professional interest. That left Chris and I to bring up the rear of the group and enjoy each other's company.

'Nearly there, folks,' Gordon encouraged us as we walked purposefully along Evans Street. 'Operational briefing please, Squadron Leader?' This latter was, somewhat informally, aimed at Paul who thus far had not let us in on the precise sequence of events he expected to put in place. The pause before his reply suggested to me that our Glorious Leader might not have gone into the necessary amount of detail in his game plan.

I didn't need to ask Danny what his expectations were; they were written all over his face in an expression of amused cynicism. He asked Paul 'Is there a plan then?'

'Of course there is,' our fearless leader told him.

'Oh good. What is it?' I thought Danny was pushing his luck somewhat.

'Well, erm, we've got two pickups really. Potters times

206

three from number eight and just the one, Dai Harris, from number nineteen. Best start at number eight; we can always come back for Harris another time if necessary.' A simple plan, though lacking depth in its method, I thought.

'How are we going to get three of them at once?' I asked.

'Depends on what they are up to, I suppose. We could electrocute them, or something structural perhaps?' Paul had clearly not thought this one through. Then another idea occurred to him. 'Poisoning. That might do it. We can slip something in their tea. Rat poison, perhaps or weed-killer. There must be some in a shed round here somewhere.' Gawd, I thought, be afraid, be slightly afraid.

'Danny,' I ventured. 'Did you bring your stun gun?'

'But of course,' he replied. 'I never leave home without it.' To prove the point, he briefly drew it from his pocket before concealing it again. No need to bother with that, I considered. We were invisible so he could run up and down the street waving it at all and sundry and no one would have noticed.

'Three simultaneous coronaries, then,' announced Paul with evident satisfaction.

'And a fourth when we catch up with Dai Harris, don't forget,' I encouraged Paul, somewhat ironically. He didn't bite.

The local Coroner, I realised, might have some questions about such a tragically unfortunate coincidence, but from our point of view at least this was not a problem. There'd be no one around to answer any awkward questions.

We let ourselves into number eight, where Eddie slumbered in his armchair in front of the rugby on television, whilst Anne leafed through an inane magazine devoted to true-life stories of unlikely personal horror. '*My Vampire Husband Ate Our Babies*', was the unlikely title of the two page piece that presently engrossed Anne as she shoved another chocolate into her mouth. With the boys all out and Eddie having drunk himself nearly comatose, at least no one else would be scrounging the sweets from her on this occasion.

We did a thorough check of the house, satisfying ourselves that three next-generation Potters weren't hiding behind the sofa or lurking under any beds in anticipation of our arrival. They weren't there, and Eddie and Anne were of no interest to us, on this occasion at least. 'Probably gone out,' offered Paul by way of stating the bleeding obvious.

'Why don't we go and see if Dai Harris is in? We can always send one of us back with him in the transport if we have to wait for these other three numpties,' Danny suggested. With action in the offing, he was suddenly taking more of an interest.

'Number nineteen it is then,' agreed Paul. 'Let's go.' We left the Potter parents to enjoy their evening; if things went to what we had of a plan, they wouldn't be enjoying another one for some considerable time.

Did I feel sorry for these two who, after all, were parents about to lose their entire clutch of male offspring? A few months previously I would have done, no matter how unsavoury their nature. It never felt right to deprive parents of their children. However, I was by now accustomed to existence in the other dimension; in fact I was having the time of my next life. Therefore I knew that the Potter brothers, and indeed Dai Harris, would soon adjust and probably have a much better time than their earthly existence represented. I couldn't see that any of them were bad enough to go to an RU; a short while of reflection about the effects of their actions on others would almost certainly suffice before they enjoyed their forthcoming entry to Paradise. I bore them no ill.

CHAPTER TWENTY-FIVE

We weren't entirely prepared for what we found at number nineteen. Walking through the front door, closed as ever, we knew there was some nefarious activity occurring in the kitchen, so went to have a look.

'Tommo and Wayne Potter,' decided Paul, having consulted the ubiquitous manilla folder. 'What on earth are they doing here, I wonder?'

'Looks like they're stealing the boiler,' Rachel pointed out. We loitered at various points around the kitchen; there was plenty of room as we were insubstantial.

Oblivious to our presence, Tommo had removed all the pipes, unscrewed the mounting points and he and Wayne were in the process of removing the new boiler from the wall. As they did so, there was the discernable hiss of escaping gas from the pipe as it emerged from the wall. Wayne mentioned this, but Tommo was confident that they would be well clear before it became a problem. Unfortunately, Tommo had failed to take into account that the gas had started leaking quietly as soon as he had started to loosen the connections to the boiler, and in the last twenty minutes it had accumulated in levels that, although unlikely to suffocate, would be explosive if a naked flame was present. Fortunately, Tommo and Wayne had no intention of introducing one.

'Where the fuck's Gaz got to?' Tommo muttered. 'He should be back with some gear by now, and we need the bloody car to shift this thing.' Paul looked thrilled at the possible arrival of a third target; he clearly loved it when a plan came together, even if he hadn't bothered to prepare one in the first place.

As if it had acquired powers of telepathy, Tommo's phone warbled to fanfare the arrival of a text message. Wayne checked it for him. 'It's Gaz. He wants to know where we are, thick pillock,' he said to Tommo.

'Don't say we're at the Harrises, that puts us at the scene if we get nicked and my phone seized,' Tommo hissed.

'Oh, right,' replied Wayne. 'I'll just say number nineteen. That could be anywhere.'

'Oh for fuck's sake, just get on with it.' Tommo was getting seriously pissed off now as he hurried to get the job completed. His phoned trumpeted the next message from Gaz's phone.

'He'll be here in a minute,' Wayne announced.

'Thank fuck for that. I've just about got this free. Give us a hand with it, mate.'

Meanwhile, Dai Harris had grown bored with the rugby. Unlike so many of his compatriots, the game didn't do much for him, if the truth be told. The fact that, by half time, Wales were trailing by twenty points did nothing to sustain his interest. The atmosphere in the Club was decidedly muted and he felt listless. Dai decided that he needed a fix, not an option in his present surroundings, but no problem if he slipped home. He murmured something about feeling under the weather, but no one was listening or particularly interested, so he slipped out and walked back up Evans Street towards his appointment with Destiny.

He reached his family dwelling and let himself through the front door. Already having enjoyed three or four beers at the Club, his befuddled mind registered some scuffling from the kitchen and a flickering light that was suddenly extinguished. He turned the light on, but it didn't work. This mystified Dai; the electricity shouldn't have been cut off even though the family had long since ceased to pay its bills. In anticipation of the utility company getting its own back, Owen had bypassed the meter to ensure an uninterrupted and totally free access to the National Grid. At least Dai was prepared for just such an eventuality. He took from his pocket his cigarette lighter and, as he pressed its plastic button, he heard a knock on the front door behind him.

Summers recalled Gaz telling him that number nineteen would be further along the same street the Potters inhabited, so he did not need phenomenal powers of deduction to locate the address. He got out of Gaz's car and walked along Evans Street towards the Harris dwelling, noticing as he went that someone had just gone into a house down near where he thought number nineteen stood. Reaching the Harris residence, he knocked loudly on the front door.

The Potters could clearly hear the front door open, then close again. Even they could work out the implications. 'Oh fuck,' said Tommo, stuck with the boiler dangling precariously from one remaining wall screw. He and Wayne froze, undecided as to what to do next. Two things then happened almost simultaneously. There was a knock on the front door, followed by a large, powerful and very loud explosion.

CHAPTER TWENTY-SIX

Ellie Jones had lived in Evans Street for most of her sixty-eight years. As she never tired of telling her husband Ifor, the place had gone right downhill. Gone were the days when neighbours would look out for each other, where doors could be left unlocked and children grew up in the security of an extended community family. Living in the no-man's-land between the Potters and the Harrises had left Ellie at her wits' end. Barely a day passed without her praying for something slightly unpleasant to happen to her warring neighbours. Her prayers were shortly to be answered more spectacularly than she could have imagined.

Ellie, much to her chagrin, hadn't managed to get down to the Club to watch the rugby. Her chilblains had been playing up something awful and she couldn't be guaranteed a seat that afforded a view of the television. With due consideration, Ifor had offered to stay at home with her, but she wouldn't hear of it. He would only have wound up playing the martyr and Ellie preferred the peace and quiet that his absence conferred on the household, so encouraged her husband to go and enjoy himself. This was a shame, as it went, because what she was about to witness would have been so much better shared.

The Harrises lived almost though not quite opposite Ellie and Ifor. Short of a bottle of stout to accompany the rugby, Ellie treated her chilblains to a short walk to the shop and back. As she passed No. 19, the house in darkness, she was certain she could hear a faint clinking of metal on metal, and some muttered cursing, as if something wasn't going entirely to plan. She didn't see us walking along Evans Street towards the Harrises' house as we were, of course, invisible.

Ellie peered through the window into the front room. Although there was no sign of life, she noticed a slight flickering reflected off the walls where the interior door was ajar. It suggested someone was moving around the kitchen by torchlight. Ellie presumed that the Harris family had failed to pay their electricity bill and, as a result, the power supply had been disconnected. This pleased her immensely; she and Ifor struggled but always paid their way, so why should these freeloaders get their energy for nothing? Ellie limped across the road to her own tidy home, and settled back to enjoy the Harrises' payback time from the comfort of her sofa.

She was reminiscing about the nice old couple who used to live at number nineteen before their unfortunate demise had led to the arrival of the uncouth and revolting Harris family. Noting that someone who looked unsavoury was even now banging on their door, she was wishing the whole damned lot of them would just disappear in a puff of smoke, when their house did just that. With a thunderclap and bright flash shining through every window, the roof and upper floor were obliterated, the windows blew out showering glass all over Evans Street, and the front door flew across the street carrying with it the figure of the hapless caller. The door flattened itself against the streetlamp across the street, instantly and fatally snapping the neck of Summers who had joined it on its first and only flight.

Dai Harris, Wayne and Tommo Potter died instantly, the heat and pressure causing multiple percussive injuries and burns. We sat in awe as the building collapsed around us.

Across the street, Ellie Jones could only stand at her window, her jaw dropping, as she gawped at the cataclysmic realisation of her wish.

I have to say that I was impressed with the devastation a simple gas explosion could cause, though it might seem somewhat insensitive to say so. The blast had occurred on the ground floor; the windows and doors being less robust than the brick walls, these had blown out allowing some of the high-pressure gas to escape. Even so there was a delay due to the narrow apertures which was sufficient to cause a build-up of pressure inside the rooms of the ground floor. The next weakest point was the ceilings and the floorboards of the first floor bedrooms and loft, then the roof tiles. So, at pretty much the same time as Lee Summers was meeting a sticky end wrapped around a lamp post, the roof and sundry contents of the bedrooms were briefly airborne before falling back and forming a large pile of rubble. The rapid expansion of the air and its being forced out of the building resulted, microseconds afterwards, in a vacuum which drew the surrounding air just as forcefully back in to the building, causing the badly-damaged brickwork of the outer walls to collapse inwards. There was, therefore, the complete destruction of number 19 whilst the adjoining premises appeared to be miraculously unscathed, to the amazement and relief of their temporarily-deafened occupants.

Evans Street was, notwithstanding the tidy dynamics of the gas explosion, awash with rubble outside the random collection of bricks, wood, furnishings and body parts that now comprised the former Harris residence and its erstwhile occupants. As the last half bricks and fragments of roof tile respectively thumped and clattered their way back to terra firma, a brief silence ensued. No burglar alarm shattered the silence; had the occupants bothered with such a facility it would have been obliterated in any case.

Being incorporeal, none of the physical rearrangements had affected us. We sat on top of the pile of rubble that had fallen back onto the remnants of the ground floor and surveyed the effects of the cataclysm. We were joined by the now-spiritual forms of our targets, the Potter brothers and Dai Harris. They all bore the confused looks of the newly dead, struggling to come to terms with the life-cancelling events of a few seconds before.

Across the street I saw the familiar figure of Lee Patrick Summers staring in disbelief at his broken body. Wondering where on earth that muppet had come from, I decided I would go over and reacquaint myself with him in a moment, once the dust had settled. It suddenly dawned on me that, perhaps, his own time really had come. How richly ironic, I felt, that it was down to me to welcome him to the Afterlife. I was going to enjoy this.

Danny, Gordon and Chris had each latched on to a new arrival. A nice one to one introduction to the Afterlife was exactly what the Grim Reaper ordered. Rachel had cleared off somewhere, presumably to arrange our pick up.

Tommo and Wayne Potter sat disconsolately with Chris

and Danny. Chris was comforting Tommo with her most sympathetic manner whilst Danny was explaining his new circumstances to Wayne. Neither brother looked all that pleased to be with us, not that that was unusual. Gordon, meanwhile, was enthusiastically explaining the dynamics of explosive building deconstruction to Dai Harris, who was struggling to take in what had happened to his house, the Potter brothers who had been burgling it, and his mortal body, which was under several feet of rubble. Gordon was just impressed at seeing the results of an explosion up close and personal, rather than from a Lancaster bomber at twenty thousand feet. As a one man weapon of mass destruction, Gordon had few equals. His planning skills certainly outshone those of our Grim Leader.

Paul was left to strut around like he owned the place, a rather smug expression manifesting itself on his comprehensively-bearded face. Of course, he couldn't keep quiet for long. 'Good work, everyone,' he boomed, his stentorian tones in stark contrast to the eerie silence that had fallen once the echoes of the explosion had died away and the rubble had untidily rearranged itself.

Danny was the first of us to respond. 'How the hell did you do that?'

'I told you I had a plan,' said the Grim Reaper.

Unable to put off the inevitable I went over to greet my murderer. Given the months of surreptitious effort I had put into haunting him and ensuring that he was identified as the perpetrator of my own demise, our reunion might reasonably have been marked by a memorable quote: 'So, Mr. Summers, we meet again,' in my best Bond-villain accent perhaps. Typically, that idea only occurred to me once the moment had passed, and all I managed was a rather feeble 'Hello, Lee'.

His reply was equally succinct.

'You bastard'.

EPILOGUE

There isn't one. Yet.

We'll see you in due course.

Don't keep us waiting…

GLOSSARY

Being mainly for the benefit of overseas readers, those who are not police officers, and anyone else who might not understand British police jargon.

Admin people: Bureaucrats

Advanced Level: High level of driver training allowing an officer to drive powerful police vehicles quite quickly, under the right circumstances of course.

Advice given: Sometimes when there are no charges against a criminal, they are let off with a 'friendly warning'. This is recorded as 'Advice given'. It does not usually specify what advice was given, or how assertively it was delivered.

ANPR: Automatic Number Plate Recognition. A camera-based system which electronically reads the image of a vehicle's registration plate, compares it with a list of vehicles of interest to the police, and alerts the operator. Sometimes requires a bit of professional guesswork when only part of the registration is known.

Authorised Firearms Officer: Only a small minority of British police officers carry a firearm. AFOs do. Others have to talk their way out of trouble.

ASAP: As Soon As Possible.

Assisting an Offender: Helping a criminal evade justice, for example by hiding them or disposing of their car or firearm.

Backing up: Assisting another unit.

Bail out: To leave suddenly.

Beat: Area worked regularly by a local police officer.

Blag / Blaggers: Armed robbers.

Blue on blue: A clash between policing or military operations by units on the same side, resulting in disruption to the smooth progress of one or both operations. Similar to a 'Friendly Fire Incident'.

Bobby: Police officer.

Bought into: Accepted or supported.

Brief: Lawyer.

Call Centres: Customer contact centres.

Caution: A minor sanction resulting in a criminal being given a not-very-severe telling-off by police. See Pink and Fluffy Policing.

Cash-in-transit: Delivery of large sums of money to businesses such as banks and supermarkets.

CCTV: Closed circuit television, monitored by the local council to see what the public is up to.

Chief Superintendent: The rank of most divisional / district commanders. See 'British Police Rank Structure'.

Chief Constable: Senior police officer in a county police force, i.e. any force other than the Metropolitan Police.

CID: Criminal Investigation Department. Detectives.

Circulated as wanted: Wanted for questioning.

Clean car: Vehicle not previously involved in crime so not previously of interest to the police.

Clocked: Seen or recorded.

Cloud base below limits: The cloud base is too low for the helicopter to fly. This usually happens when the helicopter is serviceable, fully-fuelled and the crew has plenty of duty time left.

Come on-side: Cooperate.

Coming clean: Making an admission of guilt.

Compromise: Expose an undercover officer or operation.

CPS: Crown Prosecution Service, responsible for prosecuting criminals. Universally derided by police officers who believe (possibly unfairly) that the CPS is only interested in dropping cases and letting criminals walk free, hence its alternative title, the Criminal Protection Service.

Commendations: Awards by senior officers recognising good work by their subordinates. Used sparingly in order to avoid devaluing them.

Cough to it: Admit guilt.

Cough or nothing: An admission in the absence of supporting evidence sufficient to support a charge.

Couldn't keep his vehicle shiny side up on the tarmac: Managed to crash his car.

Counter Terrorist Unit: Separate policing unit responsible for countering terrorist activity.

Crim: Criminal.

Crime group: Criminals acting together as an enterprise.

Crimestoppers: Charity which runs an anonymous reporting system, encouraging people to pass information indirectly to the police, thereby reducing the likelihood of being identified and victimized by wrongdoers.

Crimewatch: Television programme which features high-profile unsolved cases.

Custody office: Charge room.

DCI Gene Hunt: Leading character in the original (British) series, *Life on Mars* and *Ashes to Ashes*; an abrasive, hard-talking and assertive Detective Chief Inspector who treated criminals with contempt. A hero to many older-in-service present-day police officers.

Death Message: Notification to the soon-to-be-grieving relatives that their loved one has died.

Desk jockey: Office worker, especially one who is also a police officer. Sometimes known as the *Station Cat*.

Disciplined organisation: An organisation where staff are legally obliged to obey lawful orders, such as the police or military.

Divisional Commander: Head of a police division, typically a city.

Divisional Office: Where local police officers work.

Divisional unit: Police vehicle tasked with very local patrol rather than operating across the whole force area.

Domestic: A family argument, often verbal, frequently violent and always a nightmare for cops because as soon as we turn up and arrest one party, the other party forgets about the initial argument and just gives us a hard time anyway. Still, it's the most common scenario resulting in murder so we've got to try.

Door ram: A heavy metal bar used to force entry via a locked door. It can be used against an unlocked door, but this is generally discouraged by the force solicitor who would have to pay compensation for unnecessary damage.

D/Supt.: Detective Superintendent.

Duty roster: Rota for work.

Emergency transmitter button: A button that allows the user to send a continuous message in desperate circumstances. Useful if they are fighting with an assailant and couldn't keep stopping to press the transmit button every time they wanted to say something.

Enhanced payments: Higher than normal payments for information.

Fair game: A reasonable target.

Filth: Police officer (term used by the scumbags against fundamentally decent, hard-working and dedicated officers).

Fingertip search: Very thorough search usually carried out by staff on their hands and knees.

Firm: Organised gang of criminals.

Fit the bill: Match the description.

Five grand: Five thousand pounds.

Fixed penalty notice: Citation for a traffic offence requiring the payment of a fine and incurring a set number of penalty points on the driver's licence. Generally, if you incur twelve penalty points in three years, you are banned from driving for six months.

Force boundary: The limit of the area of responsibility for a particular police force. Officers' powers do, however, extend beyond the boundary. The law applies all over the place just the same, at least in England and Wales.

Force Control Room Supervisor: Person in charge of the centre dispatching officers.

Forensic: Physical evidence of crime capable of being scientifically analysed and used in a criminal case, usually before being excluded due to a minor irregularity exposed by the defence.

From the office: Turning out from the police station.

Gear: Property subject of crime, usually drugs but could also include the tools of the trade.

Go a bit postal: US term originally. Suffer an adverse emotional reaction resulting in the application of violence, sometimes to fatal effect.

Grassing up: Passing information to the police

Have a crack at him: Make an attempt to secure his cooperation.

Have a ratch around: Have a look around, explore.

Heavies: Thugs.

Help Desk: Customer contact centre, renowned for not being particularly helpful.

High visibility jacket: Bright yellow jacket designed to make the wearer obvious to drivers.

Home Office: The Government department responsible for policing the UK. Universally derided by police officers who do not perceive it as having our best interests at heart.

Host forces: Police forces where persons of interest actually live.

In play: A legitimate target.

In the job: Employed as a police officer.

In trade: For sale in the hands of a car dealer.

Inside: In prison.

Inspector Clouseau: Film character, played by Peter Sellers. A spectacularly inept Detective Inspector who, despite his best efforts, always wound up winning.

Job's a good'un: Everything will be OK.

Joe Soap: The average person in the street. The female equivalent is Mrs. Miggins.

Juicy shout: Interesting job.

Late shift: Afternoon into early evening work period, usually 2pm till 10pm.

Leant on: Persuaded.

Licensing visit: Occasional visit by police to a pub, to see how many archaic licensing laws are being broken. These are less frequent now that pubs are open virtually round the clock, and under-age drinkers are out drinking vodka or cheap cider in the local park with their mates.

Lie down: Prolonged period in custody, enabling further questioning to take place.

Life was pronounced extinct: Declared officially dead, by a medically-qualified person. We tend to know when someone is dead, but can't actually say so officially.

Likely to prove fatal: The person is likely to die. Usually shortened to 'Likely to Prove' as we don't like upsetting faint-hearted people listening in, such as management.

Lingua Franca: Common language.

Loan-sharking: Unregulated money lending at exorbitant rates of interest. Non-payment of debts is often rectified by the application of violence.

Lock ups: Private shed or similar facility, used for storage.

Locked up: Arrested or imprisoned.

Lodge: A branch of the Freemasons, reputedly frequented by community figures such as senior police officers and politicians. The author has never been invited to join.

Low level dealers: Suppliers of drugs to individual users, usually in order to fund their own habit.

Major result: Securing evidence to bring serious and/or numerous charges against members of a crime group.

Making off without payment: Leaving without paying for a service or certain goods, such as fuel.

Matey boy: Informal term for an unnamed individual, usually male.

Mental Health Act: Legislation to allow people with mental health issues to be dealt with promptly and effectively, before being released back onto the streets.

Met: Metropolitan Police Service, looking after London. Other areas of the country are also available, but that is of little interest to the Met. Allegedly.

MI5: Branch of the Security Services dealing with internal threats to the security of the state.

Mike Whisky Seven Six: Phonetic call sign of police vehicle. Although this call sign is fictitious it is typical of those used in reality. M (Mike) indicates a car, W (Whisky) is Western Division, Seven would indicate the station where the car is based and Six is the vehicle's number at that station. In reality, we would struggle to find six vehicles at one station these days.

Minder: Bodyguard.

Mob: Gang of criminals.

Mobile ANPR: An ANPR camera mounted in a vehicle allowing it to be moved from place to place.

Mole grips: A pair of adjustable, spring-loaded pliers, favoured by burglars as a tool for breaking into houses.

Moving traffic offences: Infringements of the Road Traffic Act 1988 and similar legislation.

Mugged: Robbed in the street.

Mug shot: Official photograph.

Muppets: Persons of low worth.

New Scotland Yard: Former headquarters of the

Metropolitan Police Service (Met), held up to other forces as a paragon of experience and best practice (usually by the Met themselves). They've moved now and New Scotland Yard has been demolished.

Nick: Police Station.

No comment: In Britain you do not have to say anything when interviewed by the police, but if you subsequently come up with a defence, the court can infer that it's a load of bollocks. They probably won't.

Nonces: Sex offenders.

Numpty: Idiot.

OCG: Organised Crime Group.

Of interest: Something or someone that the police would like to know more about.

Old shed: Decrepit or unreliable car.

Organised crime nominals / Criminals: Persons involved in organised criminal enterprises, like Mobsters.

Outstanding: Not yet traced.

Partial forensic lifts: Traces of evidence that might help to indicate that a certain person was involved, or might not.

Pay As You Go: Non-contract mobile (cell) phone. Use is enabled by paying a sum of money, especially cash, to buy a certain amount of talk time. This is usually done anonymously.

PACE: Police and Criminal Evidence Act 1984. Comprehensive legislation governing the securing of evidence including by questioning.

Partial registration: Part of a vehicle registration number, the rest not having been recorded.

PC6204: Typical identification number for a police officer. PC denotes a police constable and the numbers are the officer's unique identifier.

Pedestrian knock-down: Someone on foot on or adjacent to the road, getting run over by a vehicle that coincides with them in time and face.

Personalised plates: Non-standard vehicle registration, often intended to read like the owner's name.

Performance indicators: Things for the bosses to count and get worried about. These tell us what our policing priorities are, hence the phrase 'What gets counted, gets done', an essential feature of British policing.

Performance culture: The working environment whereby we are told what is being counted and therefore what we have to do. Nothing else seems to matter.

Perverting the Course of Justice: Offence whereby the offender sets out to stop the law being enforced or justice being properly enacted. Maximum sentence is potentially (though hardly ever) life imprisonment.

Picked up: Recorded.

Pinged: Alerted a computer system, such as ANPR. See above.

Pink and fluffy policing: Derogatory term for a policing style that apparently puts being nice to people ahead of robust enforcement of the law.

Plain car: Fully equipped police vehicle which is not in the police force livery, so can be used to sneak up on criminals and offending drivers without them realizing they are about to be caught.

Plate: Registration number.

Plods: Police officers, in uniform, usually rushing around like maniacs to get to all the shouts. See CID, who don't.

PNC: Police National Computer, containing details of criminals and vehicles.

PND: Police National Database. A national system for sharing intelligence about criminals between forces.

Politically-correct commissars: Humourless individuals intent on preventing people (usually police officers) enjoying themselves.

Potted: Arrested and charged.

Priority nominals: Most wanted criminals.

Probationer: Trainee police officer. The UK doesn't have Police Academies. We are trained in force. Now called 'Student Officers' to make them feel valued. They still get to make the tea though.

Professional Standards Department (PSD): Department of police force responsible for hunting down and dealing with police officers who have erred. Formerly called Complaints & Discipline or similar. *Pink and Fluffy Policing* does not feature in the PSD ethos.

Pursuit trained, not: (Not) trained or authorised to chase fleeing vehicles.

Ran the local area: Organised crime activity in a particular neighbourhood, usually reinforced by violence.

Rank hath its privileges: Ironic expression that bosses can get away with more than lesser mortals.

Registered keeper: The individual registered with DVLA as the legal guardian of a particular vehicle. This is usually, though not always, the owner.

Release without charge after 24 hours: Legal requirement if there is insufficient evidence to charge. N.B. There is scope for Superintendent to extend detention for a further twelve hours, or for Magistrates to do so for a further sixty beyond that, but let's keep it simple.

Request back up: Ask for another police car or officer to assist.

Resident loony: A crank, living locally, pre-disposed to contacting the police in connection with their particular delusions.

Rest period: Eight-hour period in which the suspect is allowed a bit of peace and quiet.

Road Traffic Act 1988: Lengthy piece of legislation covering almost all aspects of driving vehicles on the British road network.

Roads Policing Unit: Police team tasked with patrolling the road network.

Rozzers: Police.

Sawn off: Shot gun, shortened by having most of the barrel cut off with a hacksaw so it can be concealed more easily.

Scientific Support: Forensic evidence collectors and investigators attached to the police force. Like CSI

Scrote: A criminal. This wonderful term was apparently coined by American novelist Joseph Wambaugh in *The Choirboys*. It has since passed into everyday parlance in the British police service, except when the bosses are listening, in which case we talk about 'clients' or 'suspects'.

Security Services: Various government agencies dealing with different aspects of state security, including MI5 and Counter Terrorist Units.

Sectioned: Detained under the Mental Health Act (usually under Section 136).

Shooters: Guns

Shouted control: Called dispatch.

Single-crewed: Police officer patrolling alone.

SIO: Senior Investigating Officer; the lead detective in a serious crime case.

SNAFU: Situation Normal - All Fucked Up. RAF expression of resigned acceptance that all is less than perfect.

Sneak in burglaries: Burglary effected by the burglar walking into a house through an unlocked door.

Social housing: Housing provided at low cost as part of the benefits package paid to the unemployed or indolent.

SOCO: Scenes of Crime Officer.

Spontaneous and preplanned jobs: Firearms jobs come in two types; those that come as complete surprise (to us) and those that are planned in advance (by us). They are known, respectively, as spontaneous and pre-planned. This novel features the former type.

Sound like a police trainer: Utter meaningless platitudes designed to sound supportive and caring.

Stash: Quantity of illicit goods (such as drugs) or money.

Stop-checked: Stopped by police for the purpose of verifying identity and reason for being at that location.

Straight cough: Full admission.

Straight up: Open and honest.

Sudden death: Unanticipated and rapid onset of not being alive any longer.

Sun's well over the yardarm: Time for a drink, the sun having apparently past the yardarm (on its way to setting), part of a ship's structure.

Supervision: Sergeant responsible for the team. Any higher ranks are 'Management'.

Tactical Pursuit and Containment: A complex process to bring to a halt a vehicle that has refused to stop for a police patrol.

Targets: The numerical expression of performance indicators. Alternatively, people to chase.

Tasking of sources: Seeking information by asking informants to find out what is needed.

Taxing: Illegally relieving other criminals of their possessions or money (except when carried out by HM Revenue and Customs of course).

Team briefing: Opportunity for the team sergeant to update the incoming shift on latest incidents, wanted persons, policing priorities and directives from senior management. The team then joins hands and sings the force song. (The last sentence is a complete fabrication but the way things are going, it's only a matter of time).

Telecom enquiries: Investigations into the owner or user of telephone numbers, usually relating to mobile (cell) phones.

Thirty years minimum: Since the abolition of the death penalty, British courts have usually imposed a minimum period of thirty years imprisonment for anyone convicted of murdering a police officer. This is of little consolation to the officer's family.

To no gain: Without any result.

Toe rags: Persons of low worth.

Top brass: Senior officers.

Torched: Set on fire.

Traffic patrol: Highway patrol.

Traffic ticket: See *Fixed Penalty Notice*.

Trafficker: Drug dealer working in large quantities and supplying a network rather than a few individuals.

Trained negotiator: Police officer, usually senior, trained to talk people out of committing suicide or holding hostages.

Trawl of ANPR: Search of ANPR records to see if certain vehicles have passed the camera, and if so, when.

Trolley bus: A bus that, in times gone by, was powered by overhead electrical wires but ran along a road without rails to guide it and keep it aligned with its power supply. What could possibly go wrong?

Turf: Area regularly worked or frequented by an individual.

Unattributed phone: Mobile (cell) phone not registered to an identifiable user, to the frustration of the police.

Unclassified road: A minor road or lane, too small to be given a road number of its own.

Undercover (UC) work: Infiltrating criminal gangs by posing as a criminal. The difficult bit is not actually committing crime whilst still appearing to be a scrote, the more verminous the better.

Units: Police vehicles

Unmarked vehicle: See Plain car.

Urgent assistance: Help required immediately. The word 'urgent' is used with care as it will usually result in numerous officers stopping what they are doing and rushing to help.

Vehicle Identification Number: Identification number allocated at the point of manufacture to a vehicle and stamped irremovably to the chassis. This supposedly enables the vehicle to be identified regardless of any false registration plates or being torched. Details are stored on PNC.

Vehicle making off: Driver failing to stop for the police, usually because they would rather not speak to us just now.

Verified address: Confirmed address for a purchaser.

Warning markers on PNC: Information on PNC that a person is potentially dangerous, for example because they habitually carry weapons.

Warrant card: Police officers' identity card. We don't wave badges around in the UK.

Welfare check: Checking that a police officer is still OK even though they haven't responded to a radio call.

'Yip yip wibble' file: Place where the authorities potentially file complaints by persons who are slightly deranged.

British Police Rank Structure (In order of grovel-worthiness):

Chief Constable
Deputy Chief Constable
Assistant Chief Constable
Chief Superintendent
Superintendent
Chief Inspector
Inspector
Sergeant
Constable. (You are here)

Officers working in CID or Intelligence prefix their rank with the word 'Detective', to rub in the fact that they are better than everybody else. The senior ranks at the Metropolitan Police Service in London are structured slightly differently, but that is not relevant to this story.

SIMON HEPWORTH

THE
DARK PART
OF SKY
THE

A COLLECTION OF B⊙MBER COMMAND **GHOST STORIES**

Dead men told no tales…
until now.

Imagine setting out in a bomber, night after night, knowing that the might of the Luftwaffe is hell-bent on killing you…

…parachuting from a blazing bomber into enemy territory, having just bombed a nearby city…

…deciding, day by day, which of your crews you will send out, probably to their deaths, not knowing their fate until they let you know…

…having a date with the Chop Girl…

…spending the rest of time haunting your former airfield after failing to return from those ops.

What's not to like?

In the Second World War more than sixty thousand aircrew of Bomber Command lost their lives on operations or in training. Mostly young and energetic, they died suddenly and traumatically. No spirits could have more reason to remain attached to the places where they lived the last few weeks or months of their earthly lives before they disappeared into the night.

Simon Hepworth's latest paranormal tales put a new spin on the sightings, myths and legends of phantom airmen at old RAF stations across England.

Available from Amazon worldwide.

35160821R00141

Printed in Poland
by Amazon Fulfillment
Poland Sp. z o.o., Wrocław